BY KATE ROBB

This Spells Love
Prime Time Romance
Kitty St. Clair's Last Dance
Solar Eclipse of the Heart

SOLAR ECLIPSE OF THE HEART

THE DIAL PRESS
NEW YORK

SOLAR ECLIPSE OF THE HEART

A Novel

KATE ROBB

The Dial Press
An imprint of Random House
A division of Penguin Random House LLC
1745 Broadway, New York, NY 10019
randomhousebooks.com
penguinrandomhouse.com

A Dial Press Trade Paperback Original

ISBN 978-0-593-73414-8
Ebook ISBN 978-0-593-73415-5

PRINTED IN THE UNITED STATES OF AMERICA

1st Printing

BOOK TEAM: Production editor: Cindy Berman • Managing editor: Leah Sims • Production manager: Meghan O'Leary • Copy editor: Rebecca Maines • Proofreaders: Pam Rehm, Kristin Jones, Judy Kiviat

Dotwork eclipse art by swillklitch/Adobe Stock

Book design by Kim Henze Walker

The authorized representative in the EU for product safety and compliance is Penguin Random House Ireland, Morrison Chambers, 32 Nassau Street, Dublin D02 YH68, Ireland. https://eu-contact.penguin.ie

For anyone looking . . .
this is your sign!

SOLAR ECLIPSE OF THE HEART

Prologue

April 2024

THE WEATHER FORECAST CALLED FOR OVERCAST SKIES, or at least that was the excuse I gave my Uncle Larry as his motorcycle idled next to where I stood on the sidewalk. When he didn't say anything, I offered two more. I had a job interview the next day and needed to review my notes, and I was feeling a little queasy from eating three-day-old Szechuan leftovers for breakfast that morning. There were also a few excuses I kept to myself. Riding on the back of his Harley terrified me, even though he promised to take only the back roads, and I had cramps.

"I'll be able to see the eclipse just fine from here," I told him. "Seriously, you go on without me. They said on the news that traffic is backing up already. It might take you a few hours to get there."

I stepped back as if the motion might convince him my decision was final, but Uncle Larry just shook his head. "We're not in the path of totality here, Beans," he said, tilting his head toward the sky. "You want to miss a solar eclipse in your own backyard? It's a time for spiritual awakening." He patted the empty space on the seat behind him. "Come on. Let the universe take you down a path. Trust it to guide you where you need to go. I dare you."

"I'm fairly confident my spiritual needs can hold on for the next one," I said, certain at least of that fact. "And I do want to experience it in my own backyard. My actual backyard." I gestured at the alleyway next to the building that led to a small scrap of grass in the back. "I'm sorry, really I am. Next one, I promise."

Larry sighed, and I knew he was done arguing with me. He lifted the lapel of his black leather jacket and reached inside to pull something out. "Okay," he said, holding out a strip of brightly colored cardboard, which he unfolded. It was a pair of those cheap solar eclipse glasses you can buy online.

"August twelfth, 2026. Peñíscola, Spain. It's a date." He bent across the handlebars of his bike and held out the glasses until I leaned forward and allowed him to slip them over my eyes.

"There's a great little spot called Restaurante El Peñón. It's the best suquet de peix you'll ever have. We'll make a week of it."

I tried to roll my eyes, but I couldn't see anything through the lenses. "Really? Spain."

"You promised next time," Uncle Larry said, laughing a little as he slipped the glasses from my face, leaving me to blink rapidly until my eyes readjusted to the daylight.

He reached out as if to hand me back the glasses but stopped himself. "On second thought, maybe I'll hold on to these." He tucked them into the inner pocket of his leather jacket. "Keep 'em safe."

This time, I managed to roll my eyes. "Always looking out for me."

Larry smiled and turned his wrist, revving the engine of his motorcycle twice. "Always will, kiddo. No matter what." He brought his hand to the brim of his black helmet in a mock salute before cranking the radio on his bike as high as it would go. "If you like piña coladas . . ." blasted through the speakers as he pulled out onto Queen Street and made a quick U-turn. I heard the faint traces of the chorus as his bike became indiscernible from the rest of the traffic heading toward Bathurst, many of them also on their way to Niagara Falls to watch the solar eclipse.

If this were the tragic part of the story, I'd tell you he rode off, and I never saw him again. That it taught me that life is short; you need to seize the moment. Carpe diem or whatever that expression is. But Uncle Larry came back about seven hours later—high on life and possibly gummies, with another story of another one of his crazy adventures. No, the tragedy came a few months later when his doctor diagnosed my full-of-life uncle with stage four pancreatic cancer. Then, four months after that, we said goodbye.

"I had a good run, kiddo," he said that last day in his hospital bed, rubbing one of the many tears I shed with the pad of his thumb.

"Do an old guy a favor and chat with a stranger sometime. Take a moment to gaze up at the stars every once in a while and think of me when you're dancing to my favorite song or drinking a Diet Coke. I'll be watching you, Beans."

Beans.

He gave me that nickname when I was a kid. I was a rascal. Always full of magic beans.

I can barely remember being like that: full of whimsy and wonder. The world, in its way, prepared me early to watch it claim a beautiful spirit with not so much as an afterthought.

Larry died in his sleep a few hours later, quietly and with little event other than the absence of the *beep beep beep* of the heart rate machine.

If there were magic beans still lingering deep within my psyche, they died along with him.

1

September 2025

I CAN HEAR THE MUSIC PUMPING FROM the store's speakers as soon as I round the corner onto Queen Street. It's some obscure song by some obscure band I don't even attempt to pretend I've heard of. The store's front door is propped open by a tiny stone garden gnome painted to loosely resemble Snoop Dogg, allowing the tiny blue-haired woman to wheel out a rack of carefully curated secondhand treasures onto the storefront sidewalk.

The rack suddenly picks up speed down the ramp, then swings hard to the right. But just as it's about to flatten me, Koko Hayashida, the owner and sole proprietor of Thrift Me Baby (One More Time), gives it a hard yank, pulling it backward before she locks the metal wheel latch into place with her foot and looks up.

"Oh, hey, Lise." Koko waves a white crocheted vest in my direction. "Happy Friday."

Within twenty-eight seconds of our first encounter on this exact same spot three months ago, she gave me a nickname, immediately dropping the dowdy "Anna" half of my name for the much cooler and shorter "Lise."

"Hey." I brush my dark fringed bangs from my forehead and loop my right hand under the strap of my backpack, letting it slip from my shoulder in an effort to look more cool and Lise-like.

"Looks like you've been doing some shopping?" I incline my head and peer into her already crowded vintage shop, wondering where this rack of clothing even fit before she pulled it out onto the sidewalk.

"Yeah. That place over on Dufferin had another pop-up." Koko pulls a bright yellow beaded gown from the rack and holds it up. "I think most of the stuff came from that *Law & Order* spin-off they were filming downtown all last year, but they had some cute dresses." She turns the gown so the light makes the beading shimmer. "Fifteen bucks for this. I couldn't resist." She hooks the hanger back onto the rack.

"Are you just getting home from work?" She glances at the gold vintage Cartier on her left hand. It's another one of her secondhand finds. According to last week's sidewalk conversation, she thrifted the watch from an impromptu garage sale she happened across on her walk to work last month for forty dollars. Even from the upside-down angle, I can see that the time reads almost six.

I nod and resist the urge to slide my arm back through my strap, so it once again sits ergonomically on my back, relieving the weight of my laptop and notebooks.

"Yes. Long day." I look past her, toward the painted yellow door next to her store that leads up to my second-floor apartment—home to my sweatpants, my incredibly comfortable couch, and my premium subscription Netflix account.

"You look like you could use a drink or three," she says.

"I'm closing up in an hour or so. What are you up to later? You should come out." She says it more like a statement than a question. "My friend Lucien knows this guy who is bartending at this great new place in Ossington. He says the cocktails are a little gaudy, but that's kind of the norm these days."

I smile as if I know about the norm these days. "That sounds really great; I'm just not a drinker." Or a stay-out-past-nine-thirty-er or socialize-with-strangers-unless-I-absolutely-have-to-er.

She continues to smile at me.

We have been doing this delicate sidewalk dance for three months or so, since she opened her thrift store below my apartment, replacing the dry cleaner, who I highly suspect was using the place as a front to launder money, seeing as he only seemed to be open on Tuesdays and every other Sunday. Our conversations have slowly progressed from deliberate eye contact to casual "heys" to a friendly level of chitchat. The last few weeks she has started to invite me to things: casual drinks, free concerts in the park, her friend Ramone's autobiographical one-person show. Although I've come to enjoy our impromptu chats, I'm just not sure we're ready to take things to the next level. "And I actually have a thing tonight.

"It's a dinner at that big Polish church over on Roncey," I explain. "They awarded me this scholarship for my PhD. It's not all that much—just two grand—but they're having this big awards ceremony tonight for all the recipients. I think they will make us all stand onstage and receive those big cardboard checks. Anyway, I need to be there. Thank you for the offer, though." I take another step toward my door.

It's not that I don't like Koko—I do. It's just that humans, as a species, typically prefer forming close bonds with similar people. It's a biological instinct driven by our mammalian brains. Our personal safety is dependent on flocking with herds that are as akin to us as possible, and I cannot imagine anyone describing Koko and me as birds of the same feather.

Koko is effortlessly cool in her two-sizes-too-big carpenter pants and a tiny cropped top that looks like it once lived a double life as an elderly man's necktie. She has a glossy blue bob, and I have practical penny loafers and the same button-down blouse bought in three colors because it fits my short torso and disproportionately long arms.

We simply don't match.

Putting all that aside, there's also the fact that I have less than three months until I'm heading off across the pond to Liverpool to pursue my PhD degree in neuroscience. We would be investing in a relationship that would most likely dwindle to an obligatory sporadic text message every few months.

"What are you wearing?" Koko's question catches me so off guard that I stare down at my blouse, wondering if I accidentally said that last part out loud.

I pull at the hem. "It's a hundred percent cotton. The store had a BOGO."

Koko laughs. "No, not right now. I meant tonight. It sounds like it's a big deal. Do you have something special that you are planning to wear?"

Again, my eyes fall to my blouse, preferring the previous question to this one. "Uh . . . I don't know. Maybe like black slacks and a shirt?" My voice inflects upward as if I'm asking her the question.

She shakes her head in a way that I immediately know I've said the wrong thing. It's confirmed as she grabs my wrist and tugs me inside the store with a roll of her eyes and a "Come on."

As soon as I'm inside, Koko begins pulling clothes from three different racks, all within arm's reach.

"I have a few ideas," she says, tossing me a brightly patterned dress. "The hall will be hot this time of year. Everyone's turned their air off. You'll want something that breathes and a jacket for when it gets cold later."

She's right about both things. I find a room full of strangers stifling on a good day, let alone the mid-September heat wave we seem to be having. But there is a nice breeze once the sun goes down. It blows right off Lake Ontario, keeping the south end of Toronto a few degrees cooler than the north and thus making a commuting jacket a necessity.

Koko drops another dress into my hands along with a tube of fabric I'm not entirely certain is a skirt or a top. "Pop these on." She nods toward a tiny dressing room separated from the rest of the store by a pink velvet curtain.

I obey, slipping inside and pulling the curtain closed behind me. I take a second to breathe before I slip out of my blouse and jeans. The dress slides on easily, but there is no mirror inside, so I am forced to pull back the curtain and step back into the store and Koko's assessing gaze.

"Cute," she says, addressing the dress and not my socked feet, which I've only now realized are two black trouser socks that are noticeably different lengths.

"But maybe try the blue one next." She shoos me back behind the curtain. "It will bring out those beautiful ocean eyes."

I do as she says, grateful that, unlike the fabric tube, the blue one is a scooped-neck sundress with puff sleeves, tiny buttons, and, more important, a zipper, which makes it very easy to tell the back from the front.

When I step out again, I can immediately see from the lift of Koko's eyebrows that she approves.

"What do you think?" She turns me toward the three-way mirror and watches me appraise my reflection. The dress's cinched waist gives the illusion of curves where they otherwise don't exist, and the periwinkle does seem to bring the blue out in my eyes. I lift my arm to glance at the price tag. It's eighty dollars. I wince, knowing I would think twice about buying a dress like this new, let alone used.

"It's vintage," Koko says as if reading my thoughts. "And it's my treat." She turns my shoulders and steers me back toward the changing room. "It's my way of saying thank you for not calling the cops last weekend. We were way later than I said we'd be."

I am pretty certain she's referring to the party she held last Saturday in the store. It was her friend Ramone's birthday. The music thumped up through my floorboards until after three. Koko had invited me to that one, too. Instead, I put in my earplugs.

I glance again at the price tag dangling from my arm before pulling the velvet curtain closed behind me. "That's nice of you to offer, but I totally don't mind paying."

"No, no," she calls from what sounds like the opposite side of the store. "I insist. That dress fits as if it were made for you. It's a sign from the universe that you should have it."

A sign.

A sharp pain shoots below my ribs. It's been nine months since Larry's death and over a year since his diagnosis and still the smallest things bring painful reminders.

Uncle Larry lived his life guided by signs.

"Sometimes the path ahead isn't always clear," he would say whenever faced with a difficult decision, and on occasion when deciding what to order for dinner. "The universe will always send you a message if you look hard enough."

And Larry would always look.

Sometimes, he'd find his answer in his horoscope or the tiny leaves that escaped his Tetley tea bag. Sometimes, it was in the abstract shape of a cumulus cloud.

Sometimes, when he couldn't find the message he was looking for, he'd reach into his wallet and pull out a yellow slip of legal pad paper with the words "this is your sign" scrawled in his own handwriting in blue Bic pen.

"See, Beans." He'd hold up the paper and laugh. "I'm meant to [insert whatever wild idea he'd come up with that day]," and then he'd go right ahead and do whatever he wanted to do in the first place.

My moment of grief is interrupted by a *zip*, then a *ding*, from what I'm certain is the cash register opening and closing. It's followed by footsteps and the high-pitched squeak of metal rubbing on metal as if she's sifting through one of her clothing racks. The bell above the door tinkles as if it's been opened. I hear Koko say, "Okay, thanks," presumably to the person who walked in. The bell chimes again, and the store grows quiet until Koko asks, "Any plans for the weekend?"

It's a moment before I realize she's talking to me. "Uh, yeah . . . I guess. My new roommate moves in tomorrow. Her bus gets in sometime in the morning so I need to stick around to give her a key."

"New roommate. That's kind of exciting. What's her deal?" Koko's voice is noticeably louder than a moment ago, placing her on the other side of the curtain.

I shrug even though she can't actually see me. "I don't know too much about her other than her name is Mackenzie Smith and she's a musician from some small town up north. I guess she got a job down here. She plays the tuba, so maybe the Toronto Symphony? We've only really emailed, but she seems nice."

"I'm sure she is." Koko's arm juts through the crack of the changing room. "Here, try this on, too."

A wooden hanger dangles from her fingertips. On it is a black leather biker jacket, cracked but soft as if made from quality leather but aged with years of use.

"What size is this?" I take the hanger from her hands. The jacket looks like it would fit a large man.

"It's meant to be big," Koko says, her voice getting farther away with each word. "Oversized is in right now."

I know the moment I slip it off the hanger, the jacket will be a hard no. It's too edgy. A step too far from the nerdy wannabe neuroscientist who actually enjoys the shapeless institutional cut of her lab coat. Still, I zip back up the dress I was taking off only a moment ago and slide the jacket on. I open my mouth to tell Koko thanks for the offer but I don't think it's going to work, when the world around me suddenly goes dark.

2

MY SURROUNDINGS LIGHT UP SLOWLY AS IF giving my eyes time to adjust. Even then, it takes me a moment to recalibrate.

I'm not in Koko's dressing room.

My body floods with a feeling of panic that cools my blood. The sensation is momentarily halted as it is interrupted by a familiar sound: a high-pitched screech of metal-on-metal paired with a building *clack clack clack.*

A train is approaching.

I look around. This new realization allows me to orient myself.

I am surrounded by floor-to-ceiling tiles of a pale yellow color. The floor is a smooth, specked terrazzo, save for a bright yellow studded strip set to warn commuters of the dark tracks below.

It's a subway station.

If the letters etched into the wall are to be believed, it's Toronto's Bloor-Yonge subway station.

But how the hell did I get here?

My answer doesn't come.

What does come is the silver subway train. It grinds to a

halt in front of me with a final metallic squeal followed by a *puff* and then a *hiss* as the doors slide open.

Several people step out—not nearly enough for it to be anywhere close to a weekday rush hour. The small handful of commuters makes me think it must be very late or maybe very early.

"Excuse me," I call to a tired-looking man in a rumpled gray suit, suddenly needing to know at least the time.

He doesn't look up or give any other indication he's heard me.

I inhale and try a second attempt. This one is much louder. "Excuse me, *sir.*"

He pulls out his phone but still does not look up. Instead, he walks straight toward me, his sudden increase in pace so unexpected that I need to jump out of the way to avoid running into him.

But I'm not fast enough.

My arms come out in front of me to brace or push him away, but when he makes contact, it's in a way I am not prepared for.

He walks straight through me as if I were a ghost or made of air.

Oh, god, am I dead?

I think back to the changing room.

How? I wasn't eating anything, so I couldn't have choked. Nor was I doing anything particularly dangerous. I would have felt the beginnings of a heart attack, wouldn't I?

Maybe it was a brain aneurysm, then. A quick spark and then blackness.

But if I am dead, then why is the afterlife the Bloor-Yonge subway station? It feels . . . underwhelming.

I have more thoughts and more questions—all of which

disintegrate at the sight of a man walking down the platform ahead of me.

His face is turned away, but the slope of his shoulders, the spring to his gait as he walks on his toes, and even the reflection of the lights bouncing off the bald spot on the back of his head are so familiar that my eyes immediately fill with tears.

"Uncle Larry?" My words come out as a whisper.

"Uncle Larr—" I call again, my voice cracking this time, cutting off the last syllable.

Like the man in the gray suit, my uncle can't seem to hear me. He continues to walk, heading for the stairs.

In a few more strides, he will be on his way back up to the surface and the bustling crowds of Bloor Street.

I begin to run, momentarily grateful for the ability to pass through everyone.

"Uncle Larry. Please wait!" I worry I won't catch him in time, but he stops just before he reaches the stairs.

I stop as well as if on instinct. My eyes trace the same path as his to the man standing against the wall, guitar in hand, the open velvet-lined case at his feet.

He's wearing a threadbare yellow T-shirt. His long, auburn hair hangs past his shoulders. His beard, a brighter shade of red, is bushy and full. His eyes are closed, but his hands pluck the guitar strings with a practiced ease. Their melody is soft and familiar.

I can't quite place the song until his low tenor voice joins in, the acoustics of the tiled walls magnifying it so it fills the whole station.

It's an old Jimmy Buffett song. "Bring Back the Magic." I only know it because my uncle owned an original LP, which he played all of the time on his old record player.

"You can get that on Spotify," I'd tell him every time the record would skip.

"I know that, Beans," he'd say with a shake of his head. "But it sounds better this way."

My uncle—the one in front of me—closes his eyes and begins to sway. It's such a characteristic Larry thing to do that the tears that only brimmed my eyes a few moments ago begin to fall like raindrops on my cheeks.

The musician finishes the song. Larry begins to clap. Like me, he is openly weeping as he reaches into his wallet and tosses twenty dollars into the open guitar case.

"Thanks, man," says the busker, who drops his hand from his guitar, letting it dangle from the strap around his neck. He reaches across the case, extending his hand for my uncle to shake.

"That song means a lot to me," my uncle says, taking his hand. I can hear the sudden choke in his voice. "I had some rough news today, and I was looking for a sign to let me know it would all be all right, and here you are."

The busker nods as if sympathetic to a problem that goes far beyond him and his guitar, then juts his chin at my uncle. "That's a great jacket, by the way."

Instinctively, I look down. The jacket I pulled on in Koko's store only minutes ago engulfs me. Its sleeves are so long they almost reach my fingertips.

"You know what," my uncle says, unzipping his almost identical jacket and handing it to the busker. "This old thing has witnessed some good times, but I think it has room for a few more stories. Here. Take it."

The busker reaches out and then hesitates. "It's really okay, man. I don't want to—"

"I insist." My uncle presses it into his hands.

The busker stares at the jacket for a moment. "Are you sure?"

My uncle nods his head. "Can't take it with me where I'm headed." He smiles. "But let me give you some unsolicited advice—" His voice cracks, but he takes a deep breath and continues. "Life is a gift, and you don't always appreciate that fact until . . . well, it's too late. I guess what I'm saying is . . . don't wait to do the big thing, because there is some peace in knowing you damn well squeezed every moment out of your life that you could."

The contents of my stomach turn sour.

What is unfolding in front of me right now is not a complete figment of my imagination.

I think it's a memory.

Only it didn't happen to me.

There was a night last year at the beginning of August. After a string of hot, humid days, we had an unexpected cold snap, and Larry came home shivering.

"Didn't you take a jacket?" I chastised, failing to notice the pained lines etched into my uncle's forehead.

"Sit down, Beans," he said. "I have something I need to tell you."

He didn't tell me specifically about the busker that day, only the grim diagnosis and how, on the way home, he had heard his song in the subway. He was certain it was a sign from the universe. A reassurance that even though he'd be gone soon, I'd be okay without him.

I felt my heart split open that night, and standing here, watching Larry now, the thin layers that had started to grow back—to heal—rip right back open again.

Larry turns and moves for the stairs. I try to call out or follow, but the world around me goes black. I'm ripped away before his name can leave my lips and thrust back to reality.

3

I OPEN MY EYES AND STARE AT that pink velvet curtain. Pulling it back, I'm struck by the sight of my reflection in the store's three-way mirror.

My eyes are wide and wild, my near-black hair a little mussed, but otherwise, I look like me. Perfectly normal.

I step out of the changing room, my eyes trained on my reflection. I'm still wearing the blue dress, though it's mostly engulfed under the giant black jacket.

Koko appears behind me in the glass. "Okay, I know I said oversized was in, but that might be a bit much." She steps toward a rack of clothing and begins searching through the pieces. "I think I have a brown suede cropped one that might work better. I feel like you have the bone structure to pull off Old Western meets *Little House on the Prairie.*"

"It's fine." I wiggle out of the jacket, needing it off immediately.

I toss it onto the top of the rack, my body breaking out in a full-blown sweat.

What the hell just happened?

I reach out and grab Koko's arm. It's solid and real, and I definitely don't pass through it.

Her eyes widen with surprise and then soften. "Hey, are you okay?"

I don't know. I feel fine, I think.

"I'm just a little hot." I gather my sweat-slicked hair into a ponytail and then drop it when I realize I don't have a spare elastic on my wrist. "I think I better go. Thank you for the dress."

I shove my feet back into my shoes and gather my jeans and blouse in my hands, not bothering to change.

I need to get out of this store.

I need air.

"You should come out with us tonight if your thing ends early," Koko calls after me. "Text me! And good luck!"

I MAKE IT through dinner (and what is in fact a cardboard check ceremony) and when I finally get back home, I go straight to bed with a belly full of pierogies and a head full of questions—none of them answered. When I wake on Saturday morning, it's a little after eight. The sun is streaming through my bedroom window, leaving little square patterns on my blue-and-green-striped bedspread.

I lie there, letting my brain shift from its state of rest to an active consciousness, and as it does, memories of yesterday flood my thoughts.

I still don't know what happened with that jacket. The most obvious explanations just don't seem probable. I don't, as a rule, do drugs. I haven't been diagnosed with any sort of mental health disorder, nor have I experienced any symptoms that make me suspect I may be suffering from one gone undiagnosed. Other than last night, I usually sleep well—at least well enough to rule out sleep deprivation, and as far as I know,

I'm not sick. I lift my palm to my forehead as if to prove that fact to myself. I don't feel warm.

The only thing left is stress.

Or trauma? a little voice inside my head whispers.

Yes, I lost my mom—my only parent—when I was sixteen and then my guardian and only living relative a few years later. I could see how someone might perceive these events as traumatizing, but I've been coping just fine. I'm good.

I probably just need to exercise more—maybe finally start meditating.

Yes, I think. That's it. I'm just more stressed than usual.

I am moving overseas in just over three months to earn a very intensive PhD, which will very much determine my future in a very competitive field. On top of that, a virtual stranger is about to move in with me. It's difficult to share a space with another human, let alone one you've never met. My brain is obviously telling me I need to take better care of myself.

I pad to the kitchen, deciding my first step in taking care of my mental health is to have a nice, hot cup of coffee. However, as I open the red-and-black canister, I remember I finished the last of it the day before. I throw on my sweatpants and head to the little doughnut shop on the corner that makes their coffee strong and dark.

As I step out of my apartment onto the tiny landing, I stop.

The hallway outside my front door isn't big. It's about enough for a six-foot man to lie down comfortably and roll over once before falling down the stairs (as per my ex-situationship Lucca on a night he came over drunk and forgot I was out of town at a convention).

There are two doors: mine and my neighbor Harmony's,

and a sizable window, which makes the space seem larger and airier than the floor plan.

What has stopped me this morning is the three large duffel bags and a black guitar case. They are sitting, in a neatly stacked pile, just to the left of my door. On the very top is a note.

I bend down to pick it up. It looks like a lined page torn out of a notebook. The writing is in blue pen and sloppy.

Hey Annalise,

I got in this morning earlier than planned. Didn't want to wake you before nine. I've gone in search of some breakfast. Will be back in a bit. Look forward to meeting you.

—Mackenzie

It had taken me months to admit I needed a roommate. My uncle's life insurance had paid off what remained of the mortgage on the two-bedroom, which, as his sole heir, I inherited fully, but there are still bills to pay and annual property taxes. I could probably have made it work if I'd continued working at the lab. However, my tuition for my doctorate plus all of the expenses of living in Liverpool, UK, for the two years would mean I'd have to sell the place or sublet.

I've lost too much to let go of one of the few places with happy memories, so I put an ad online for a roommate who would live with me for the next three and a half months and then take care of the place for the two years while I'm in Liverpool. After about fifty replies (half of them making me rethink my idea completely), I found Mackenzie—a small-town girl moving to the big city to follow her dream of becoming a musician. We haven't met in person yet, but our email exchanges have been pleasant. She answered my emails promptly, in full, grammatically correct sentences. My light internet stalking turned up no red flags other than she posts a lot of cat pics and plays the tuba. Those reservations were calmed by her near-perfect credit score and confirmation that no cat would be making the move to Toronto.

I'm not one to typically rely on my instincts, but as I set the note down, I can't help but feel proud of mine. Not wanting to wake me up early on a Saturday morning—that's courteous roommate behavior.

I slip back inside my apartment and grab the spare set of keys I had made in anticipation of Mackenzie's arrival before returning to the landing, where I knock softly on Harmony's door. I, too, am a courteous person, but I know for a fact that Harmony is an early bird who gets up for a six A.M. yoga class.

After a few moments, I hear the soft shuffle of feet on hardwood, and the door opens. Harmony is still in her yoga wear: her loose patterned pants and tight black tank top show off a set of toned, tanned arms. Her long gray hair is in a thick braid that reaches past her breasts. Her eyes wrinkle as she smiles at me. "Good morning, Annalise. How are you doing, chickpea?" Her eyes search my face as if they're looking for something.

She started doing this shortly after my uncle passed away, and whatever she is looking for, I don't think she has found it yet.

Harmony and my Uncle Larry were close. I put her in her early fifties, a few years older than my uncle. I had wondered if they'd ever been more than just friends before deciding that it's best left as a mystery.

I hold out Mackenzie's keys. "I was hoping I could ask you a favor." I lean to the side so she can see the baggage behind me. "My new roommate is moving in today. I'm going to run out and grab some coffee, but if she gets back before I do, can I leave her keys with you so she isn't stuck waiting in the hallway?"

Harmony nods. "Of course. That's not a problem at all, but while you're here—" She turns and heads toward the kitchen, disappearing from my view for a few seconds. When she returns, she has a plate of something in her hands.

"I know you haven't felt like eating much lately," she says. "But I baked my famous cookies fresh this morning." She holds out a plate and winks. "It's a special recipe. You'd be amazed how the rosemary enhances the flavor of the lime. I'm not sure what your new friend is into, but consider this my housewarming gift."

I stare down at the light brown mounds flecked with specks of dark green. "You know what . . . I think Mackenzie might have mentioned a rosemary allergy." I wince at the terrible lie. "It's probably better if I don't, just in case it's aggravated by . . . um . . . air particles." I take a step back. "It's really too bad. These look . . . like they were a lot of work."

I drop the keys on the bookshelf and retreat into the hall before she can protest.

Harmony loves to bake. However, her passion is not always matched by her skills. Her unusual flavor combinations have an equal probability of becoming my new favorite treat as they do of leaving an unpleasant aftertaste that lingers for days.

Harmony follows me onto the landing, the plate still in

her hands. "Well, that's just too bad. I'll have to run them downstairs to Koko in a bit, then." She pauses momentarily, holding her breath as if deciding upon her next words. "I'm happy to see you've taken on a roommate, Annalise. It would have made Larry so pleased to see."

Her eyes fill. My stomach clenches.

Sometimes, it's as if my body has forgotten about Larry's death. Unlike my brain, it has returned to walking around as if nothing terrible happened.

But in this moment, it all comes rushing back.

"Yeah. Cool. Thanks for doing this." I sprint down the steep steps as quickly as I dare, through the door, and onto the sidewalk. I don't want to hold her grief right now. I don't even want to hold my own.

I walk the three blocks to Nana's Old Fashioned Doughnuts, a small, local chain that makes the best doughnuts I have ever eaten and a very strong Americano. I order, take a very long sip, and feel pretty much back to normal by the time I step out onto the sidewalk and begin my walk home.

I pass The Bagel Stop on my way. There is a very cute guy, with dark blond hair, eating at one of the metal cafe tables out front. He looks up as I approach and smiles. I actually smile back, which is a step up from my usual move of flushing red, breaking eye contact, and sweating.

My dating life has been more of a theoretical concept than anything else since Larry's death. Other than the three months last winter with Lucca—who was more of a friends with benefits with mixed signals (his heart was all in and mine was barely functioning)—I just haven't felt the desire to look at anyone twice, yet I find myself glancing over my shoulder, pleasantly surprised when those left-for-dead stomach butterflies stretch their fluttery wings as I catch him watching me back.

It's shaping up to be a nice little Saturday.

That is, until I stop at the light to cross and something falls from the sky above and lands on my head with an audible splat.

My hands instinctively reach for my hair before I work out what has happened.

Crap.

Bird crap, to be exact.

I gaze up and spot the offending pigeon perched on the window ledge above me.

"You have got to be kidding me." My fingers come away white and sticky.

The pigeon coos. It sounds a little like a laugh before it flies off toward another building.

When I was an undergrad, I had a professor who claimed getting shat on by a bird was a sign that good fortune was headed your way.

I, however, have never been a believer in luck. Sometimes things just happen. Birds shit. Healthy cells mutate. Bad drivers make poor left-hand turns.

After my mom died, there was a period where I thought the answer to these problems was to mitigate risk—take public transport and eat more leafy greens.

But if Larry's diagnosis taught me anything, I've learned that it's impossible to prepare for everything. Even if you carry around an umbrella everywhere, it won't prevent you from stepping in dog shit.

By the time I walk back to my building I am very much in need of a shower, so I am relieved when I climb the stairs and find Mackenzie's bags still stacked in the hallway, my note intact on top.

I shed my clothes on the way to my bedroom, throw them

in my hamper, and wrap my naked body in a clean towel before exiting to the living room, off of which is the door to the apartment's one and only bathroom.

Twenty minutes later, I emerge in a puff of mango-scented steam, the cooler air from the living room sending a rush of goose bumps up my arms.

The feeling is replaced very quickly by a sickening stab of fear.

Because there is a man in my apartment.

Sitting on my couch—eating cookies.

4

YEARS AGO, I WROTE A PAPER ON the human brain's instinctive patterns when faced with an emergency situation. Despite evolutionary advancements, when faced with danger, the human brain recesses to its primitive, mammalian roots and defaults to one of two behaviors. It either shifts into fight-mode and finds a way to battle the perceived threat, or it flees.

I have often wondered which of my instincts would kick in if faced with a bona fide threat.

Turns out, the answer is flight—it's not even a contest.

I don't even look for a weapon as I sprint at full speed toward my bedroom and slam the door behind me.

The moment I'm inside, I drop my towel and reach for the lock, only realizing as my hand closes over the cool metal handle that there is no lock—there has never been one.

Barricade.

I look at my IKEA desk, wondering how much of a fight the particleboard would put up against a man his size.

He was sitting, but he looked big.

He felt big.

My defense plan is interrupted by a soft knock on the door and the sound of a male voice.

"Annalise?" it says. "I'm so sorry I scared you. I did call out when I let myself in."

I reach down for the towel at my feet, pulling it around my naked body as if the flimsy cotton will offer some sort of protection.

"I'm calling the police," I lie, my eyes darting around the room, looking for my phone, which I realize in a moment of sickening clarity is still in the purse I left hanging by my front door.

"They hang out at the doughnut shop down the street. They will be here in minutes," I hedge, hoping I sound convincing.

"Don't do that." His voice has lost the calm of a moment ago. "I think there's been some mistake? I'm Mackenzie Smith. I'm supposed to be moving in here today. Your neighbor gave me a key."

Harmony? No. Why would she . . .

"You are not Mackenzie Smith," I tell him, getting back to the facts. "Mackenzie Smith is a woman. She is from West Lake and loves cats and plays the tuba."

There's a beat of silence. It's followed by a very soft *ahhhhh.*

"I *am* Mackenzie Smith," he says. "I swear it. I'm more of a dog guy, but cats are fine, and I think I know what might have happened here. Can I ask . . . did you google me? Or her, I guess? Is that how you know about the tuba?"

My cheeks heat. "I wasn't going to just let some random stranger move in here without knowing a few things about them first, and I don't need to explain anything to you because you are not Mackenzie Smith, and I need you to leave my apartment immediately."

There is a long moment of complete silence. I crane my neck, listening for footsteps or handle jiggling—any sort of clue about what is happening on the other side of the door. Finally, there's a quiet groan to the floorboards as if he's shifting his weight, then a pop, like a knee or hip being cracked, and then the sound of something being slid along the floor.

I look down and see a small plastic driver's license being pushed through the space under my door.

I pick it up.

My eyes immediately shoot to the name, which does, in fact, say *Mackenzie Smith.* They move to the picture. It's a black-and-white of the same man who was sitting at The Bagel Stop and then on my couch.

Now that my adrenaline has returned to adequate levels, I can study his face: the sharp, square jaw, the slightly curled dark blond hair, and the eyes that, even with the grayscale tone of the photo, I can tell are a beautiful light blue.

"I think I might know what happened," he says again, startling me so much that I drop the ID. "It's not the first time we've been mixed up," he continues. "She's a few years younger than me. Our town is pretty small, so we solved the issue by going by Mac and Kenzie. I can assure you I'm the Mackenzie Smith you've been emailing for the last month. I answered your ad online. I moved here because I got a job, playing in a band."

I try to think back to our emails. Without my phone, I can only go by memory. We had several back and forth. They were mostly transactional. There were a few get-to-know-you questions, but I don't know if I ever specifically asked Mackenzie their gender. I guess from the start, I just pictured a lanky brunette in my head.

"Wait." I suddenly recall the evidence I've been looking for. "I asked you if you played your tuba regularly." I recall the email clearly. "And you wrote back, *just a normal amount.* Why would you say that if you don't play the tuba?"

There's a notable pause before he answers. "Um . . . I thought that was a metaphor."

"A metaphor for what?"

It clicks the moment the words leave my lips.

"Oh, god."

My back presses against the door, and I slowly melt to the floor in a mortified heap.

His laughter becomes audible through the wood.

"It's not funny," I say to the door.

"It's pretty funny," he answers. His laughter begins to fade.

"Listen," he finally says. "I am sorry if I didn't clarify. I didn't realize . . . I can try to find another place if you're not comfortable living with a man, but if there's any way you'd let me stay for a bit—even the night—I'd really appreciate it. I don't know too many people in the city. I definitely don't know anyone well enough to crash on a couch, but I'm sure I can work something out."

My brain works through the ramifications of what he's proposing.

I don't really want to look for a new roommate, and I'm only here for three and a half more months. Larry and I had no issues living together and he was a man, although he was family.

"You're not like a sex pervert or anything, right?"

His laugh returns. "I promise you, I'm not, but if you're worried, I can give you a few names of some female friends. I could probably even get the other Mackenzie's phone number for you. She'd vouch that I'm a good guy."

"Okay." I pull myself back to a standing position. "Give me a few minutes."

I emerge from my room two minutes later, as promised, with wet hair and in a pair of jeans. Mackenzie is back on the couch, the plate of Harmony's cookies sits in his lap, and he freezes with a half-eaten cookie en route to his mouth.

"Your neighbor also gave me these," he says, setting the plate on the coffee table. "She said you'd tell me about them. I wasn't sold on the flavor combo initially, especially when she asked if I carried an Epipen, but they're surprisingly good."

I take a seat in the chair across from him and reach for a cookie. I could get used to a roommate who doesn't mind being the guinea pig for Harmony's baking. That was always Larry's job. He'd eat anything that showed up on our doorstep and tell me which ones were safe for consumption.

I take a bite, and the wild combination of acid and herb has me closing my eyes in a concerted effort not to moan in appreciation.

When I open them again, it's to the sight of Mackenzie watching me.

"Good, right?" he asks

My mouth is full, so I nod.

"Harmony is a really wonderful person, but the thing with her baking is that as much as it goes very right sometimes, it can also go very wrong. She once made a flan from SpaghettiOs that still gives me nightmares."

Mackenzie coughs a little, then pats himself on the chest and swallows.

His smile settles into a firm but friendly line. "So you're sure you're okay with me staying?"

I consider my decision one last time, knowing this is my one chance to get out before feeling like an asshole.

"I am, but we should probably have a bathroom schedule," I tell him. "And a few house rules, like always wear pants on the couch."

Mackenzie nods. "I can do that."

"Also, no drugs."

Mackenzie continues to nod. "No problem."

"And just so you know, I would have made that rule for the other Mackenzie, too," I clarify. "Also, I don't drink. But you are welcome to."

We stare awkwardly at each other for a full minute before he wipes his hands on his pants and then stands. "I guess I should probably start unpacking, then."

I follow him to my feet. "That's your room." I point at the door behind the couch. "It's got a bed and a dresser like we discussed. Let me know if there is anything you need."

He heads to his room, and I retreat to mine.

Once I'm safely behind the closed door, I collapse on my bed and stare up at the popcorn ceiling.

I usually spend my weekends on my couch and then treat myself to pad Thai from Sukho Thai or lo mein from C'est Bon. Occasionally, I go for a walk or run a few errands, but my time outside of the research lab is pretty low-key.

My two best friends, Magda and Gopi, no longer live in the city. We met a few years ago during our first semester at the University of Toronto. Our friendship was not forged in the traditional undergraduate ways of our peers—picking out outfits to wear to keg parties and sharing secrets on late-night poutine runs—but through a love of marathon library study sessions and our shared desire to carve out a future career in neuroscience. However, after graduation, Magda moved back home to Poland, where, like me, she works in a research lab, and Gopi went straight from U of T to Boston University, where she completed her master's and is now pursuing a PhD. Our friendship is kept up through the occasional call or message in our group chat, usually with a link to an article on the newest neuroscience breakthrough, but for the past four years, since graduation, there's been a notable gap in my social calendar.

I know I should try to fill it. Uncle Larry was always encouraging me to go out. "Humans are social creatures," he'd prod me as I lay wrapped up like a fleece burrito on the couch. "Not everyone you hang out with needs a science degree, Beans. Some of my best friends came into my life when I least expected it. The universe has a knack for pushing the right people our way when we need them. You just have to be open to it." Not only had my uncle failed to realize that he was wrong—shared mental models are a key predictor of strong friendships, as they ensure smoother communication and a greater mutual understanding—but he also discounted the fact that although he was an extreme extrovert with a knack for striking up conversations, I am an indoor cat. I don't want to join a salsa club or play recreational beach volleyball. The thought of walking into a bar by myself makes me want to shrivel up like a raisin.

I have resigned myself to the idea that the way I forge friendships is with like-minded people in forced proximity. Therefore, I just need to sit tight, wait until I move to Liverpool in January, and spend forty hours a week with a carefully curated group of individuals who also get excited about genomics.

A phone rings from somewhere in the living room. Mackenzie promptly answers it with a "Hey, man" followed by a "Yeah, things are great." Then I lose the plot of the rest of the conversation as his voice gets muffled and quiet, and I assume he's taking the rest of the call in his bedroom.

It's in this moment that I realize the mistake I've made in letting Mackenzie Smith stay.

When I had secretly stalked the other Mackenzie, I liked

that she had seemed quiet and kind of a homebody. She didn't have a ton of posts with friends. She was really into her cat. I couldn't imagine her judging me when she came home to find me passed out on the couch on top of a bag of All Dressed chips.

The Mackenzie Smith who is currently occupying my apartment clearly has friends. He just got here and already his phone is ringing. Not only that, he's in a band. And I get the strong sense it's not the orchestra type of band I had imagined for tuba-playing Mackenzie. Judging by the guitar case in the hallway, it's probably a rock band, which tracks, as Mackenzie Smith is hot. He's got that rumpled, rock band musician with puppy dog eyes look. Like he's just rolled out of bed making you wonder what he's like in bed.

Oh, god, it's been less than fifteen minutes, and I'm already thinking about him having sex.

Oh, god, we are going to live together for the next three and a half months—he probably will have sex.

Under my roof.

My roof with its very thin walls.

I make a mental note to buy more earplugs.

I flop back onto my bed and stare up at the ceiling, calming myself by remembering why I made the very logical decision to let Mackenzie stay. A roommate is not something I should be panicking about. A roommate can be managed with rules and boundaries and open lines of communication—then, if needed, gentle reminders on color-coordinated Post-it notes.

Panicking should be reserved for bigger problems.

Like the state of mental healthcare.

Or climate change.

Or maybe what happened in Koko's store yesterday.

My body breaks out in a full-blown sweat.

I roll out of bed and head back out to the living room, determined to find a logical explanation for yesterday's events.

Mackenzie isn't in his bedroom. His door is wide open, and a pink Post-it note is stuck to the back of my apartment door.

Heading out to run a few errands. Feel free to text me if you need anything
—Mac

His number is scrawled at the bottom.

I take the note, shove it into my pocket, then grab my purse and head downstairs.

The clothes racks are already out on the sidewalk when I get to Koko's store.

Koko herself is sitting behind the counter with her head in her hands and a very large coffee in front of her.

"Hey," I say softly, and she looks up.

"Lise, hey." She slumps onto the counter dramatically. "I am hanging on by a very thin thread this morning. Last night was a good time. It's too bad you couldn't make it."

I feel the tiniest pang of guilt that I forgot to text her and confirm that I wasn't coming.

"Thanks again for that dress. It was perfect." I move toward the rack near the changing room, not entirely sure of where I left the jacket when I made my quick exit.

It's not on the rack by the mirror. Or the two other racks next to it. I check the changing room just in case, but it's empty.

"Hey Koko."

She opens her eyes but doesn't lift her head.

"That jacket you had me try on yesterday, the leather one. Do you know where it went?"

She closes her eyes and lets out a long breath through her nose. "If it's not on those racks, then I probably sold it."

My heart sinks. "Do you remember who bought it?"

Koko lifts her head, her fingers grope for the paper cup, and she proceeds to drink several gulps of her coffee at an awkward angle I wouldn't have thought possible.

"Might have been the guy who came in earlier. The burrito I had after the bar last night was making a morning appearance, so I was in the bathroom. He had cash, so I told him to tally it up on his own. You know, the honor system. I'm not sure what he ended up taking."

I scan the store one last time but find nothing resembling the jacket. "Okay, well, thanks anyway."

I push open the door to leave and notice that Koko is still slumped in the same position.

"Are you sure you're going to be okay?" I ask her.

She lifts an arm to wave me off. "I'll be fine. Eventually, I'll summon the energy to make my way to the bagel place. As soon as I get some carbs in my belly, I'll be right as rain."

I take her word for it and step back out onto the street. However, when I get to my door, I hesitate.

No matter what caused that hallucination with the jacket yesterday, it was a reminder of Uncle Larry. That whole scene was a metaphor for the kind of guy he was: a man who'd give you the literal jacket off his back. He was the best kind of human.

With a clear picture of him in my head, I reverse directions and head to the other end of the block. I enter The Bagel

Stop and purchase a poppy seed bagel with extra cream cheese and another egregiously large coffee.

When I return, Koko is exactly where I left her.

"Hey," I say quietly, holding out the bag and coffee.

She opens her eyes, then immediately sits up. "You sweet baby angel girl. I'd kiss you right now if you were into it and my breath didn't smell like haddock."

I set the bagel and coffee on the counter. "Well . . . hopefully this gets you back on your feet."

She opens the wrapper, takes a huge bite, and moans.

I leave her to her breakfast and head back upstairs, a little bud of warmth blooming in my chest.

WHEN I RETURN to the apartment, Mackenzie is back. I walk by his bedroom, the door partially open, and catch a glance of him attempting to put a fitted sheet on his mattress. Every time he gets a corner on, the opposite pops off.

I consider asking if he needs help, the rush of my earlier good deed still fresh in my brain, but when Mackenzie looks up, and our eyes connect, I flush, panic, and instead walk quickly to the kitchen to get a glass of water that I don't need.

The rest of the day is a little like that: him setting up his space, me getting used to sharing mine. We run into each other as he's coming out of the bathroom. We both reach for the refrigerator door at the same time, bumping hands. It's not a cute, romantic comedy bump either, but a clash that splays my fingers with his knuckles and leaves me shaking out my stinging hand.

I start to notice things about him—little mannerisms that infringe on my personal space. He sings constantly. His voice is actually quite nice, and the volume is just a hint above a whisper, but he repeats the same parts of a song over and over as if he's fine-tuning his voice.

He also smells—not bad. It's a faint trace of aftershave or maybe deodorant. He'll walk by, and I'll catch a whiff, and every time it happens, I give the smell a different name: Thunder Rush or Iron Rebellion.

He grunts when he lifts things. There's one piece of hair that constantly gets in his eyes. His T-shirt looks too small around his biceps.

I know that my annoyance is my brain's reaction to the disruption in its predictive coding system. It's used to being quiet and alone, and all of this new information it's having to process is causing it to work harder, and it's not really into that.

There's also a tiny part of me that wonders if I've made a mistake, if I should have sent Mackenzie Smith on his way, the moment I realized the mix-up. Am I going to be regretting that split-second decision for the next few months?

My stomach begins to growl around six o'clock. On a normal Saturday, I'd be ordering Thai food right about now. I finally retrieve my phone from my purse and scroll through the menu I know by heart when it occurs to me that proper protocol might be to ask Mackenzie if he's hungry.

But what if he is?

What if I order extra tonight and then next weekend he returns the favor? But he orders from the gross place two blocks down instead of the good place three blocks up?

What if he orders generic chain pizza?

I don't know if I'm ready for a food-sharing relationship. I don't know if I'm ready for a roommate. Maybe I'll just order and eat in my room, and then—

"Annalise."

It takes me a moment to realize he's called my name. The way he's staring at me, I don't think that was the first attempt to get my attention.

He's paused with the fridge half open.

"I was going to order dinner. I don't have much in the fridge yet. Is there anywhere in particular you'd recommend, and are you hungry?"

My panic from a moment ago suddenly seems a little overblown.

"Sukho Thai. It's the best spot around. I recommend the shrimp khao soi."

He nods, "Sounds great. Is that what you'd like?"

I hold up my phone. "I can order for us. They sort of know me there."

He smiles. "Even better." Then he reaches into his back pocket and pulls out cash, tossing it onto the counter. "I'm moving all my bank stuff to one down here, so I've got cash until I get myself sorted."

I nod. How was this all so simple?

Our food arrives thirty-five minutes later. I eat mine on the couch. He leaves his plate on the kitchen counter, stealing bites as he moves around the apartment, as if he is getting ready to go out somewhere.

When he finally sits down next to me, most of his food is already eaten.

"Not sure what you're up to tonight." He spears a shrimp with his fork. "I've got my first gig with the new band. We've got a practice in an hour, but then we're playing the Gladstone at ten if you want to come and watch."

I almost tell him that I have a standing date with my couch but stop myself. "Do you think you'll be playing a lot of weekends?"

He nods and swallows his food. "We're pretty booked up, I think. Gigs Thursday through Sunday with the occasional Tuesday or Wednesday. I'll be gone most nights and home pretty late. I hope that's not a problem."

It's not a problem at all. He'll be out playing. I'll have my TV all to myself.

"That sounds great," I tell him. "Thanks for the invite, but I'm probably going to stay in. It's been kind of a long week."

He gets to his feet, his plate now empty, then reaches for my empty one on the coffee table. "You done?"

I nod. "Yeah."

He returns them to the kitchen, where he promptly washes them in the sink.

I take back all my earlier negative thoughts.

He disappears into his bedroom and emerges a moment later with his guitar case in hand.

"I was wondering how you'd manage with a tuba on the subway." I nod at his case, and he laughs.

"It gets pretty cold at night," I tell him, eyeing the T-shirt, which I've now decided isn't too tight but simply fitted. "You might want to take a sweater."

He sets his case down next to the door and disappears into his room again.

When he emerges for the second time, he's not in his T-shirt.

He's not wearing a sweater, either.

Goose bumps cover my body from toes to fingers as I realize what he has put on.

It's a black leather jacket.

5

CAUSES OF TEMPORARY HALLUCINATIONS.

I type the search into Dr. Google, which spits back a long list of possibilities. None of them are reassuring.

Drugs and Alcohol. Nope.

Lack of sleep. I sleep well enough—thank you, magnesium. Besides, my hallucination happened after a full night of rest.

Extreme hunger. I stare at the now empty plate of Harmony's cookies I've been stress eating. Not my issue. Never my issue.

Urinary tract infections. Huh . . . who knew?

I let my phone drop between the couch cushions in frustration. None of these options explain why a jacket triggers my memories. Nor does it narrow the odds that the exact same jacket is now wandering around Toronto on the back of my new roommate.

Maybe it's not the same one?

It's a black leather biker jacket. There must be thousands of them in the city. I can't say for certain it was the same one I tried on at Koko's. My memories from yesterday are fuzzy, and I was so shocked I didn't really get a good look at Mackenzie's jacket on his way out the door.

This could be a classic case of the Baader-Meinhof phenomenon. My brain is simply paying more attention to Mackenzie's jacket because of yesterday's changing room incident. I bet I've seen a dozen people walking around Toronto in similar jackets this week; I just didn't take notice.

This theory begins to calm my nerves. God, I love science: providing very logical explanations as soon as you sort through the facts.

I sink into my couch and flick on the television, feeling my tension ease as I search for something to watch.

When I started my job in the lab at CAMH: Toronto's Center for Addiction and Mental Health, they sat us down on the very first day and told us that in order to be successful in our jobs we each needed an outlet to help us de-stress. Although lab work isn't quite as hands-on as the medical or counseling positions, the subject matter can get heavy at times. The orientation leader posted a list of suggested activities, from tae kwon do classes to pottery throwing. Each option made my introverted stomach churn until the woman sitting next to me raised her hand and asked, "Can watching TV count?" And the leader smiled and replied, "Absolutely."

So TV has become my go-to coping mechanism when it comes to stress relief. My preferences lean toward unrealistic holiday rom-coms where all of the world's problems can be solved with a cup of candy cane hot chocolate, but on occasion I'll swing in the complete opposite direction and turn on an overdramatized crime show with well-timed melodramatic soundtracks and effortless forensic pathology.

Tonight, I'm feeling murder more than meet-cutes, so I settle on the first episode of *Mindhunter.*

Manson, Kemper, Rissell. The episodes blur together with a glamorized take on behavioral science sexed up for television.

I fall asleep somewhere between the fourth and fifth episodes.

I AWAKEN AGAIN sometime later. A siren blaring from the street below startles me back to consciousness.

I'm on my couch. I am somehow covered in a blanket. *Did I get up and grab it?* The TV is off. *Did I turn it off?*

I reach between the cushions for my phone. The time reads just after six in the morning.

Now fully conscious, I feel the lumpiness of the couch on my outstretched body and long for the cozy, soft mattress of my bed. On my third attempt, I will myself up and back to my room, where I tunnel under the covers like a hibernating hedgehog.

Despite wanting to, I can't fall back asleep. I try counting back from one thousand, then clearing my mind completely, but all I do is toss and turn.

I used to have trouble sleeping when I was a kid. It was usually timed to the beginning of one of my mom's relationships. She'd start dating someone new and become obsessed. It would be *Chris. Chris. Chris.* Or *Wayne. Wayne. Wayne* for weeks on end. Although she'd physically still be there, sleeping in the bedroom across the hall, it would feel like she had disappeared, and my anxious brain would worry all night that I'd never get her back.

My mom loved to fall in love. "Best drug you'll ever try, kiddo," she'd tell me. She'd describe it as a rush. A lovesick high only to follow with the low that would inevitably come when things didn't work out.

I started sleeping normally again by my teen years as my prefrontal cortex developed further, and I depended less on my mom to fill my days as I became busy with school and studying. However, my sleepless nights returned with a vengeance after she died and I moved in with Larry.

Unlike my mother, Larry always seemed to sense when I couldn't sleep. I wouldn't even have to tell him. He'd just take one look at my face and put a pot on the stove. He'd melt real chocolate into milk and make the richest, most luxurious hot chocolate.

"The secret to good hot chocolate is that you need to heat the milk slowly," he'd say. "Don't cheap out on the chocolate, and add a pinch of salt." I'd roll my eyes, and he'd cross his arms. "Someone needs to carry on my legacy," he'd tease. "This is a secret recipe. When I'm an old man living in your spare bedroom, Beans, I'll expect you to be able to make it for me when I forget how."

He'd wink like it was all a big joke, but I liked that image. Old man Larry living in my spare bedroom. What I wouldn't give to see that now.

Eventually, I give up on sleep completely and climb out of bed to head to the kitchen. There is a half bar of random dark chocolate in my cupboard, so I make my cup of hot chocolate just like he showed me. I know I follow all the steps correctly—even the salt—but it doesn't taste quite right.

I return to the couch and the discarded blanket I abandoned. Picking it up, I fold it and place it back in its spot on the back of the couch, and as I do, I notice the door to Mackenzie's room is half open.

It's probably because the apartment gets hot at night, but there's a nice breeze that comes off the lake through the window. I often do the same thing.

I know I shouldn't, but I find myself gazing into his space.

I can see his things. His chair. His bed. Even the outline of his sleeping body under his sheet.

All of a sudden it's all too intimate. I'm about to turn away, but something catches my eye.

The jacket.

It's tossed over the back of his chair, next to his discarded jeans. It's just an arm's reach from the doorframe. I could lean in and grab it without setting foot in his room—technically.

And that would be totally and completely creepy, Annalise, I chastise myself. *Not to mention an invasion of his privacy.*

If the roles were reversed and I woke up to his upper torso in my space, I'd throw him out. It would be unforgivable.

My rational brain knows what I'm thinking is so wrong on so many levels, but I begin to walk toward his room as if the jacket itself is a siren, calling to me, luring me toward rocky shores.

I linger just outside his door. I am so close that I can now hear the soft and even rise and fall of his breath. In and out. In and out.

He is very much asleep.

I reach out my hand. My fingers stroke the soft leather.

Then it feels like a jolt goes up my arm. A tiny spark. As if I've touched something forbidden.

I listen again. His breath is the same.

I hold mine as I lean forward and slowly slip the jacket from the chair.

My heart is pounding like a jackhammer as I stand, still in my pajamas, right outside his bedroom, and slip the jacket on.

It stops completely as everything around me, once again, goes black.

6

I'M NOT ON THE SUBWAY THIS TIME.

There's grass under my feet and a soft breeze. It's warm and so sunny that I need to lift my hand to block out the rays so I can see what is going on.

I am surrounded by people—lots of people. It appears to be a festival of some sort. A big stage is set up in the distance, and a band is playing some folky rock song I don't know. A few people are gathered at the base of the stage, but for the most part, people are lounging on blankets or lawn chairs.

It's less Coachella and more of a small-town country festival.

I look around, frantically searching for anyone or anything familiar. There's a street with shops that I don't know, and a large body of water in the distance that could be an ocean or maybe one of the great lakes.

The festivalgoers are a mix of families, elderly, and a few people my age. I get a sinking feeling and realize that I was hoping to see a glimpse of Larry again, but I don't see him anywhere.

"These guys aren't bad," says a guy a few feet to the left of me. He's sitting in a lawn chair, his feet outstretched in front of him, an open beer in one hand and a nose covered in a layer of white zinc.

"They aren't good, either," says his friend, leaning over to grab his own beer from a little red cooler. As he does, his fisherman's hat slips off and falls to the grass. His long red hair catches in the sunlight, and I realize I do recognize him. It's the busker from the subway.

"Hey," I call out, stepping toward them. Neither turn. It's as if they don't hear me. Sure enough, when I reach out to shake the man's shoulder, my hand passes right through as if I were a ghost.

"I'm definitely not dead," I tell myself.

But I'm also not dreaming. At least, it doesn't feel like a dream. I feel like me. I have complete agency over my whole body, and everything around me seems so . . . normal.

Except maybe for the watermelons. There's a disproportionate amount of watermelon-related paraphernalia. Watermelon tablecloths. Watermelon decorations. There's even a group of elderly women in watermelon-themed clothing dancing next to the stage.

I'm distracted by the busker standing. He shoves his hands into his ripped khaki cargo shorts and nods along with the band onstage. "For such a shitty band their drummer is decent. More than decent."

As if to illustrate that point, the drummer bangs out a rhythmic solo that has the crowd cheering.

The song ends with a final clash of the cymbals. The crowd claps and whoops loudly. The lead singer calls out a "thank you, everybody" before waving to the crowd and running offstage.

"I'm going to go talk to him." The redheaded busker turns to his friend, who shrugs before leaning back in his seat.

"I'll be back in a bit."

He reaches down toward the cooler and rummages through a bag next to it. When he stands, he's holding a black jacket—Mackenzie's jacket? Or Larry's? He reaches into the pocket and pulls out a pack of cigarettes. He removes one from the pack, then tosses the rest along with the jacket into his now vacant seat.

I want to stay and examine the jacket more closely, but the busker is walking away through the crowd, which has dispersed some since the band walked offstage. I give up and follow him toward a crop of white tents, next to which there is a small carnival with a temporary Tilt-A-Whirl, and a giant slide you ride down on in potato sacks. I can smell French fries and hear the collective cries of happy children. It's so vivid and real and yet I know that it's very much not.

"Hey, man," the busker says to a guy in a black T-shirt and jeans who is smoking next to a black amp with a guitar case on top. He looks like the singer from the band.

"I'm looking to talk to your drummer. Is he around?"

The singer shakes his head. "He had to head back to work."

The busker looks around. His eyes settle on a small blue tent with a table underneath that has a sign that reads ROYAL CANADIAN LEGION, 50/50 DRAW. He jogs over to the table, speaks with one of the men behind it. The man hands the busker a pen, then tears off a piece of the white paper plate in front of him. The busker scrawls something down on it, hands the pen back to the man, and jogs back over to the singer and hands him the piece of paper plate.

"Would you mind giving this to him and asking him to call me? I'd really appreciate it."

The singer eyes the torn piece of plate, the grease stain above the phone number clearly visible.

He takes it and nods, then opens his mouth as if he's about to say something, but before he does I'm sucked right back out and plopped down in the middle of my living room.

"What was that?" I say aloud, momentarily forgetting about Mackenzie sleeping just an open door away.

Hallucinating about my uncle in the subway at least feels logical. I miss him. I think constantly about how I wished we had more time.

But hallucinating about some random band in some random field with people I've never met before—that makes no sense.

What if I'm sick?

My brain pivots to that horrible thought.

That's two episodes now. It's not a fluke.

What if it's a brain tumor?

I should get an MRI.

Yes, that's exactly what I need. Proof that something is or isn't going on inside my head.

My panic is temporarily halted by the sound of a creaking mattress.

Shit.

I had almost forgotten that on top of my possible brain trauma, I've stolen my brand-new roommate's clothing from his room.

I freeze and listen, trying to decipher the sounds. Is he awake?

Slowly, I slip the jacket from my shoulders; the entire time my eyes are fixed on the single corner of his mattress visible from where I'm standing.

I step toward his open door.

The floorboards beneath my feet creak.

Then I hear a single grunt, then more sheet shuffling.

Shit shit shit. In a panic I fling the jacket over the back of the couch and then sprint tiptoe, as quietly as I can, to the kitchen, my heart beating so loudly in my ears that I almost don't hear him behind me when he yawns and pads into the kitchen with a sleepy-sounding "Morning."

I busy myself with the tin of Folgers. "Morning," I return the greeting but can't yet bring myself to turn. Instead, I stare at the empty canister I have yet to replace until enough time passes that I am left with no other choice than to turn around and face him.

He's sitting at the counter, a red bowl in front of him and a yellow box of cereal opened beside him.

"Corn Pops?" he offers, tipping the box toward me when he catches me eyeing it.

He does not look distressed.

Not at all like a man who has caught his roommate trying on his stolen clothes in the middle of the living room.

"Good first night?" I manage to speak and shake my head to decline the cereal.

He nods, his mouth clearly full, and he promptly chews before answering. "The bed is really comfortable. It just took me a little while to get used to the city sounds."

I nod sympathetically, although as a born and raised Toronto girl I've never had this problem. "I can sleep anywhere," I tell him. "My brain has learned to filter out the noise."

He nods at the couch. "Yeah, I noticed."

My mouth goes dry. A memory surfaces from the night before. The sound of someone coming home. A blanket being placed on top of me.

"What are you up to this morning?" I ask, desperately needing a new topic of conversation.

He leans back and stretches his arms out with another grunted yawn. His white T-shirt rides up. It's just an inch, but my eyes immediately fall on the strip of tanned skin.

He clears his throat. My eyes snap up, and my cheeks grow hot as I realize I've been openly gawking.

"Want coffee?" I hold up the canister as if presenting evidence that it was coffee that occupied my thoughts just now.

Mackenzie gets to his feet. "Yeah. I'd love some, but do you mind if I watch how you make it? I don't want to screw it up when it's my turn."

He reaches me just as my brain clues in to the problem. We stare down at the empty canister together.

"Do you have any more?" Mackenzie looks up, puzzled.

I turn around quickly, using the need to find the lid as an excuse to hide what I'm sure are two cheeks now fully on fire. *What the hell is wrong with me this morning?* It's as if my brain is functioning at 40 percent.

"Sorry." I whip back around. "What I meant is, do you want to *go* for coffee? There's a good spot at the end of the block. We could get to know each other better . . . as roommates."

Mackenzie nods and laughs as if the misunderstanding is entirely on him.

"Yeah, sure. Sounds good," he says. "Let me just throw on my jeans. Give me two minutes?"

I nod, and he disappears into his room. I follow suit and change into a pair of jeans and a T-shirt and grab my U of T hoodie in case it gets cold. I beat him back into the living room but only by a few seconds.

He emerges wearing a pair of loose jeans and a dark gray crew T-shirt. Like yesterday, it clings to his arms. And like yesterday, I don't know how I feel about it.

We walk toward the front door, our hands bumping awkwardly as we both reach for the handle at the same time.

"After you—"

"Sorry, I—"

He takes a step back. "Actually I'm going to grab a jacket." He runs back into his bedroom. I stand at the door, my heart hammering so hard that I decide to put my hoodie on because I'm convinced he will be able to see my chest pulsate beneath my shirt.

He pops his head out of his room a few moments later, looking around the living room, a confused ridge forming between his eyebrows.

"Ah, there." He steps back out as he spots the jacket, hanging off the back of the couch. "Sorry about that," he says as he pulls it on. "I swear I'm usually pretty neat."

I watch him and wait.

But nothing happens.

He doesn't get sucked into an alternate reality.

He doesn't even flinch.

"Ready to go?" he asks, but I am too preoccupied with trying to figure out what the hell is going on to answer.

Clearly there's nothing wrong with that jacket. Which means something must be wrong with me.

"Annalise?"

I snap out of my stupor with a shake of my head. "I'm fine," I tell him. "I think I really just need that coffee."

7

"SO YOU'RE A DOCTOR OF NEUROSCIENCE?" Mackenzie reaches out and presses the button for the crosswalk, waiting patiently for the little white stick figure to light up.

It's early on a Sunday morning, which means the traffic on Queen is minimal. I glance both ways to make sure I'm not going to get smoked by a Prius, or the more likely culprit, a cyclist, then cross the street while the light is still red.

Mackenzie runs to catch up, a sheepish smile on his lips.

"I don't have my doctorate yet." My arms swing as I walk, as do Mackenzie's. As we pass a garbage can, he steps toward me to avoid it, which once again causes our hands to hit at an awkward angle, prompting both of us to respond with a very Canadian "sorry."

"I am a research lab tech at CAMH: The Center for Addiction and Mental Health," I explain. "But yes, a doctorate in neuroscience is the end goal."

Mackenzie nods. "So that's what you're studying in January. In Liverpool, right?"

"Yup." I am surprised that he remembers my very first email. In it I explained I had been accepted to a two-year PhD program at the University of Liverpool. I was looking for a roommate to live in my second bedroom from September until January, then, when I moved out, look after the apartment while I was away.

Mackenzie claimed to be the perfect fit. He was going to be new to the city. His job paid enough to get by, especially with a roommate. He wasn't keen on the high-rises of the downtown core or the basement apartments in the Annex. A small walk-up right on a streetcar line was exactly what he was looking for.

I push open the door of Nana's, enjoying the blast of warm, yeasty air. There are a few patrons drinking coffee and eating doughnuts at tables, but no one is in line as I read through the menu board, even though I've already decided what I'm going to order.

"So what's good?" Mackenzie asks, his eyes skimming over the glass case of colorful doughnuts.

"Everything," I say at the same time as the tiny redheaded woman behind the cash register.

She works here every morning. Since Nana's moved into its spot on the corner, she has rung through my coffee order every Saturday and Sunday and sometimes during the week when the Folgers won't cut it. She has never once smiled at me.

It's never bothered me before. A woman should smile only when she feels like it. I'd probably be grumpy, too, waking up every morning at the butt crack of dawn to service lines of customers who can never make up their minds. But this morning, she beams at Mackenzie. Her shoulders press back, her pupils grow big, and her voice rises an entire octave higher than her usual grunt as she says, "But my favorite is the strawberry sunshine."

Mackenzie nods. "Can't argue with that. I'll take one and

a black coffee, please." He turns to me. "What about you? My treat."

I startle at his offer. "Oh . . . okay . . . thanks. Maybe just a coffee? An Americano would be great."

The barista gives me her usual glare but begins to make my coffee order. Her smile only returns as she hands us our drinks, and Mackenzie stuffs a five-dollar bill into her tip jar.

We look around for a place to sit, only now realizing that there is only one available table, which is fine, except there is only one available chair.

Mackenzie sets his coffee and doughnut down and motions for me to take the seat. Scanning the shop, he catches the attention of a guy at the table for two working on his laptop.

"Hey, man, do you mind?" Mackenzie points to the empty chair across from him, and when he realizes the guy is wearing headphones, he makes a motion as if asking if he can take it. The guy pulls out his earbuds, and the two of them proceed to chat for a few moments about something presumably not chair-related until Mackenzie holds out his fist, and the guy bumps it back.

I have never had a fist-bumping relationship with anyone I've just met. In fact, had I been here on my own today, I would have noticed the lack of seating and simply turned around and left. It's almost fascinating to watch not only the way Mackenzie seems almost to welcome an impromptu conversation with a complete stranger but also the way that stranger seems to welcome it right back.

When I was in graduate school, we studied the "halo effect" in my cognitive psychology class. It was a laboratory-based experiment done sometime in the seventies. Its core finding was that humans have an innate cognitive bias toward appealing physical characteristics. In layman's terms, people like hot people.

It was a facet of human behavior that I cataloged and filed away along with the other fascinating facts, but this morning it's as if I am being treated to my own real, live case study right here in this doughnut shop.

There's no question that Mackenzie Smith, by conventional standards, would be considered attractive. He's tall, and the clingy T-shirts he seems to favor make it very obvious he's well muscled. His skin is clear and slightly tanned. His dark blond hair is shiny and thick. He ticks all the boxes biology and evolution and *Vogue* magazine have deemed desirable, and it's fascinating how perfectly symmetrical facial features can have such an effect on complete and total strangers.

I can see it in the two women sipping coffee near the window, the way their eyes follow Mackenzie as he returns to our table, chair in hand, declaring, "Problem solved."

I can see it in the baby being bounced on its tired mother's lap, who keeps catching Mackenzie's eye and cooing.

I start to notice it in me, too. The way I lean in just as he does, resting my forearms on the edge of the table, how I blow on my coffee and sip, perfectly in time with him as if we are opposite reflections in a mirror.

I find my insides warming as he holds my gaze, his lips slipping into a smile that is wide and inviting, making me acutely aware of the tiny dimple in his chin and how his lower lashes are almost as long as the top ones and—

I stop myself just as the tip of my tongue swipes along the edge of my lower lip.

Oh, god, I'm flirting. Sure, it's almost entirely subconscious, but my mirror neuron sensors are firing on all cylinders.

That, on its own, would be awkward enough, seeing as we are meant to be sharing a very small living space for the next few months, but when I sneak a glance his way, I'm mortified to find him . . . wincing?

He sets his cup down and does, in fact, pinch his eyebrows into what would most accurately be described as a wince.

"I think she accidentally added sugar," he says, glancing at his coffee and then the cash register.

All of the blood that drained from my humiliated face just a moment ago returns in a rush.

"Oh." I reach for his cup, needing to do something productive with my hands. "Let me take it back, then."

He shakes his head, clasping both hands around his mug. "It's fine. It was just a bit of a shock, that's all."

I stare at him. "I really don't mind. It will just take a second."

Again, he gives a slight head shake. "All good. I was already in for a sugar rush from the doughnut anyway."

He takes another sip as if unbothered.

Although I am fully aware I am mirroring him again, I take another sip of my perfectly unsweetened Americano.

I can't stand sugar in my coffee. If that were my cup, I'd go back to the counter, politely explain the mix-up, and ask for a new one. But if he seems fine dealing with it, I will just add that piece of info to my small arsenal of Mackenzie Smith facts.

"Um . . ." I hesitate, wondering where to start. "I've never actually done this before."

He raises an eyebrow and grins. "Had coffee?"

"Had a roommate," I correct him. "I'm not really sure what I am supposed to ask you."

He sets his cup down and thinks. "You're actually my first

roommate as well. If you don't count my brother Clive, and I can tell you already you're a significant upgrade based solely on the fact that nothing is living in your fridge and that you have a toilet paper holder installed in your bathroom." He takes a big bite of his doughnut and nods his head approvingly as if he likes it before setting it down, swallowing, and continuing on. "What else is important? Um . . . I'm from West Lake—which you already know. I do *not* play the tuba—which you learned yesterday. I have *two* brothers, actually, and a sister." He grins and then reaches for his doughnut again, but stops right before he bites. "What about you? Big family?"

"Just me, actually," I answer, then take a long sip of my coffee. He doesn't need to know that I never knew my dad, and my mom died in a car accident three days after I turned sixteen. Then, my one and only living relative took me in, only to pass away seven years later from pancreatic cancer, leaving me completely alone.

"So . . ." I change the subject before he can ask a follow-up question. "Were you a musician back in West Lake as well?"

Once I've said it, I realize I've asked him while he is mid-sip. He shakes his head, but I have to wait for him to swallow before I get his answer.

"I was a mechanic," he finally says. "Not your most logical step to a soft rock cover band, so this is all a little new for me. New job. New city. New roommate." He lifts his cup toward me in a cheers-ing motion.

"That's a lot of news." I pick up my cup and knock it with his.

He leans back in his chair. His fingers absentmindedly drum out a beat on the tabletop. "It is, but I have a feeling it's going to work out."

He smiles, and I note that his teeth are both very straight and very white.

"You said you work in a research lab. What do you research?"

I open my mouth to answer his question, but the two women who were looking at him earlier walk by and pause just as they reach our table. The taller of the two seems to be looking for something in her purse, but also keeps sneaking glances at Mackenzie. He, however, either doesn't notice or doesn't care, and his eyes stay fixed on me.

"I am studying substance abuse and its impacts on the brain," I say once the two women move on.

Mackenzie sets his coffee down next to his half-eaten doughnut. "Did you always want to be a neuroscientist?"

I think about his question. "I guess I always enjoyed science but maybe started thinking about it more as a career toward the end of high school."

It was about a year after my mom passed away. Larry had made me see a grief counselor to help me process my emotions. My counselor's name was Hal, and we spent six very long months together working through my "parental grief and resulting depression." For Hal, this meant guiding me to embrace my emotions by lighting candles, taking bubble baths, and going on long walks in nature, where I gave each of my feelings a name. Well, I can understand how this might be an acceptable and even therapeutic method for some people, but it absolutely did not work for me. I begged Larry to let me quit. I pleaded. I argued and even gave him the silent treatment for weeks. Eventually, we compromised. Larry agreed I could ditch Hal if I found someone who better suited my personality. That's how I started working with Dr. Kelly Koppelman. She was a doctor at CAMH in the Family Resource Center, and her approach to working through grief could not have been more different from Hal's. She spoke to me like an adult and explained that during periods of grief, our brain's reward system is disrupted, and dopamine is cut off, which leads to a feeling of numbness. For the first time since my mother's passing, I understood what was happening to my body, how chemical reactions were making me do and feel things I didn't want to do or feel. For the first time I felt like I had control over what was happening to me. The more I read, the better I understood my grief, and in doing so my love for neuroscience was born.

Mackenzie finishes the last bite of his doughnut, then crunches the paper it came on into a ball in his fist. "Do you think you will go back to your job once you finish your doctorate?"

I consider his question. "Maybe. I mean, I'd need to be offered a job first, and I really like CAMH, but I'm not sure . . ." I don't feel pulled to my work right now. It's almost as if the fire that was in me a year ago has gone quiet. "I'm hoping a little time away will help me figure out what I want to do next."

He leans forward, his forehead catching a beam of sunlight streaming through the front window. "Well, I guess then cheers to new beginnings for both of us."

He lifts his cup and waits for me to clink mine with his before downing the last of his coffee in one gulp.

We toss our empty cups in the trash and walk back to the apartment. As we pass Koko's store, I pause just as we near the coatracks.

"This place has a lot of great stuff if you're ever looking for something special." I'm not satisfied with my Baader-Meinhof theory. I need to know if his jacket is the same one from yesterday.

Mackenzie reaches out and picks up the sleeve of a denim shirt, examining it for a moment before letting it go. "Yeah, it's great. I actually popped in yesterday. Picked up a few things."

My heart rate quickens. "Really? Anything good?"

He shrugs. "A pair of jeans. A couple of shirts." He pauses as if it's the end of the sentence. "Oh yeah, and this." He holds out his arms, showing off his leather sleeves. "I'm not normally a leather jacket kind of guy, but this one called to me."

I stop, unsure if his word choice was intentional. "Did you . . . happen to notice anything weird when you put it on?"

The hesitation before he answers has me holding my breath. Maybe there *is* something wrong with the jacket. It's laced with a pesticide or traces of some topical LSD.

Mackenzie pulls open the front door to the apartment and waits. "I guess it had a bit of a funky smell at first, but maybe I've gotten used to it." He holds the lapel up to his nose and sniffs. "Is that what you mean?"

"Yup," I reply.

Although it's not what I mean at all.

8

I WAKE ON MONDAY MORNING A FULL hour before my alarm. The apartment is quiet as I get ready for work, and Mackenzie's door remains closed as I lock up and head down the stairs.

Normally, in the mornings, I welcome the fresh air and city sounds as I walk to my streetcar stop, but this morning I am jittery and anxious, having spent most of Sunday night coming up with new theories on what is causing my hallucinations (none of them good).

I did, however, come up with a plan—one that requires the assistance of exceptionally delicious pastry, so I make a quick pit stop at Nana's for a Boston cream doughnut before heading on to work.

For anyone looking to study the brain, CAMH is a pretty great place to spend your days. They have two cyclotrons, seventeen hot cells, and a state-of-the-art medicinal chemistry lab. After getting my job, my nerd heart fantasized for weeks about the brains I'd be able to see in the center's very own MRI machine. Never in a million years did I ever think that one day I would hope to be one of them.

My streetcar arrives just as I get to my stop. As I board, my brain shifts from MRIs to Mackenzie's question about plans after my PhD.

When I started working at CAMH, I saw it as the perfect place to spend my career. The people were passionate, the facilities were top-notch, and it was a great commute from my apartment. However, this past year, my own passion for my work has dimmed from what was once a raging bonfire to a flame barely big enough to heat a fondue pot.

And I feel guilty about it.

I wish I were still that girl who looked at the world and believed she could change it for the better. A girl who turned her grief from her mother's death into an inspirational charge to put an end to one of the leading causes of death in young adults.

But after Larry died, all my hope morphed into a big, exhausted "what's the point?"

Even if I did everything I set out to do, there would always be another disease, or accident, or mutating cancer cells waiting to wipe out innocent lives.

Part of me wonders if, when Larry left this world, he took my spark with him. My more pragmatic side, however, suspects that I've simply grown up—finally learned the hard lesson that real life isn't a fairy tale; my purpose is simply to get through it the best way I can.

When I arrive at the center, my lab partner, Dr. Phillip Button, is already in our shared office—a windowless room, not much bigger than a closet, suitable for paperwork and drinking coffee. Phillip and I have been working together for the last year and a half. Although he is only three years older than me, he is in the process of completing his second PhD.

Phillip is what my Uncle Larry would have called "a bit of a different duck." On the outside he blends in easily in a hospital or research setting with his thick black glasses and light brown bowl cut. Someone once gave him a Lego figurine from their Child's City Scientist set that looks so much like him I've never been able to unsee it. He's not one for small talk and is so blunt when you do engage him in conversation that he sometimes comes across as rude if you don't know that he doesn't have a mean bone in his body. He's also brilliant. I once asked him why he pursued two different PhDs. A doctorate is a doctorate is a doctorate. I'm all for furthering your education, but why go through the pain of defending a thesis twice? His response was to tap his temple with his index finger and reply, "Who knows why we do the things we do, Annalise. But one day I'll figure it out."

This morning he has a large Tim Hortons double double in his hand, which is excellent for me because it means he didn't have time to stop at the fancy place three blocks out of the way of his streetcar commute with the French pastries I know are his kryptonite.

"I picked you up something this morning," I tell him. "Hope you haven't eaten." I toss the Nana's bag into his lap. He eyes the grease-soaked paper before pulling out the doughnut, lifting it with two hands, and smelling it as one might sniff a Cuban cigar.

"How was your weekend?" I ask, hoping to ease into things with a casual question.

His eyes remain on the still-to-be-eaten doughnut. "Uneventful. I read a book. Did some calisthenics, then I ate a very nice peach."

"Oh." I pause, not sure how to respond. "Well, that sounds like fun. Would you like to hear about my weekend?"

Phillip shakes his head. "Not particularly." He then proceeds to bite into the doughnut, making no indication whether he likes it or not other than a quick, successive second bite.

"Well, I had a bit of a weird one," I say, knowing his mouth is full and there is now little he can do to stop me. "I had a hallucination," I tell him. "Actually I had two. The first one happened when I was trying on a leather jacket in a thrift store. One minute I was in the changing room and then *poof!* I was in the middle of the Bloor-Yonge subway station."

Phillip begins to chew rapidly. I can tell he's trying to force a very large dough ball down his throat, because he's turning a maroon shade of red. Finally, he swallows.

"What about the second?"

"I was in my apartment, trying on the same jacket." I leave out how I stole it from my new roommate's room. "I'm not sure where the second one was. Some small-town festival. I don't think I've been there before. There were a lot of watermelons."

"In the hallucinations?" Phillip asks.

"Just the second one," I clarify. "I think watermelons might have been the festival's theme."

Phillip hums. It's his thinking hum. He does it when he is working out a problem.

"Were you consuming alcohol?" he asks. His tone is not the least bit judgmental.

"Nope. I considered the idea that maybe the jacket was laced with something, but the substance would have had to work quickly and last on the fabric for at least twenty-four hours. I can't think of what it could be."

Phillip nods. "Not impossible, but I agree, it's improbable. Any history of mental illness?"

I shake my head.

"What about in the family? Parents? Grandparents?"

That little twinge between my ribs returns, but again I shake my head. "Nothing that I'm aware of."

"And you have no other symptoms?"

I shrug. "I feel great. Totally normal. It's bizarre, right?"

Phillip scratches at his chin while staring at a spot just above the bridge of my nose. "Very."

He reaches out his hand, almost as if to cup the top of my head with his fingers, but stops himself before making contact. "We should do an MRI."

Exactly what I hoped he would say. No judgments. No questions. Just Phillip and his straight-up curiosity, trying to figure out the solution to a complex puzzle.

"How soon do you think we can fit me in?"

Phil swivels around in his chair and opens up his laptop. Neither of us is working on projects that require MRIs right now. But since Phillip is a PhD candidate, he has privileges to book the MRI machine for his doctoral research as long as it isn't in use. However, with the demand for MRIs in Toronto far exceeding the available time slots, openings are hard to come by.

"Looks like there is a cancellation at two," he says.

"Wow. Seriously?"

"Two A.M.," he clarifies, and my heart sinks a little.

"Could you be persuaded to come in and run it for me?" I ask. "I can bribe you with doughnuts."

He reaches out and this time does lay his hand on the tip of my skull, his thumb softly stroking my temple. "I have always wanted to see the inside of your head," he says very matter-of-factly until he meets my gaze as my eyes widen.

"Oh." He removes his hand with a jerk. "Too creepy?"

I nod. "Yes. But this time I'll let it slide."

9

MACKENZIE ISN'T THERE WHEN I GET HOME from work. But on the kitchen counter is a plate of what look like chocolate brownies and a note:

May contain beets. Not terrible but not good either. 5/10. If you need the good stuff, there's some in the cupboard. Help yourself. —Mac

There is a very large corner brownie missing from the pan.

I am starving, so I cut myself a small square and take a bite. It's chewy and chocolaty at first, but there is a very distinct aftertaste that most closely resembles dirt. Mackenzie was being very generous with his five. I grab a pen.

That was edible at best. I think I need to knock two

points off your scale to match mine. Excellent guinea pigging though. —AL

I can't get the weird taste out of my mouth. I try water. I even brush my teeth. Finally, I open the cupboard, hoping Mackenzie's "good stuff" might do the trick but freeze the moment I lay eyes on the foil-covered chocolate bar.

It's a Ghirardelli 72 percent dark cacao bar. Definitely the good stuff. It's also the same brand Larry used to buy for his hot chocolate. Since his death, I haven't been able to bring myself to buy it.

However, now it's within arm's reach.

I unfold the foil paper. Just like with the brownies, there is a single square missing from the bar. I break off its matching square and put the entire piece into my mouth.

The moment it hits my tongue, it begins to melt, overwhelming my taste buds with cacao and a hint of sugar and overwhelming the rest of me with such a strong wave of nostalgia that when I close my eyes, a single tear rolls down my cheek.

"You are crying over a chocolate bar," I chastise myself, wiping the tear with the back of my hand. It's just chocolate. Good chocolate.

As I place the bar back where I found it, I am pleasantly surprised that the weird dirt-like aftertaste is completely gone. I return to the note, needing to append to it.

Chocolate saved the day.
Thanks.

The rest of my evening follows my usual, familiar pre-Mackenzie pattern of reheating the weekend's takeout and eating it on my couch while watching a blissfully predictable Hallmark movie. The only difference is that I go to bed an hour and a half earlier than my usual eleven-thirty bedtime and set my alarm for one-fifteen. I get dressed in my usual pajamas, which are an old U of T T-shirt and a pair of sweatpants. I plan to wear them to the MRI since no one will see me in the dead of night, other than Phillip, who will be so preoccupied looking at my brain that he won't even notice the sizable hole in the crotch.

It takes me a little longer than usual to fall asleep, but when I do, it's hard and deep. When my phone alarm rips me back to reality, I wake with a physical jolt, then have to wait for a solid minute for my poor confused heart to slow to a regular speed before I can sit up.

My room is dark, as is the main living area of the apartment. I don't bother turning the lights on as I tiptoe past the couch, using only the flashlight from my phone, to find my purse and hoodie and put on my shoes.

However, as I reach to unlock the door, the knob begins to turn on its own. My still-half-asleep brain doesn't fully clue in to what is happening until the door swings open and I'm standing toe to toe with Mackenzie Smith.

"Whoa." He drops his guitar case on the floor with a loud thud and grabs my arms, although I'm not sure if his intention is to steady me or the other way around. My next thought is of how warm his hands are and if they just came from his pockets or if he naturally runs hot. That, in turn, sends an unexpected rush of heat through my body.

"You scared the crap out of me." I press my hands to my

now frantic heart, which did not sign up for this much late-night activity.

"Sorry, about that." He reaches down and picks up his guitar. "I was trying to sneak in, didn't think you'd still be up." His eyes do a quick scan of my outfit. "You heading somewhere?"

I fiddle with the ponytail I went to bed with and didn't bother to brush out. "I am just meeting someone . . . a colleague."

"Oh." His face breaks out in a knowing smile. "Enjoy, I guess." He steps to the side, letting me pass. It isn't until I'm on the landing that I realize what he's thinking.

I whip around. "I'm not—we're not—It's not a booty call."

He holds up his hands. "I wasn't judging."

I do not want to explain to him where I'm actually going.

"It's just a meeting . . . at work." I wince as soon as the words leave my mouth.

Mackenzie nods. "Okay." He glances at his phone. "But you're not *walking* there, right? I mean, it's after one."

I had planned on walking. Spadina is a main street, and I do carry two different types of bear spray, though I've never had to use them.

"Let me walk you." Mackenzie steps back into the hallway. "I'm sure you're totally capable of getting to where you need to go, but I am still a guy from a small town, and where I am from, if it's after midnight, we live and die by the buddy system."

I try to tell him that I'm fine, that he should go to bed, and that only one of us needs to be up in the dead of night for an intensive brain scan because only one of us is having vividly intense visions while wearing his leather jacket. But before I can find a believable way to communicate this, he has closed and locked our door, and we are walking down the stairs, and then we're out on the sidewalk heading east.

"So." Mackenzie drops behind me, then steps around, putting himself between me and the road. "Do you normally have work meetings in the middle of the night?"

I decide to keep my answer as close to the truth as possible. "No, but my colleague and I need to run an emergency MRI, and the machine is booked basically all day, every day. This was the only time slot we could get."

Mackenzie nods as if what I've just said makes sense before he turns his head away and brings a fist to his mouth, trying unsuccessfully to stifle a yawn.

"You know you really don't have to walk me. You must be tired."

He's yawning again, but he doesn't try to hide it this time. He lets it out with a rushed exhale and smiles. "It's all good. Got that post-show adrenaline pumping, and this is the perfect way to burn it off."

"How are the shows going?"

"Good, I think," he says. "We get a big crowd, and they seem to be having a decent time, but honestly, it's hard to tell if it's the music or just the beer. You should come check us out one night. I feel like you're the kind of person who would tell me the truth."

"I am?"

He smiles and tilts his head. "Yeah. I get the sense you're pretty straightforward—I like that. You always seem to stick to the facts."

I think he thinks he's complimenting me, but also—"You kind of sound like you're describing my colleague Phillip right now, and that scares me a little."

Mackenzie laughs. "So, is he the one you're meeting tonight?"

I nod. "He has MRI privileges. In my world, that makes him kind of a big deal. Plus, he's a very brilliant scientist."

Mackenzie gives me a sidelong glance. "Are you two . . . ?"

"No!" The word comes out like a squawk as I accidentally picture it for a second. "Oh my god, no. I don't even know if Phillip *has* feelings; if he does, they are definitely not for me. We are just colleagues . . ."

I drop my eyes to the sidewalk, wondering why I couldn't have answered with a simple "no."

"So . . ." I look up. "What about you?"

His brow lifts. "Am I dating any of my colleagues?"

My jaw drops open, at first to protest, and then in horror.

"Nope"—he grins—"I haven't dated anyone in a while—at least not seriously. The last few months have been busy with the move, and I kind of like the idea of focusing on my music for a bit." He kicks a small stone with the toe of his shoe, sending it skittering over the curb.

I welcome the turn in topics. "Did you always want to be a musician?"

He shakes his head and laughs a little to himself. "Not really. I kind of . . . stumbled into it. When I was little, I was torn between being a garbageman or, like, an Avenger. But then puberty hit, and suddenly I fell head over heels for Becky van Ghelt . . ." He draws out her name, smiling. "Becky . . . she was the captain of pretty much every sports team—volleyball, rugby, women's hockey—you name it. She sat right in front of me in biology but, of course, had no idea I even existed. So, I'd go home and write these angsty, soul-crushing poems for her—which I stealthily kept hidden under my mattress until my older brother Aaron found them and made copies for all of his friends."

My stomach twists, mortified on his behalf. "Oh, god."

He nods. "'Oh, god' is right. He and our brother Clive tortured me about it. One night, while I was sleeping, they drew a mustache on me with a permanent marker. And every time I tried to say anything, they'd snap their fingers like they were some kind of coffeehouse poets. Then, one day, Becky came up to me and asked if my poem was a song. I, of course, panicked and said yes, but it turns out tortured teenage poets are not cool, but angsty musicians do fairly well with the ladies."

I feel a weird stab of jealousy for no logical reason. "So you got the girl in the end?"

He laughs, shaking his head. "Not even close. She started dating one of her assistant captains. They got married eventually and now run a cheese shop in Collingwood."

"Good for Becky." I smile at this ending.

He grins, nodding. "Great for Becky and for me, I guess. I found out I love composing music."

"Wait. You write music as well as play?"

He gives a casual shrug as if it's no big deal. "The writing is actually my main thing. The playing is just what pays the bills. I'd love to be able to compose full-time, but the music industry isn't exactly known for hiring random unknown mechanics off the street. So I joined the band, figuring my odds are better if I'm a *slightly* known musician." He raises an eyebrow. "It's a solid strategy, right?"

I am not entirely sure if he's joking. "I mean, it's definitely *a* strategy."

He knocks his elbow into mine. "See, you tell it like it is." He sighs, closing his eyes for a second. "So, yeah . . . Zee seems pretty connected, and part of our deal when I agreed to move here was that they'd play some of my songs. I've already met a few people in the industry, and I don't know . . ." His voice trails, and I think he's lost his train of thought for a moment, but then he stops and turns to face me. "Have you ever had a moment in your life where you know, for no other reason than a feeling in your gut, that something is just . . . *right*?"

I assume his question is rhetorical, but I shake my head anyway. "This may come as a shock, but I am more of a follow-the-facts kind of girl. Who makes carefully curated lists of pros and cons—ideally on color-coordinated Post-it notes."

He gives a little half laugh. "I know it sounds a bit out there, but last spring, I got this . . . random sign from the universe, I guess, and it got me thinking about my life and how I'd never be happy unless I at least gave the whole music thing a shot, and I just . . . *knew* I was supposed to be here."

I almost tell him that the closest I've come to following through on a whim was picking up a box of strawberry Pop-Tarts while cruising the cereal aisle, which I promptly put down after reading the sugar content. I can't imagine moving to a new city without thoroughly conducting research.

The rest of our walk is quiet but easy, and we arrive with fifteen minutes to spare.

"This is me." I stop on the sidewalk, holding out my arm as if showcasing the building behind me, even though the College Street campus of CAMH is just big, brown, and institutional-looking. Really, the only redeeming architectural quality is the numerous windows that, during the day, let in ample natural light. Tonight, they act as a beacon, pointing to the parts of the center that are still up and running and those that shut down for the night.

Mackenzie inclines his head in the direction of the brightly lit lobby. "So . . . do you want me to wait until you're done?"

I shake my head even though I like the idea of him wanting to. "It's okay. This might take awhile. I'll call an Uber when I'm finished. Thank you, though, for the company."

I linger on the sidewalk, unsure of the protocol here. I can't recall ever having been walked anywhere before and it's nice . . . really nice. My weight shifts, and I consider opening my arms because maybe we are roommates who hug. I swear I see Mackenzie's arms flinch like he's thinking the same, but at the last minute, he changes his mind and brings his arm up, making a fist.

I knock my fist into his, the motion anticlimactic.

Mackenzie tucks his hand into his pocket. "Good luck with everything tonight. Hope whoever it is you're meeting is okay."

I have to bite my lip to prevent myself from commenting back, *That makes two of us.* Instead, I watch him as he walks backward, waiting until I'm inside the front doors before turning around with one last wave.

I WIND UP using my extra fifteen minutes to make coffee in the tiny machine we keep in the office for days when we're too lazy to walk downstairs to Tim Hortons.

"Two cream, two sugar." I hand Phillip a steaming mug when he steps out of the elevator at one fifty-five. Unlike me, Phillip is dressed as if he is ready for work in a pressed dress shirt and chinos.

He takes the coffee and nods his head to follow him down the hall, not bothering to wait for me as he pushes open the double doors to the MRI room.

There's a tired-looking nurse behind the glass. She gives Phillip a curt nod when they make eye contact, but her eyes skim right over me. She either doesn't recognize me or doesn't care.

I've been in the MRI room many times. It's a simple, clinical space with white floors and white walls, save for the far wall, which is made of a Plexiglas coated in copper wire, which protects the control room on the other side from the magnetic fields of the MRI machine.

Phillip picks up a hospital gown and hands it to me. "You can change in there." He points at the door that I know leads into a small examination room.

"I came dressed," I counter, taking off my hoodie to reveal the plain U of T shirt underneath. "No jewelry or metal of any kind." I hold up my hands as if to show supporting evidence. "I promise."

Phillip sighs and rolls his eyes. "Fine, get in."

I lie down on top of the table, familiar enough with the process that I don't require direction.

We conducted more than fifty MRI scans in the first four months of our research. Each patient had been diagnosed with some form of addiction ranging from alcohol to heroin, opioids to porn. Our study was focused on the frontal cortex—the part of the brain that controls logical thinking, goal setting, planning, and self-control—and we wanted to determine if the changes incurred during extended periods of abuse could be reversed with an intensive rehabilitation program supported by the CAMH outpatient program.

However, lying on the narrow table now is a very different experience, especially as Phillip slides me in and I'm forced to lie completely still, suddenly noticing itchy spots on my scalp and nose and under my armpit that were not there a moment ago, when scratching was an option.

The machine kicks up with a whirling sound, then begins

to bang with an even metallic *thunk.* The first two minutes are excruciating. I want out. I want quiet. I want to be cozied up under the covers in my own bed.

Eventually, I get used to the noise. The rhythm becomes relaxing even.

When the machine finally goes quiet, I am considering asking Phillip if he can just bring me a blanket and tuck me in right here, but he pulls the table back out with practiced efficiency. When I finally sit up, he meets my eyes with a stoic gaze and a very clinical "Come."

I feel short of breath as I follow him into the control room. The nurse is gone, but on the screen are two black-and-white images—my brain.

"Take a look for yourself," Phillip says, standing aside. My eyes skim over the screen, once then twice, looking for any signs that things are not right. I find nothing.

"What is it?" I ask Phillip, still not sure what he saw that I didn't.

"You're fine," he replies, crossing his arms over his chest.

"Then why did you say it like that? You made it seem like you saw something."

Phillip shakes his head. "I simply told you to come and see your results for yourself. This is a good learning opportunity. Sometimes patients are convinced they have a physical ailment, but the science proves the contrary."

I scan the screen one last time. "There's really nothing wrong with me?"

Phillip shakes his head, "I never said *that,* but yes, your brain looks fine." He squints his eyes and stares at me. "If you're still concerned, we could do some bloodwork. It will take a few weeks to get the results back as I'll have to submit it with my next round of test samples, but if the issue is due to an ingested substance, it would—"

"It's fine," I cut him off. "It's probably just my brain balancing too many things at once."

Phillip nods. "A logical explanation."

I grab my purse and pull on my hoodie, then use my app to call an Uber.

"Thanks again, Phillip," I say to him as he wastes no time in pulling on his coat.

He gives me yet another curt nod. "I'll look forward to the honey cruller tomorrow morning."

By the time I get home it's almost three-thirty. The apartment is quiet as I unlock the door, but as I step into the living room, it's filled with soft blue light. The television is on. I stand for a moment and watch. It's an old episode of *Carson's Cove.* For a moment I think I must have left it on by accident, but then I hear a soft snore coming from the other side of the couch.

I peer over the back and down at the cushions. Mackenzie is fast asleep, legs straight out in front of him, arms crossed over his chest as if he were a vampire. The TV remote is tucked underneath his arm.

I reach for it. Moving slowly, I slip it out of his grasp, then click the power button, leaving us both in almost blackness.

I start to tiptoe toward my room, but I stop. I pull the fuzzy Hudson's Bay blanket from the back of the leather love seat and cover him with it. He doesn't wake, but his lips form a small smile and then let out a little puff of air.

I turn to tiptoe back into my room but stop as I spot something black hanging from the back of my kitchen barstool.

It's the jacket.

I consider my options. Mackenzie is fast asleep. I could try once again and put my mind to rest. Once bitten, twice shy, but thrice can't deny that something is seriously wrong.

"No," I whisper to the dark. "Stop feeding this stupid fantasy."

It's nothing.

To think otherwise would be ludicrous.

10

TWO WEEKS GO BY, AND I BARELY see Mackenzie.

We communicate almost entirely by Post-it notes left in the kitchen next to Harmony's latest baking experiment.

On Monday it's a pink note left next to a loaf pan.

> *Summer Squash pound cake.*
> *The squash had me going in with*
> *low expectations. Was*
> *pleasantly surprised 9/10*
> *—Mackenzie*

Wednesday, I leave a green note on a paper plate covered in cornflower-blue flowers.

> *Chickpea Blondies. They taste*
> *as beige as they look. 4/10 —AL*

Saturday, I come home from the library to an empty apartment and a blue Post-it above the garbage can with an arrow pointing down. Inside the can are what look like brownies again, and on the counter is a second blue note.

These didn't come with a name
but I am calling them
Slow Death by chocolate.
—Mackenzie

I laugh loudly as I read it and then reach for a pen to write him back.

Anyone ever tell you, you have
a way with words. You should
write angsty poetry. —Al

I fall asleep on the couch later that night, and when he comes home late from his gig, I wake just enough to hear his footsteps as he walks to the kitchen, then his soft laugh as he reads my note. I fall back asleep with a smile on my face.

Harmony takes a baking hiatus until the following Tuesday, when I come home from work to find an orange plastic container in the fridge that looks like it was purchased at a Tupperware party in the seventies. We have made a full rotation and are back to pink Post-its.

You are not going to try this
if I tell you what's in it but
it's a solid 10/10
—Mackenzie

I open it to reveal a seemingly normal-looking chocolate cake complete with frosting.

I sniff it, because nothing is ever "normal" when it comes to Harmony's baking, but it smells . . . good?

I take a small forkful. It's moist and rich and incredible. I cut off a sizable piece and skip dinner to go back for a second.

Mackenzie isn't home again by the time I fall asleep, so I scrawl back my thoughts on the Post-it note:

> I cannot figure it out.
> Sour cream? Avocado?
> Black beans? I know she put
> something weird in it but I
> can't deny that whatever it is,
> I'm into it. I can't stop
> eating.

I wake in the morning to no sign of Mackenzie but another note.

> Left you the last piece.
> I'll tell you when you're done.

I eat every last crumb and even lick the lid of the container before I wash it.

My MRI feels like a lifetime ago. I haven't had a single vision since the weird watermelon festival and have almost, *almost,* convinced myself I imagined the whole thing. And since Mackenzie and I have been on opposite schedules, I haven't even seen the jacket in weeks, so there has been no temptation to test my theory—that is, until I'm walking home from Liberty Village at eight-thirty on a Saturday night. I happen to cross the street so I can window-shop my favorite painted pink bookstore when I pass the Gladstone with its big street-facing windows.

The jacket is just sitting there, slung over the back of a chair next to the stage.

I know it's the jacket.

Not to mention Mackenzie's guitar case is propped up next to it.

He is nowhere to be found. In fact, the entire stage is empty. The bar isn't busy. There are a few occupied tables: a small group of twentysomething guys with pitchers of beer and an older couple that look to be on a date. Without thinking, I slip inside, avoid eye contact with the bartender, and make my way over to the jacket.

I stop just short of the chair and stare, realizing I have no actual plan. It's not like I'm going to slip it on right here. It's one thing to test my wild theories in the safety of my own living room, but in a downtown public bar? No thank you.

What else can I do? Steal it? That would be ludicrous. Almost as ludicrous as standing here staring and—

"Annalise?"

I haven't heard his voice in days, but I know without a doubt it's Mackenzie behind me.

"Hey . . ." I pivot slowly to face him. "There you are. I was just thinking, that looks like your jacket."

I point. He nods, a smile breaking across his face.

"I'm so glad you finally made it out."

"Oh, I—"

"Zee!" he calls to someone behind me. "Come meet my roommate, Annalise."

I shake my head, but Mackenzie is high-fiving some guy in a tan-colored toque. He is tall and broad-backed, and his very tight, slightly transparent shirt shows off a set of muscles that have obviously seen ample gym time. He's clean shaven with a strong jaw, and out of nowhere I am struck with the sudden sense that I know him somehow.

I blink twice, but can't place his face. Nor can I imagine where our paths might have crossed before. Bars are definitely not my usual scene, and although the academic crowd comes in all shapes and forms, they don't typically look like him.

Larry would have called this moment a glimmer and told me that this stranger and I must have crossed paths in a past life. He'd say something like the familiarity I am experiencing is simply my soul recognizing his energy. I would have rolled my eyes, yet I can't deny the rush of déjà vu as he pulls me into a hard hug, squashing my cheek against his collarbone.

"Ah, Annalise!" he says. "Glad you could make it out. I'm Zee. Mackie," he barks, "get this woman a beer!"

Again, I shake my head, but it's ignored because Zee has released me and is steering me toward a high-top table. "We reserve this one for our groupies," Zee says, pulling out one of the chairs with a wink.

"Which is why it usually remains empty," says a different guy with a British accent and a very long beard. He carries a bass guitar and also wears a T-shirt that's lacking in thread count.

I sit, mainly because I don't see another way out other than to pretend that I am actually here to see the band play.

Zee jumps up onto the stage, picks up one of the guitars,

and strums it, sending an electric twang through the entire bar.

Someone toward the back of the bar lets out a *whoop,* and people begin to pour in from other rooms.

The bearded man jumps up onto the stage just as a tall blond bartender sets a Diet Coke in front of me.

"Just so you know, I don't do table service unless you have a face like this one." She turns to Mackenzie, who has appeared behind her, and cups her hand around his cheek, giving it a light smack as he flashes her a grin. "But if you need a refill in a bit"—she turns to me—"come see me at the bar."

"Thanks, Jodi." Mackenzie lifts his glass, giving her an air cheers, then when she turns to go, he clinks my Diet Coke still on the table with his water glass.

"Thank you for this," I say.

"No worries. I'm glad you're here." He squeezes my shoulder before setting his half-drunk water glass down next to me and following the rest of his bandmates up onto the stage and, to my surprise, sliding behind the set of drums.

Mackenzie picks up his drumsticks, and like straight out of a music video, he hits them evenly with a *one, two, three, four.*

The band slips into their first song. Zee's voice fills the bar, and although I'm about as far as you can get from a music critic, I can tell they're good—really good.

My toe taps against my stool as the band moves seamlessly from one tune to the next. With every new song, the bar gets a little fuller.

Twice, I'm asked if I need the three empty chairs at my table. Both times, I panic and then contemplate if Zee's groupie comment was a joke or if I should save seats for these other late-to-arrive groupies. When the third person asks about the empty chairs, I give up one and then spend the next song staring self-consciously at the other two as I debate the best way to sneak out unnoticed. However, whenever I scrounge up the courage to go, I somehow catch Mackenzie's eye, and he gives me a smile.

At first, I think it's the same one he uses to charm, well, everyone, apparently, but then something shifts. Maybe it's that he holds my gaze a little longer or the way his lips curl up ever so slightly when our eyes lock, but I get the strange sense he likes having someone here just for him—and so I stay.

When the guy who took my spare chair has another friend show up, I know I'm seconds away from losing another seat. I pull out my phone to avoid him and see a text from Koko on my screen.

> You home? I'm just closing up.
> We should grab a drink.

She sent it eight minutes ago. For a moment, I consider using Koko as my excuse to leave, then think: If she wants a drink, why not come here? It's not too far from my apartment.

I text her back.

> I'm at the Gladstone
> watching my roommate
> Mackenzie play. Join me?

A minute later, I get her reply.

> Be there in 15

Twenty minutes later, she plops down beside me. "Wow. They sound great," Koko says, shaking her shoulders to the music. "I do not remember Mac being that hot. However, I was very hungover when we met. And he wasn't wearing the hat."

She lets out a *woo,* raising her drink above her head. Zee looks over, winking at her as she takes the tiny cocktail straw between her lips and drinks.

"Uh, that isn't Mackenzie," I tell her as I put it together.

"It's not?" She turns to look at me.

"No, he's the one on drums."

She tilts her head as if trying to get a better look. "Then why do I always see him carrying a guitar case?"

I shrug. "I actually thought the same thing and do not know the answer."

We solve the mystery ten minutes later, as Zee announces they will slow it down for one more before they break.

Mackenzie gets out from behind the drums, grabs his guitar, and pulls up a stool next to Zee. The two of them begin to play. The song is slower tempoed than what they've played so far. The even strum of Zee's guitar is a stark contrast to Mackenzie's quick, melodic fingers. When Mackenzie's baritone meets Zee's honey tenor at the chorus, the resulting sound is hauntingly beautiful.

You said your name and I forgot mine
Like I'd dropped it at your feet
Every piece fell in line
Like it knew just who to meet.

"Ohhhh, I'm into this," Koko says, tipping her head toward mine.

I am, too. And I'm almost sad when the final notes play, and Zee announces, "Okay, folks. We're gonna take a little break. Don't go too far."

A techno mashup thrums through the speakers as they step off the stage. It sounds almost offensive in comparison to the moments before. So when Mackenzie slides into the seat next to me and asks, "So, what'd you think?" I'm not lying in the least when I answer, "You guys were incredible."

Zee plops down next to Koko. Within seconds their heads are tipped together, Zee's arm cradled around her backrest. Mackenzie introduces me to Benjamin, the bassist with the beard, and Rocco, the rhythm guitarist, who, upon closer inspection, is dressed head to toe in black leather.

"It's a pleasure," Benjamin says, shaking my hand. "Rocco and I are headed to the bar for a pint. Can we get you anything?"

I shake my head, still nursing my Diet Coke. Mackenzie must do the same, because the two turn and disappear into the crowd, which has grown relatively thick with bodies.

"You can go with them." I swivel around to face him. "Don't feel like you have to sit here on my account. I'm fine hanging out with Koko."

No sooner do I say it than Zee and Koko stand. We both watch as he takes her by both hands, pulling her onto the dance floor, where he lets go of one arm to twirl her in tight. She laughs as they connect, then runs her arms up and down the front of his chest as he begins to sway to the music.

I don't know Koko that well, and I have talked to Zee for all of five minutes, yet I have a strong suspicion that if things continue, they will be doing a whole lot more than dancing by the end of the night. I can practically see the dopamine releasing from their pores.

"Do you want to?" Mackenzie's voice interrupts my thoughts.

"Want to what?" I ask, wondering if he, too, is speculating about Koko and Zee.

"Dance." He points at the empty patch of dance floor between Zee's back and a high-top table.

"Oh, no. Absolutely not."

I turn my head just in time to see his smile slip.

"Sorry." I shake my head. "That didn't come out right. I'm just . . . a horrible dancer. The chances of you stepping onto that floor perfectly fine and then leaving with a serious injury are way higher than you'd want them to be. You have a show to play tonight, and I have a conscience."

Mackenzie flashes a smile. "I do use all ten of my toes pretty regularly."

His eyes slide back to the dance floor. Mine do the same, just in time to see Zee drop Koko into a low dip. She laughs, throwing her head back, and I feel a tiny stab of jealousy. I wonder if I made the wrong call too fast.

"Thanks again for coming out tonight." Mackenzie leans forward so the sides of our arms touch. "I get the sense this probably isn't your scene, but I'm glad you're here."

My heart, which I assumed had long ago morphed into a solid, impenetrable lump, softens enough to feel a small pang of guilt at my earlier lie.

"Was that one of your songs? The slow one?"

Mackenzie nods as he takes a sip of the water he abandoned earlier.

"It was really good," I tell him honestly. "I know you weren't sure about the band, and I'm not, like, super into music or anything, but I think it's actually working out—really well."

He leans back in his seat, surveying the bar. "What do you think the odds are that some big music producer in the crowd tonight is looking for a songwriter to sign?"

I incline my head toward a guy in a Leafs jersey, chugging

a full pint as his two friends pound in unison on the table. "You never know—could be that guy."

Mackenzie watches him down half a beer, spilling most of it down his chin.

"Or that guy." He points to a man with a side part and a thick black mustache.

I follow his finger. "I'm pretty sure that's my dentist."

The guy looks over as if he can sense we're talking about him. We make eye contact, and he waves.

"Hey, Dr. Foster," I say softly, waving back.

Mackenzie laughs beside me. "So *not* him."

"Nope. But if you need a good dentist in the city, he's usually taking patients."

Mackenzie grins and opens his mouth, and I get the sense that he is about to say something, but then he stops as three women approach our table.

They are around my age. Pretty. With tiny tops that show off toned arms and flat stomachs and make me very aware I am wearing a five-year-old T-shirt I got for free from a charity walk-a-thon.

"Hey," says one with very red lips and dark eyes fixed only on Mackenzie. "We were here last weekend."

He smiles and nods. "Right, yeah . . . Good to see you. Thanks for coming out again." His tone is friendly, but as he leans back in his seat, he stretches out his arm, letting it rest on the back of my chair.

I am aware of it both by the heat from his skin, which I can feel through my shirt, and the dagger eyes I am getting from two of the three women.

"Hey, listen," Mackenzie says to them. "We are going to start back up in about two minutes." He nods at the bar. "In case you want to grab a drink."

The women leave, but his arm stays. I'm sure I'm just a tactic to fend off what was clearly an unwanted advance, but I like it. I also like that when he leans in, he drops his voice, so I have to tip my head toward him to hear.

"Zee usually switches us over to the crowd favorites right about now. If you're not feeling Journey, I'll understand if you head out, but if you stay, maybe you can walk me home?"

It's late—way later than I ever planned on being out tonight, and my sheets are freshly laundered and calling to me. Still, I find myself turning toward him so he can hear me over the music.

"I'll stick around. I may be a born and bred city girl, but I have become a recent recruit to the buddy system."

He smiles like this was the exact answer he was hoping for.

Benjamin and Rocco return less than a minute later, handing Mackenzie one of their beers with a "You ready to get back up there?" and a firm pat on his back. I get a shoulder squeeze from Mackenzie as he follows the two, grabbing Zee on their way and returning Koko to the table, where she drops back into her seat with a sweaty sigh.

"I thought tonight was going to be low-key," she says, and I'm not sure if I should take it as an insult or a compliment. "I love it when the universe tells me otherwise."

She smiles, and although she looks nothing like him, something about her expression reminds me of Larry. That's two glimmers in one night.

Two glimmers too many.

The band starts up again. It's a classic rock song I actually do recognize, and there are a lot of drums. I find myself watching Mackenzie and realizing that drumming isn't just about the beat. It's strong hands and forearms and contracting abdominals—movements that are hard and precise and—

"He *is* very hot." Koko leans in, interrupting my thoughts. I can smell the tequila on her breath as it mixes with the florals of her perfume.

"Yeah, you said that earlier." I switch my gaze from Mackenzie to Zee and am once again struck by the feeling that I know him from somewhere.

"No, I'm not talking about Zee." Koko pokes me in a soft spot between my ribs. "I'm talking about Mac. I can totally see why you're into him."

I feel my stomach bottom out. "I'm not *into* him. He's my roommate. That would be . . . completely inappropriate." I stare at my now empty Coke glass, swirling the ice cubes as they clank against the sides.

Koko tips her head so it comes to rest on my shoulder. "Are you sure? You at least have to admit the man is sexy. Look at that broad chest all slick with drummer sweat."

Against my better judgment, I look.

Mackenzie's eyes are closed now. A small, contented smile splays across his lips as he tips his head toward the stage lights as if lost in the music.

"Hmmmmm?" Koko pokes me again, finding that same spot from before.

"Of course I find him attractive." He is arguably the hottest guy I've ever exchanged more than a passing sentence with. "But that's just biology. It doesn't mean anything."

Koko manages to give me a side eye while also simultaneously watching the band. "If you say so."

Before I can further argue my point, Mackenzie breaks out into a drum solo. His arms beat out a wild rhythm that ends the song with one last clash of the cymbals. The whole bar breaks out in shouts and applause.

Mackenzie looks up and twirls his sticks around his fingers before setting them down on top of the drums. He wipes a sweaty lock of hair off his forehead, which immediately falls back to the same place as he leans back in his stool and scans the still-cheering crowd. His eyes catch mine for the briefest of moments—just long enough for him to smile and wink.

Koko leans toward me, waiting until the clapping dies down just enough so I can hear her.

"So banging your roommate . . . completely inappropriate? Or just incredibly convenient?"

11

It's almost three when we leave the Gladstone. The streets are still busy with late-night clubbers heading home from the bar or loitering on the sidewalks to eat foil-wrapped shawarma and cardboard containers filled with poutine.

As predicted, Koko and Zee leave together. The moment they slide into a cab, their bodies are a tangled mess of legs, lips, and arms, leaving Mackenzie and me behind on the sidewalk to exchange awkward glances.

We walk slowly down Queen, heading east toward Spadina. The relatively warm evening and my Converse high-tops make the experience rather pleasant, as the city's subdued sounds at night relieve my still-ringing ears.

Mackenzie walks at the pace of someone out for a late-night stroll, stopping to wait at every red light, sending me smiling side-eye glances as if daring me to roll my eyes or call him out for it.

"I *will* make a jaywalker out of you." I tug the handle of his guitar case as I pull him across a quiet side street with no sign of traffic. "I am making an exception tonight for the slow walking since it's after midnight, but you should know that all of your walking etiquette needs work to meet the minimum Toronto standards."

He lifts his hands as if acknowledging his lack of defense. "What can I say? I am enjoying my evening."

My head wants him to clarify this statement. What specifically is he enjoying? The exercise? The unseasonably warm air? Was it the sizable crowd at the bar earlier? The music? Or something else?

"The show was really great," I say. "I know you want to be a songwriter and everything, but honestly, you kind of pull off the whole rock star thing pretty well." He turns his head just enough that I can see his eyebrow lift. "I mean, that's what Koko said. She seems to know what she is talking about. I think she goes to a lot of concerts."

He nods as if what I've said makes sense, but then he clears his throat and asks, "So, did *Koko* enjoy the show?"

My gaze, which was on his face only a second ago, suddenly becomes very interested in the cracks in the sidewalk. "Uh, yes. She definitely did."

I am still watching my feet, but I can somehow sense him smiling.

"And what was her favorite part?"

We are both very much aware of the lack of actual Koko in this conversation, but I shrug and keep it going anyway. "I think she loved all of it, but if she had to pick, it would be the song you wrote."

I look up long enough to sneak a quick glance, and I'm just fast enough to see the brief curl of his lips at my answer.

It really was a beautiful song. The harmonies, and the melody, and the way he described falling for someone not as a series of pheromones and hormones and chemical reactions but as an act of surrender that made me consider that maybe I had been thinking about love all wrong.

"Who is it about?" I only listened to the lyrics once, but they gave me the sense that whoever he wrote about was meaningful to him.

"You want me to name names?" His voice teases, and I realize that not only have I asked something that might be very personal, I am also unsure what answer I want to hear.

"Sorry," I apologize.

"I'm kidding." He knocks his elbow into mine, but instead of pulling away again, he stays, the side of his arm brushing against mine as we walk. "The song is not really about anyone. It's more about that rush that comes when you know you want something badly, and you're kind of terrified both for it to happen and also for it not to."

We hit another light. He stops, and I stop, too, but instead of facing the road, we face each other. Toe to toe. It's a wide sidewalk, and yet we are close enough that I can feel the warmth of his exhale and smell just the faintest trace of drummer sweat. *Percussion rush.*

"High blood pressure," I whisper as if in response.

His forehead wrinkles.

"That rush you're describing. It's a sympathetic nervous system response. The spike in adrenaline increases your heart rate. It makes you both excited and jittery at the same time."

I am feeling both of these things right now. My palms are sweaty, and my stomach seems to be throwing tumble passes inside me, and yet I like everything about this moment.

"Sorry," I apologize again. "You were being poetic, and I went and made it very literal."

He laughs. "It's okay, I like that. Both things can be true, right?"

I nod. "I guess they can."

The light turns, and we walk again until we reach a spot in the sidewalk that looks to be under construction due to a broken water main. There is a small gap big enough for a single pedestrian to cross with a large step or a small leap. Mackenzie goes first. His long legs allow him to cross with low effort, and when he is safely on the other side, he stops and turns, holding his hand out to me.

I take it, noticing the strength of his grip and the slight scratch of his calluses as he helps me across. My shorter legs require a bit of a hop to make the gap, and when I land, I teeter slightly, relying on him to keep me steady.

He keeps hold of me until I'm still, but even then, he doesn't let go. His hand stays firmly holding onto mine.

I know it's entirely in my imagination, but I feel a slow heat seep out from where his fingers meet mine. It climbs up my arm and down my body, pooling low in my belly, where it multiplies as Mackenzie's eyes meet mine.

I can see the reflection of the streetlights in his pupils. Gone is the ocean color—replaced with a darker, deeper blue.

His tongue skims along his lower lip, and I think, contrary to what I said to Koko earlier, that I wouldn't hate it if he leaned in and kissed me right now. But then he hesitates, and I find myself needing to fill the resulting silence.

"You're really good."

He blinks twice, and I realize that I'm making a habit of starting conversations where the first half has occurred only in my head.

"At writing," I clarify. "Your song was the best one, and just in case it's unclear, that's *me* talking this time, not Koko."

He laughs, and the way he smiles at me makes me think I have long surpassed the ones he reserves for baristas.

"I am glad you liked it," he says. "Zee wasn't sold on it at first. He thinks it brings down the crowd. I guess he has this whole vision for what he calls the 'Midnight Station experience,' and what I'm writing doesn't exactly fit." He shrugs. "But hey, he agreed to play it tonight, so fingers crossed the response is good enough that he'll let me try again." He kicks a rock, which stutters across the sidewalk, bouncing off the curb and disappearing down a sewer grate.

"I didn't realize that was the name of your band," I say.

Mackenzie shrugs. "Yeah, apparently, something happened to Zee in a subway that he says changed his life and made him realize he wanted to start a band. I don't know if any of it is actually true, but it's not the worst band name I've heard."

Something tickles the back of my brain.

"Remind me, how did you meet Zee again? You answered an ad, right?"

Mackenzie shakes his head. "No, I was playing this festival back home. One of the bands had a fight with their drummer, and my brother Clive volunteered me to fill in. I guess Zee was in the crowd and liked what he heard. He got in touch a few months later."

He stops again because we need to cross Queen, and this time, we have actual traffic to contend with. As he waits for the crosswalk to signal, an unsettling feeling washes over me as a rush of goose bumps prickles up my arms.

It's impossible. It can't be.

A chill rolls down the back of my spine. I shiver.

"Are you cold?" Mackenzie asks.

"Yes." I nod. "But—"

Before I can explain that the bigger problem is that I am having an existential meltdown in the middle of the sidewalk, he slips off his jacket and places it on my shoulders, and everything around me goes black.

"WAIT!" THE WORDS leave my lips as the light around me begins to brighten. The street is gone. So is Mackenzie. I'm standing in the middle of a crowded bar.

I blink and turn, scanning the crowd of people. Just like the last two times, it's as if I'm a ghost.

I breathe in the smell of chicken wings and immediately orient myself to where I am. I recognize the long wooden bar, the televisions embedded in the walls, the leather booths and the wooden tables. It's a pub on King. The name escapes me. It's two juxtaposed words like the Crown and Dagger or Princess and Pauper.

My ex, Lucca, loved this place—or anyplace with Monday night football and half-priced nachos, so as the crowd thins and I have a clearer view of the bar, I'm not totally shocked to see him sitting there, sipping a pint as if he hasn't a care in the world.

I begin to walk toward him. Lucca and I hung out for just over three months. He worked at CAMH as a counselor. We'd always end up in the elevator at the end of the day until one particular day, he asked if I wanted to grab something to eat. We didn't have much in common, but we had the same work schedule, and he was kind and sweet. We fell into a pattern of sleeping together after work, then a couple of months went by and he was asking if I wanted to meet his parents.

"Parents? Aren't we missing a few steps?" I had asked. His response was to laugh. "It will be three months in April that we've been doing this. Aren't you ready for something more?"

I wasn't. Although I was regularly putting on clean pants

in the mornings, I was far from the mental place where I felt ready to open my heart up to someone else who I might one day lose. And, if I was being perfectly honest with myself, I wasn't sure if I'd ever get there with Lucca. After he put the idea of an actual relationship in my head, I started to notice little things—how his nose whistled while he slept and how he spat his toothpaste out with the accuracy of a cartoon character and then never wiped the sink. More important, I knew I wasn't in love with him. I was lonely and using him as a distraction, and it was unfair to string him along.

A few days later, I took the opportunity to make a clean break and ended it.

I never did meet his parents.

I'm still not regretting that decision as I move through the crowd, wondering if I possess the physical ability to slide into the empty seat beside him. I worry that my ghostly body will slip through the chair like it does everything else.

I don't get a chance to test my theory. Before I reach Lucca, someone else slides into the seat. He is tall and holding hands with a woman with braids. I don't recognize either of them until he turns his face toward me and removes his black leather jacket.

I know that jacket.

This isn't Baader-Meinhof this time, because I have been studying this particular jacket for weeks. I know the thickness of the zipper and the way the leather is worn to a place where it's almost white around the edges of the lapels.

It's Mackenzie's jacket. The one I am wearing right now. And that thought overwhelms me until it's replaced with one even more alarming as the jacket's wearer turns to give Lucca's back a friendly slap, and I catch his profile.

His hair is long and not covered by a hat like it was earlier tonight, and he has an auburn beard trimmed short and neat, and when he smiles it's as if my worlds collide, two thunderclouds clashing so hard they strike a bolt of electricity so intense my whole body shakes.

It's Zee.

No, not only is it Zee, it's the busker.

They are one and the same.

My heart begins to pound hard and fast, and even in my ghostly body, I find it hard to breathe.

I don't know how I didn't see it before.

The bushy beard and the scraggly hair created some kind of Clark Kent–like magic. But I knew Zee looked familiar. I just never in a million years expected him to be a fictitious figment plucked from somewhere deep within my subconscious, and yet, here he is.

"You guys are late," Lucca says, nudging his almost empty pint glass with his fingers.

"Sorry, man," Zee says. "Auditions went long."

"Find anyone good?" Lucca asks. Zee's date makes a quick, sharp shake of her head, her mouth stretching into an expression that says, nope and don't ask.

"I just can't get that guy out of my head," Zee says. "He's exactly what the band needs, if only I could find him, but he's Cinda-fucking-rella."

Lucca signals to the bartender, who pulls three new pints from the taps and sets them down in front of him.

"Who's he playing with now?" Lucca asks.

"That's the thing," Zee says. "I have no idea. I tracked down what I was sure was the same band, but the drummer definitely wasn't the right guy. I have half a mind to drive back up there and start roaming the streets. West Lake isn't that big. It would probably be more effective than anything else I've tried."

Zee's date sits up straight. "Wait a minute. That band was from West Lake?"

Zee nods.

"I just met someone from there. She's in my anatomy class. I can text her and see if she might know anything."

Zee grabs both her hands. "You find him for me, I will give you anything you want. Anything."

She removes her hands from his grip with a laugh. "You can start by buying my beer." She pulls a phone from her back pocket and begins to type.

I don't know why I'm here, why the jacket or my brain has brought me to this particular time and place. I wonder if it's even real. Lucca, Zee, even this bar exists somewhere in my subconscious. Could it be that I'm simply creating a story around what Mackenzie told me only moments ago? But what about the last hallucination at the festival? I hadn't met Zee yet, and I definitely didn't know about Mackenzie and the drums. It's not adding up.

My thoughts are interrupted as the woman smacks her hand down on the bar and then holds it over the mouthpiece of her phone, turning to Zee. "I would like to point out that I just accomplished in mere minutes what you failed to do in weeks." She holds out her hand. "Someone hand me a pen."

Both men look at each other.

She rolls her eyes. "You two are a waste of good pockets," and she reaches into her purse and pulls out a black eyeliner, then, pressing her phone between her cheek and shoulder, scrawls something on the coaster in front of her. When she's done, she pops the liner and phone into her bag and slides the coaster along the bar to Zee. "His name is Mackenzie. My girl Jules knows his cousin."

Zee picks up the coaster with the number and kisses it. "You are a tremendous woman." He shoves the coaster into the pocket of his jacket before kissing her next. One kiss becomes two. Two becomes three. I catch Lucca looking over and rolling his eyes twice.

The make-out continues until Zee gets up, and the two of them head off to somewhere else in the bar. I watch Lucca for a while, then look around to see if anything notable is going on. I don't recognize anyone. Nothing else is happening that looks out of character for a night at the pub. I can't even see Zee.

Finally, after about ten more minutes, Lucca gets up. He flags down the bartender and pays his tab. He turns as if he's about to leave but stops.

Zee's jacket is still hanging off the back of the barstool next to him.

Lucca looks around as if he's deciding what to do.

Finally, he picks the jacket up, tucks it under his arm, and begins to walk toward me.

For the briefest of moments, we make eye contact, and I swear he's going to recognize me, but just like everyone else, he walks right through me.

I turn to follow him out the door, but just as I do, everything around me goes dark.

I BLINK THREE times at the bright red hand on the crosswalk sign across the street. On the fourth blink, the little white stick figure appears.

Mackenzie steps off the curb and then stops. "Are you coming?"

He's not looking at me strangely.

Well, maybe a little strangely, seeing as it's time to walk and I'm frozen in place, but he's definitely not looking at me like I transported myself to another dimension and then reappeared out of thin air.

Still, I need confirmation.

"What just happened?"

Mackenzie looks from me to the light. "I'm not sure I understand the question."

I shake my head and rephrase. "Did anything weird happen to me just now? Did I go anywhere?"

A deep line forms between his eyebrows. "No?"

I was in that bar for at least thirty minutes. Long enough for Mackenzie to notice something.

"I didn't zone out? Even for a second?"

Mackenzie blinks back at me. "Like a seizure?"

My pulse quickens. "Yes!"

He shakes his head. "No. At least not that I saw."

My insides deflate. Although I'm grateful it wasn't a seizure, that would at least be a logical medical explanation.

"Hey, are you okay?" The crease between his eyes deepens enough to see it from where I'm standing.

I nod, more out of habit, but then notice the crosswalk countdown has started.

"We should go." I leap off the curb and pass him, taking off in a jog-walk. Mackenzie catches up just as I reach the other side.

The rest of the walk back to our apartment is free of unwanted hallucinations. We are both quiet as we climb the stairs and search our pockets for our apartment key.

Mackenzie finds his first, sliding it into the lock. He turns the handle and holds open the door to let me in.

I head straight for my bedroom, feeling like lying down is probably my best course of action, but he calls just as I reach my door.

"Hey, Annalise . . ."

I turn and, for a moment, ignore what happened with the jacket. "Yeah."

He takes a step toward me but then stops. "Tell Koko 'thanks for coming.' It meant more than she probably realized."

The warm, fluttery feeling from before returns. "I will be sure to do that."

He smiles, and then his gaze dips momentarily to my chest. I feel a slow heat bloom beneath my ribs until it occurs to me that there is a real, bona fide reason why he is looking at me that way.

"Oh. Your jacket." I slip it from my shoulders, turning my face so he can't see my expression.

"Don't worry about it," he protests, but I'm too quick.

It's in my hands, and I'm crossing the room, practically throwing it into his arms. "Thanks for letting me borrow it."

"No problem." He takes it from me and then, after a moment, turns to hang it on the hook next to the door.

I linger in the same spot, not expecting him to turn back around so quickly, but he does, and it becomes apparent that we are standing unnaturally close.

"Whoa—"

"Sorry, I—"

We both stop mid-sentence and laugh.

His eyes meet mine, and although my instinct is to look away, I don't.

"I should . . . probably go to bed." He bites his bottom lip and then releases it. "Good night, Annalise."

"Good night, Mackenzie." I turn and make it all the way to my room before he calls out my name.

"Hey, Annalise?"

I stop, but this time, I don't turn around. "Yeah?"

"My jacket . . . it looks good on you. You're welcome to borrow it anytime."

12

THE BRAIN SCAN ON THE COMPUTER SCREEN in front of me shows several concerning markers. Its gray matter volume is significantly reduced in both the prefrontal cortex and temporal lobes, not to mention the notable shrinkage in the hippocampus and thalamus regions.

It presents clear, scientific evidence as to why the patient is suffering from delusions. Put simply, the brain is damaged and therefore misinterpreting sensory inputs that simply aren't there.

My brain scan, on my other screen, is fine. There are no markers—not even a concerning shadow—as I study it yet again over coffee and a half-eaten coconut dream doughnut on a napkin beside me.

I have a literal mountain of files I am supposed to be reviewing this week, but it's Friday, and my head has been in another place since last weekend at the Gladstone and my latest leather jacket hallucination.

Phillip bends over my left shoulder, studying the screen that I'm doing a terrible job of hiding. "Ahhhhh, now I see it."

"What? What is it?" My heart climbs straight up into my throat.

Phillip picks up the remainder of my doughnut and takes a bite. "I'm seeing the reason we are backed up on our lab inputs. Mithra called up an hour ago and asked why we were running behind. I insisted you'd been at it all morning and her system must be the issue. Now I'm afraid you've made me a liar."

My stomach twists with guilt. "I'm sorry. I got a little distracted."

Phillip nods, chewing and swallowing the last bite. "I presume they're still happening? The hallucinations, I mean."

I nod, figuring there's no use denying it. "I had another one on Saturday. It happened when I put on the same jacket. I'm wondering if we overlooked something?"

Phillip scratches his chin. "Do you have it with you now?"

He steps toward the door where my denim jacket is hanging on a hook.

"That's not it." I shake my head. "It's a leather jacket, and it belongs to my roommate."

Phillip turns and studies me, his eyes narrowing into tiny slits. "Has your roommate experienced the same phenomenon?"

I shake my head, knowing in my heart he's about to say that my theory is more than flawed.

"Well, I am sending out another round of blood samples. If you want to check and see if it's a toxin, we can have you tested easily enough."

"No. I really don't think it's that." I attempt a reassuring smile. "I'm fine. Really."

"Have you considered seeing a counselor?" There's no judgment in his voice. His tone is the same clinical one he uses when he asks for a second opinion on a case or if I'm feeling like Mother's Dumplings for lunch, and yet I immediately feel defensive.

Before I can say anything, though, he continues. "PhDs are intense. They require focus and discipline, both of which I know you have, but if I could make a suggestion . . ." He pauses, as if waiting for an answer, and doesn't continue until I nod.

"Figure out whatever it is that's going on before you go." He points at the monitor with my brain still on the screen. "Even if it is nothing, it's still a distraction you don't need."

He's right. I am about to embark on the most intense and important two years of my professional career. I can't afford to be worrying about the health of my brain.

"Those labs you're running, are they a full tox workup? Heavy metals included?" I ask, and Phillip nods.

I push up my sleeve. "Okay, then. Let's do it."

Phillip grabs a syringe. He draws blood so effortlessly that I only feel a tiny pinch. When he's done, I feel silly about my earlier hesitance. We will get to the bottom of this and clear it up well in time for Liverpool.

I get to my feet feeling like I've at least done something to remedy the situation. But when I reach for the door to leave, Phillip clears his throat.

"Ahem. I need one more sample."

He tosses something at me, and I catch it more out of instinct than skill.

"Throw it in the deep freeze when you're done."

I stare down at the empty urine collection cup and sigh.

IT'S STILL LIGHT out when I leave, and so I decide to walk home. By the time I round Queen Street, I can see Koko pushing the racks back into her store for closing.

I wave when she looks up and spots me.

"Lise, hey." She smiles as she places the last two hangers onto the rack. "Come inside with me. Mac is here. I've taken advantage of his precious small-town heart and exploited him as free labor."

I don't fully understand what she means until I follow her inside and look up to see Mac sitting on top of one of the wooden rafters that spans the length of the store.

"Hey," I call up to his dangling feet.

He leans forward, smiling as he sees me. "Hey."

It's been an entire week since we said good night after the Gladstone. His late-night schedule and my early mornings have limited our contact to Post-it notes and the occasional creak in the floorboards when I hear him come home after his gigs.

"Whatcha doing up there?"

Beside him is what looks like a makeshift storage space I never really noticed before. It's made from a piece of particleboard long enough to bridge two of the rafters. Sitting on the board are several cardboard boxes, what looks like a broken piece of a clothing rack, and several discarded mannequin parts.

"Well." He picks up one of the boxes and pulls it into his lap. "I thought I was up here getting boxes for Koko out of storage, but now I'm worried she's trying to keep me here as a store greeter."

"He's very cute," Koko calls out from behind the cash register. "I know more than one customer who wouldn't mind taking him home."

She looks from him to me and winks.

My cheeks immediately flare red, and I sneak a glance upward to see if he saw that, but he seems preoccupied with whatever is in the box, only looking down at us again when I ask, "But how did you get up there in the first place?"

I try to judge the distance between the rafter and the floor. It has to be easily twelve feet off the ground.

"A miscalculation." Mackenzie kicks his shoe toward a pile of toppled boxes behind one of the clothing racks. "There is a very good reason I am a musician and not an engineer."

"You are lucky you didn't break your neck." I walk around to the fallen boxes, clocking the concrete floor that does not look like it would cushion any fall.

"Here." I attempt to restack the pile. "Let me see if I can get you unstuck."

I do my best, but I, too, lack structural engineering skills. Even when I put them back in their proper place, there's still a notable gap between the top of them and the bottom of Mackenzie.

"Koko," Mackenzie calls once I'm done. "Catch!" He leans forward and drops the box from his lap into Koko's awaiting arms. Once she steps out of the way, he flips onto his stomach and lowers himself slowly, treating us both to a display of his flexing biceps and a view of his abs as his shirt snags on a sliver of wood, lifting his hem like a slow striptease.

Koko catches me watching him and clears her throat. My face immediately turns from what I assume was a red shade before to one that I'm sure is deep maroon. However, that feeling is immediately replaced with an icy bolt of fear as Mackenzie drops from the rafter with a "Look out below."

I hold my breath until he lands perfectly balanced on the top of the boxes.

Koko lets out a sharp but appreciative wolf whistle and then clasps her hands under her chin and, in an exaggerated southern drawl, calls out, "My hero."

Mackenzie bows and then jumps from the boxes to the floor.

"You are better than a Boy Scout." She hands him back the box and turns her attention to me.

"You look nice. Big plans for tonight?"

I stare down at my casual Friday outfit, not remembering what I put on this morning and realizing she's referring to my jeans and plain white tee.

"My plans are to go upstairs, put on my sweatpants, and order enough takeout that they send two forks. What are you guys up to?"

Koko pulls off her sweater to reveal a tight black leather crop top underneath. "I have a date with a very hot wannabe rock star who finally has a night off." Her eyes meet Mackenzie's, and she winks.

"Oh." I feel a sudden coldness grip my body as I look from Koko to Mackenzie.

"Her date is with Zee," Mackenzie cuts in, and I feel the muscles in my back immediately relax.

"Of course it is," Koko says, "who else would I be talking abou—oooohhhh." She waves me off with a dramatic swipe of her arm. "Don't even sweat. This one is far too functional for my tastes. I only date men with glaring red flags . . . or men who own boats, which, in its own way, is also a red flag but super fun when they let you drive them in the summer."

She laughs, picks up the cardboard box, and disappears somewhere into the back of the store.

I stare at my feet, wondering if I should explain that I wasn't sweating. He can date whomever he likes and I'm good with it, actually, I'm great with it. But when my cheeks finally feel cool enough to look up, I simply say, "I think I'm going to head upstairs."

I don't wait for Mackenzie to respond before I beeline for the front door and practically throw myself out onto the sidewalk. I am acutely aware that there are no sounds of footsteps or door slams or anything else to indicate Mackenzie is on his way up to the apartment, too, as I climb the steps, let myself inside, and throw myself onto my bed with the kind of force that makes me applaud the strength of my IKEA bed frame. I lie there for a few minutes, staring at the ceiling, until I eventually hear the door open and close and a series of creaky footsteps cross the hardwood, followed by a knock.

"Hey." Mackenzie's voice is soft. "You in there?"

"One sec." I roll to my feet, straightening out the wrinkles in my blouse and fluffing my hair with my fingers before opening the door.

"What's up?"

Mackenzie stands cradling a bottle of Diet Coke in his hands as if it were an expensive champagne. "Well, I also happen to have the night off, and I was wondering if there was room on the couch for two tonight?" He holds out the Diet Coke as if it were a peace offering. "We could order chili chicken from that place you like. Or get something else if you're not into—"

"No," I interrupt. "Chili chicken would be great." My stomach does a double flip, which I tell myself is a response to the chicken and not the man proposing it.

Our doorbell rings thirty-five minutes later. Three minutes after that, we're sitting side by side on the couch, plates filled with delicious Hakka food next to two wineglasses of Diet Coke.

"Cheers." Mackenzie holds out his glass.

"To making it through the week." I pick up my glass and clink it against his.

"To being exactly where we should be." He brings his to his lips and takes a long sip.

As I tip my head back and drink, I dwell on that thought. Am I where I should be?

Metaphorically speaking, I am in a good place. I am weeks away from starting a PhD—a goal I've been working toward for years. My life plan is playing out to the exact schedule I set when I was nineteen: finish my undergrad, then complete a master's degree, followed by two to four more years of work until I accumulate enough experience to get into a top PhD program and enough money to support my way through it. Everything is exactly as it should be.

"Don't you want to see where the universe takes you?" Larry would ask as I ticked off every milestone. "You could see the world, Beans. Fall in love with a Spanish sunset? Or maybe a local guitarrista?"

I laughed at the idea at the time, but as I lift my glass to my lips again, I catch sight of Mackenzie's guitar case leaning against the wall—and I choke.

"Easy there." Mackenzie's palm finds my upper back and taps it hard until I can draw a deep breath.

"Sorry." I set my glass down. "I was thinking about something and then drinking and breathing at the same time. Not recommended."

He removes his hand, but the concerned look stays etched across his forehead. "What were you thinking about?"

I am not about to tell him that my uncle may have predicted my penchant for guitar-playing men, so I go with the first plausible lie that pops into my head. "Just that cake."

Mackenzie stops halfway to picking up his plate.

"Harmony's," I clarify. "You said you were going to tell me the secret ingredient once I finished. I thought for a moment it might be anchovies."

He swallows whatever is left in his mouth. "No. But you're not as far off as you might think."

I pick up my fork and stab a piece of chicken. "You're going to leave me in the dark?"

He mirrors me, spearing his own piece but also pops it into his mouth, creating an air of suspense as I watch him chew and swallow it down.

"It wouldn't be a secret ingredient anymore if I told you."

"You are playing a very dangerous game here, Mackenzie Smith. You're going to regret this decision when you bite into a bologna pie that I could have warned you about."

He laughs. It causes his nostrils to flare and the corners of his eyes to crinkle, and somehow those tiny flaws work to make him even more attractive.

"Anyway." I pick up the remote in front of me. "What do you want to watch?"

We've yet to have this critical conversation. Communal TV preferences can make or break a relationship. Lucca and I could never agree. He liked guns, wars, and movies with dark Dustin Hoffman. I like comedies and romances and movies where Dustin Hoffman is a lovable intern or father-in-law with questionable personal boundaries. We didn't have a middle ground, so we'd either argue or avoid the activity altogether or settle somewhere in the middle, leaving neither of us fully satisfied.

Mackenzie stares at the Netflix options displayed on the television screen. "I usually like something a little lighter. No snakes, or planes, or snakes on planes. Bonus points if everything works out in the end."

I almost blurt out, "What about *A Princess for Christmas*?" But it's still October, and I think that is several steps too far from what he's actually thinking.

We settle on *Schitt's Creek,* and we laugh our way through three episodes and an entire two-liter bottle of Diet Coke. When it's time for episode four, I'm on an aspartame high and my cheeks hurt from all of the smiling.

"You up for one more?" I hold out the remote and aim it at the onscreen message confirming we're bingeing and not forgetting to shut Netflix off.

Mackenzie glances twice at his phone, and my heart sinks a little. *Does he have plans tonight?* It's not even ten. He's used to late nights. Maybe he has a date?

I hate how much I dislike that thought.

"I have another idea." He picks up his phone and clicks the screen a few times, then turns it around so that I can see. "I don't know if you're into astronomy, but the Orionid meteor shower is happening tonight. It's a pretty clear sky. We could go up to the roof and see if we can see anything."

On any other day, the cold, hard roof could not even begin to compete with my warm, squishy sofa, but tonight the idea is appealing.

"I could be into that."

"Great." He gets to his feet. "I'll find something for us to sit on, and you might want to grab a jacket. It's pretty cold tonight."

An idea strikes just as I stand. "Do you want hot chocolate?" My insides fill with a nostalgic longing. "I have a secret recipe."

Mackenzie nods. "I could be into that." He turns toward his bedroom door but stops and whips back around. "Wait. You're not adding anchovies or anything weird, right?"

I widen my eyes as I make an exaggerated shrug—the picture of innocence.

"If I shared my secret recipe, then it wouldn't be a secret."

13

TO GET TO THE ROOF WE NEED to go out the front door of our apartment, open the window on the landing, and climb out onto a narrow fire escape with a wrought iron ladder that extends up to the roof.

Mackenzie takes two trips.

The first is to bring up a big wool blanket, and a second to carry his hot chocolate, which I've poured into a Tim Hortons insulated cup with a lid.

"Careful. It's a lot slicker than it looks." He waits on the fire escape below me as I climb. The back of his hand hovers above the small of my back. My stomach doesn't like the way my running shoes don't quite grip the thin rungs nor the fact that I'm holding my own hot chocolate and therefore only have one free climbing hand. But a part of me knows that if I do slip, Mackenzie will be right there, and he won't let me fall.

When I'm safely on the roof I look up. The sky is as clear as Mackenzie promised. In the middle of the concrete roof is a red wool blanket spread out enough for two people to sit—that is, if they are very, *very* close.

"Here, lemme take that for you." Mackenzie holds out his hand for my drink, assuming I'm worried about spilling my hot chocolate and not the way my brain is playing Tetris, trying to figure out how both of us are going to fit while also not being awkwardly on top of one another.

"Thanks." I hand him my cup and opt for a cross-legged position with my butt to the absolute edge so my left knee hangs off.

"Here." I hold out my hands. Mackenzie hands me both cups, then plops down beside me, stretching his long legs out in front of him.

He takes his cup back to take a small sip and then smiles. "Mmmmmm, anchovies. Ten out of ten." He sets the cup down beside him and lies back, stretching his hands behind his head.

I take a sip of mine and then follow his lead, pulling the hood of my puffy jacket behind my head to cushion it against the concrete.

"My brothers and sister and I used to do this all the time when we were kids," he says, his eyes on the sky. "We'd climb up onto the garage roof back home—terrifyingly steep moss-covered shingles, sheer drop—my mom would have murdered us if she found out. But the sky out in West Lake? Man, you can see everything."

I consider how different our lives were growing up: his big family and small town, my big town and small family.

"Technically, this might be my first stargazing experience," I tell him. "Unless you count my eighth-grade trip to the Science Centre. They had a planetarium."

He turns his head toward me, and I catch the slightest whiff of his aftershave. "You've been missing out. Stargazing is the ultimate reminder that we are tiny, insignificant blips. The universe has been doing its thing for billions of years, and yet, somehow, you and me—we ended up right here, right now. What are the odds?"

It's something my Uncle Larry would have said. And something that would have definitely made me roll my eyes at him, then promptly remind him that that feeling of awe he's experiencing is just his brain trying to make sense of the incomprehensible scale of time and space.

However, tonight, listening to Mackenzie say it—the sentiment somehow hits me differently.

"Hey." He points to a bright light flashing through the sky. "Shooting star. Quick! Make a wish."

I catch a glimpse of the streak of light right before it fades.

He turns to me again, this time letting one of his arms drop so it rests between us.

"Did you go big, or take the altruistic route and wish for peace on earth?"

I roll my head so I can look at him. "Neither. I don't really believe in wishes."

His eyebrow lifts. "Really? Why not?"

I shrug, the nylon of my jacket making a rustling sound as I move. "I just don't think that a hot rock flying through space has any ability to alter my life in any meaningful way—unless it's about to clock me on the head."

Mackenzie turns to face me. "Is it just hot rocks you're against, or do you feel the same about birthday candles and turkey wishbones?"

I shake my head. "The whole gamut. I also call bullshit on astrology, predestination, reincarnation, and Santa Claus."

His jaw drops in a mock attempt to look shocked, then he schools his face and narrows his eyes. "Question for you, when is your birthday?"

"September first, why?"

He nods as if that was the answer he was expecting. "Typical Virgo. Too logical for your own good."

He grins, and I actually do roll my eyes this time.

We watch the stars in silence for a while longer until there's another streak of light. I glance over in time to see Mackenzie closing his eyes. His mouth moves as if he is whispering something. I'm so intent on watching his lips that I'm caught when his eyes open again without notice.

"You're obviously not a Virgo, then," I tease.

He stretches his whole body out long, then brings his hands behind his head again. "I guess I'd like to believe there's something more than what we can see—that there might be a little magic out there, as improbable as it might be."

He sounds so much like Larry again that it makes my heart ache. Even until his last days, Larry was making wishes every time the clock read 11:11 or psychoanalyzing his feverish dreams, insisting they held good omens.

Those habits drove me crazy when he was alive, and after he was gone, they just made me angry. Where was this unseen force he was so keen to believe in? Where was his miracle?

"You don't think you're just assigning meaning to things that are purely random?" I ask.

Mackenzie glances over at me, and I think he's trying to determine if it's a serious question. The smile he had a moment ago presses into a thoughtful line, and he pauses a moment before saying anything.

"In some cases, yeah, sure. But I kind of like the idea that the universe is out there making little miracles happen."

I squint up at the night sky, letting the lights from the stars blur in an attempt to see them as anything other than what they are. "I think my problem—aside from the obvious lack of any scientific evidence—is that I just can't get my head around the idea that we're supposed to invite some obscure third party to meddle in our lives."

Mackenzie shrugs. "You say that like it's a bad thing. Don't you like the idea that the universe has your back—nudging you along your path or sending the right people into your life?"

I wouldn't be a good scientist if I were to completely refute the theory before at least examining the evidence first. But it takes only one contrary fact for me to completely shut down his idea in my head.

"My mom died when I was sixteen." I don't mean to say it so bluntly, but all these years later, I have yet to master the delivery. "She was in a car accident. Some truck ran a red light. He was fine. She didn't even make it to the hospital."

Mackenzie doesn't say anything. I'm glad because I've already heard all the obligatory platitudes, and although I know they come from a good place, nobody understands. They can't.

"I moved in with my Uncle Larry after that. He was this big, burly guy, full of life, and I was the moody, angry teen full of angst, but somehow, we managed to form a weird little family."

The heaviness returns to my chest. It hasn't dulled like they said it would. I'm just used to it now.

"He passed away last December. Pancreatic cancer."

Mackenzie places his hand over mine. His fingers press onto my palm as his thumb strokes the back of my hand: back and forth, back and forth.

"I miss him," I whisper.

Whoever told me this would get easier with time was a liar. It hurts as bad right now as it did that day he told me he was dying, and I realized I was on my own forever.

Tears prick my eyes and begin to fall, sliding sideways off my cheeks.

"He was the best kind of person." My voice cracks. "He helped people, but when no one was looking, with no expectations that you'd ever do anything for him. And he was nice. He'd shovel the snow off the neighbor's stairs or help people he barely knew move apartments. But in the end, it didn't matter how good or kind he was. He was just gone."

My tears fall harder. I let go of Mackenzie's hand to sit up and wipe my cheeks. He leans away, and when he pushes back to sit next to me, there's a Kleenex in his hand.

"Promise it's clean. Just a little crumpled."

"Thanks."

Mackenzie's arms come around me, pulling me into his shoulder. "Is this okay?"

I close my eyes and rest my head against him, hearing his heartbeat through his shirt.

"That's why I don't believe in any of it. If there is some magic force out there like you say, it's not looking out for me."

He strokes my back with his hand until my tears stop. When I finally pull away, I feel 30 percent better and 70 percent like I regret the last five minutes.

"I'm sorry I ruined the meteor shower. I haven't sobbed on a roof in a very long time." I swipe at my tears. "I'm definitely not one of those dainty, beautiful criers."

He reaches out and wipes a rogue teardrop with his thumb. "I don't trust a cry that doesn't require at least one honking nose blow."

He finds another tissue in his pocket and hands it to me. He rubs my back in slow, comforting circles, and when I secretly try to blow my nose, he laughs and then nestles me under his arm.

When he pulls away, a few minutes later, he does so with a concerned lowering of his eyebrows: "Hey, I'm sorry. What I said—it came out all wrong. I don't buy into that whole 'everything happens for a reason' thing. I just like the idea of there being something more out there."

I swipe at my now dry eyes. "I get what you're saying. And I know I just made a whole speech about vehemently disagreeing with you, but I like that you think that way. Larry was like that, too. You both have that same . . ." I wave my hand haphazardly in his direction.

His eyebrow cocks. "Delusions?"

I shake my head. "More like a sense of optimism—and faith that your *Toronto Star* horoscope holds all the answers."

He laughs, tipping his head to the sky. "Was your uncle a Pisces?"

I don't know the answer. "Maybe. His birthday was March fifteenth."

Mackenzie knocks his elbow into mine. "Well, that explains everything. I'm the twelfth. We're dreamers. The cosmic whisperers. Born with an all-access pass to the universe's deep thoughts and prone to write moody poetry."

A laugh escapes my throat. I join him, looking at the sky.

I close my eyes, not exactly listening to the cosmos but also wondering what exactly I'll hear if I do.

I don't expect to hear a repeated *buzz, buzz, buzz* coming from somewhere nearby.

"Do you hear that?" Mackenzie looks around, confirming the universe is talking to him as well.

The answer takes a moment to click. "I think that's our doorbell."

Mackenzie scrambles to his feet and holds out his hand. I take it, and he pulls me up. As we near the fire escape, the buzzing gets louder, confirming that it's the doorbell to our apartment.

Mackenzie climbs down the ladder first. Waiting at the bottom, he calls up, "Hey, be careful. It's still a bit slick."

I fling one leg over the ledge and flip around, lowering my feet onto a rung as I grip the sides of the ladder. The first and second rungs present no issues, but when my shoe finds the third, it slides off completely. The motion causes my other shoe to slip, and I'm left dangling by my arms, which hold out for all of two seconds before they give up and let go.

My entire life flashes before my eyes as I fall. It's too brief and a little too sad. But just as I get to the end—my lifeless body splayed out on the pavement below—two strong hands grab me and pull me to safety.

"Whoa, easy there. You okay?"

My feet are on solid ground. Well, at least the steel grating of the landing.

My stinging hands are clenched in front of me. I open them slowly, the shock of my slip still driving adrenaline through my body.

"Oh, shit." Mackenzie turns my shoulders so I am facing him. Reaching for my hands, he cradles them in his, peering down at the red mess coating my palms.

My head is woozy, and I sway. For a second, I think my knees are going to come out from under me, but then Mackenzie's arms come around me to hold my elbows and keep me steady.

My vision clears, and I find the nerve to open my hands again.

They are covered in something, but it is not quite red, more of a brown or a—

"Rust." I rub my thumb with my index finger to confirm

the theory. "It's just rust from the ladder. I don't think it broke the skin, and if it did, then it's a sign from the universe that I should probably make sure I'm up to date with my tetanus shot."

Mackenzie takes both my hands and presses them to his chest, where they leave rust-colored handprints on his shirt. I can feel the wild beat of his heart. The speed matches mine.

We stand for a moment, both of us just breathing, and I wonder if he is waiting for me to pull my hands away, but then his thumbs stroke the backs of my palms.

I can't tell if it's meant to be a soothing gesture or if he is doing it subconsciously.

What I do know is that I like it.

Just as I like the concerned crinkle of his forehead as his eyes skim my body from top to bottom, only relaxing as they return to my face.

And how it feels as if there is something vibrating between us that wasn't there before. Not even a moment ago when we were on the roof.

It's invisible . . .

Intangible . . .

And yet . . .

Slam.

The loud bang of a door closing acts like a pin to a bubble.

I pull my hands away with a jerk, ignoring whatever it is that just passed between us to crouch down so that I can see through the window into the hallway.

It's empty, but there is a large orange Tupperware container sitting on my doormat.

"Looks like Harmony's been doing some baking," Mackenzie says, hoisting the window open. He holds out his arm, letting me step through first.

Sure enough, when I pick it up, it's the same container from the other day with a scrawled note on top.

I heard you loved my extra special chocolate surprise so I whipped up another. I really think the practice has made perfect with this one –H

I tip the cake so Mackenzie can read the note, wondering what he wants to do next.

He reads my mind and nods at the still-open window. "I think the show is mostly over. Why don't you wash up, and I'll grab the rest of our stuff?"

I open the lid and take a peek, finding a cake identical to the earlier one. "Are you hungry?"

Mackenzie smiles. "I'd be lying if I said I didn't strongly encourage her to make one tonight."

"I will cut you a slice, then."

Mackenzie hoists a leg through the open window. When he's back out on the landing, I'm struck with a sudden urge to finish our earlier conversation.

"Hey, Mackenzie . . ."

His head pops back through the window frame.

My eyes shift upward in the direction of the roof. "Thank you for that." Then, the landing behind him. "And that. For all of it."

He dips his chin, another smile spreading across his face. "I got you, Annalise."

I walk back into the apartment and into the kitchen, where I turn on my sink, waiting for the water to warm, before I run it over my dirty hands and confirm that I won't need to take a late-night trip to the ER.

I cut two slices from the cake and lay them on plates. As I place the cover back on, I glance up and catch my reflection in the microwave door, and I'm smiling.

I can't remember the last time that happened.

Tonight did not turn out like I expected.

Mackenzie has not turned out as I expected, either.

He's still a musician with a love of late nights, indie music, bars, and being unapologetically charming to anything with a pulse that stumbles into his orbit. But he's also kind, funny, and easy to talk to—not to mention his excellent reflexes in life-threatening situations.

See what happens when you're open? Larry's voice is so clear in my head that I almost expect to see him standing in my living room.

But it's Mackenzie who walks through my front door, kicking it closed behind him with a backward flick of his foot. He drops the blanket from the roof on the floor and carries our two empty hot chocolate mugs into the kitchen, where he places them in the sink, eyeing the pieces of cake.

"I will be on a sugar high for the rest of the night. I've got at least two more episodes in me—maybe three if we pretend responsibility doesn't exist. You in?"

I was about to convince myself to eat my cake then head to bed, but instead, I carry our plates to the coffee table, and he settles down beside me on the sofa.

I can feel his thigh press into mine as he leans forward to pick up his cake. As he begins to eat, I swear that his Thunder Mountain Man smell is mingling with the sweet scent of the chocolate.

He laughs at something on the screen, and I realize the

episode has started, but I'm barely watching it. Instead, I'm noting how his Adam's apple bobs as he swallows. How that stupid lock of hair keeps falling into his eyes and how the tips of his eyelashes are blond and much longer than I ever realized.

There's a lot about him I never realized.

As I lift the last piece of cake to my mouth, I miss it completely and shovel it into the side of my face.

I set my plate down and search for something to wipe the glob of icing clinging to my lower lip but instead of finding a napkin, I draw Mackenzie's attention.

"You've got a little something . . ." His thumb swipes at the icing at the same time I try to lick it from my lip, and instead I lick him.

"Sorry." He laughs as he pulls his hand away. "That one's on me."

His eyes are on my lips and then my tongue as it darts from my mouth a second time, this time finding the chocolate.

His face is inches from mine, yet he doesn't pull back or away.

For one terrifying moment, I wonder if he's about to kiss me. Until another, even more terrifying thought follows: I wouldn't be mad if he did.

So when he doesn't lean away, I don't either.

Chocolate frosting is coursing through my veins, giving me a sugar rush that clouds my common sense.

He closes his eyes, and so I close mine, too, knowing that if I lean a little more forward, his lips will be right there. I can smell the chocolate on his breath and something else, too.

"Sauerkraut," I whisper as the connection clicks.

My eyes fly open. His do as well, a fraction after mine.

"It's sauerkraut. Isn't it? The secret ingredient in the cake?"

"Yeah." He leans away. "You got it."

Externally, I nod. Internally, I kick myself. Mackenzie leans back in his seat, turning away from me and our almost kiss.

I follow, breathing slowly and painlessly through my nostrils to calm my frantic heart, and try my best to seem totally cool with this situation.

We watch the rest of the episode in silence. I'm not sure either one of us moves at all. When it's over, he gets to his feet.

"It's probably a good time for me to head to bed."

I want to ask him what happened to the sugar high that was supposed to keep him up for at least another episode, but instead, I stand as well. "Yeah, me too."

I turn off all of the lights in the kitchen. When I reach my bedroom door, there's a creak in the hardwood near his room.

"Night, Annalise," he calls across the dark. "Sleep tight, okay?"

"You too," I call and head into my room.

14

I DON'T SLEEP TIGHT.

Instead, I toss and turn, twisting my bedsheets into one giant knot. I must fall asleep eventually, because when I open my eyes again, it's almost nine, and there's a pounding coming from somewhere in the apartment. I jump out of bed and run straight out of my room, reaching the living room at the same time as Mackenzie.

Shirtless Mackenzie.

With rumpled hair.

And little tiny creases on one side of his face from the folds in his pillowcase.

"What's going on?" He reaches up and runs a hand through his hair, disheveling it even more. The motion flexes his biceps, and my entire body reacts by breaking out into a head-to-toe sweat.

I open my mouth—whether to answer or gape, I don't entirely know, but then the pounding resumes again, and it snaps my brain like an elastic—*Wake up, dummy. Someone is here.*

I run to the door and fling it open.

Harmony stands on the other side, eyes wide and hair rivaling Mackenzie's.

"Oh, thank heavens," she says when she sees me. "Come quick. I need your help."

My body shifts into autopilot, altogether abandoning my brain and its rational questions like, *What is happening here?* And *Where are we going?* And *Why isn't Harmony wearing pants?*

All my answers come when we reach her bathroom.

"I don't know what happened," she says. "I was just brushing my teeth, then poof! Niagara Falls."

It isn't quite Niagara Falls, but at the rate the pipe under her sink is spraying water into her tiny bathroom, she is not too far away from getting an indoor swimming pool.

"Whoa." Mackenzie appears over my left shoulder.

I know I should be formulating a plan of action right now, but as he leans into the bathroom to get a better look, he braces his arms against the doorframe, putting his biceps right at eye level, and I somehow become fixated on the tiny smattering of three freckles right on the cutline of his muscle. They make the most perfect equilateral triangle and—

"Annalise—"

Mackenzie stares at me as if this isn't the first time he's said my name. "Toolbox? Do you know if you have an adjustable wrench?"

My brain reverses right out of wherever it was a moment ago and back to the task at hand. "I do. It's in the closet. I can get it."

He nods, and I run back out of Harmony's place and into mine, where I find Larry's old aluminum red toolbox at the back of the closet. I locate the adjustable wrench, then give myself a mental high five for knowing it's the adjustable wrench before running back to the other apartment.

"Here she is!" Harmony yells as I appear in her doorway

with the wrench held above my head as if it were an Olympic torch.

I leap past her to the bathroom, only stopping as I fully take in the scene before me. Mackenzie is on his knees. His gray sweatpants are drenched and clingy. His hair is soaked and slicked back as if he's just pushed it from his eyes, and there are droplets of water running down his chest.

It is straight out of a romantic fantasy.

Or maybe a porno.

I guess the distinction lies in what happens next.

He holds out his hand and takes the wrench. His other hand retracts enough for me to see that he's also holding a flashlight.

"Any chance you can hold the beam here?" He shows me where to aim the light and then hands it to me, but I can't quite get the right angle from where I'm standing.

"Can you move a little to your left?" I say as I drop to my knees beside him, drenching my sweatpants. He scootches over enough so I can see inside.

"Yeah. Right there." His thighs press against mine as he leans forward. "You got it." He shifts so his entire upper body is inside the vanity. It requires me to brace my non-flashlight-holding hand against his back to hold the correct position.

His back flexes under my fingertips.

My rational brain knows this is a motor response to the task at hand, but the rest of me wants to slide my hand down his back and feel the strength of each and every muscle.

I don't know what is wrong with me.

It's as if last night reworked my brain.

I unplugged the wire that attached "Mackenzie" and "forbidden" and reinserted it into "possibility."

Before I could ignore the overly handsome wannabe rock

star walking around half naked in my apartment, now I can't look away.

Mackenzie shifts, and the water sprays me hard in the chest. Within seconds, my entire body is soaking wet, everything except my mouth, which has gone completely dry at the sight of Mackenzie's forearms as he clasps the wrench and begins to pull—abs flexing with every tug.

His last yank comes with a groan.

And although my body is aware that we are sitting in the middle of the bathroom floor, my associative priming has me thinking about what he sounds like in bed.

Arms flexing.

Drenched in sweat.

Giving me the same focused concentration he's giving that pipe.

"Ahhh, there we go, nice and tight." He pulls away from the sink, leans back, and rests his head on the wall.

He pushes his wet hair back with a laugh and sets the wrench down beside him. "For two people who were mostly winging it, we did a pretty great job."

He holds out his hand. I clap mine on top, assuming this is a post-emergency high five, but when my palm meets his, he clasps my hand and squeezes.

It's a friendly gesture. But the heat that zips up my arm to my core is far more than friendly and makes me grateful for the curtain of wet hair hiding my face, giving me a moment to recover from whatever that was.

"You two are my heroes," Harmony calls from the hallway. She holds out two towels, which requires me to pry my hand away to grab them and pass one to Mackenzie.

"How bad are we talking about out there?" he asks, swiping at his face, then giving up and tossing it over his shoulder.

Harmony steps back into the hall. "Not so terrible. I managed to fashion a bit of a dam with my tablecloth. It held up surprisingly well, but I am going to see if Koko still has that shop vac she borrowed from Mr. Taylor after her party the other week. I think it will do the trick. Be right back."

Harmony disappears, and a moment later, I hear the sound of her door opening and closing. Then the apartment gets quiet, making me aware of the even *drip drip drip* of the last of the water trickling off the pipe and the sound of Mackenzie's labored breathing.

My eyes drop to his chest, watching it as it rises and falls, almost hypnotizing me. I manage to tear my eyes away in time to see his eyes drop to mine. I wonder if I, too, am breathing heavily, but as I look down, I realize it's not my breathing that has drawn his attention.

I am not wearing a bra.

It's usually the first thing I do when I get up in the morning. My T-shirts are well loved and therefore a little threadbare. They aren't technically see-through, but at the right angle, they also don't leave much to the imagination. But wet—I might as well be naked right now.

"Oh, god—"

I scramble to my feet, completely ignoring the inch of water on the tile floor. He pushes up from the wall as if my sudden movement has startled him to stand, too, but the moment I get my feet underneath me, they come right out from under me again.

I flail. My arms and legs shoot in four different directions as my life flashes in front of my eyes for the second time in twenty-four hours, and for the second time, two arms reach out and catch me seconds before my head cracks against the tile.

"Whoa. You all right?"

I peer up at a concerned Mackenzie leaning over me. My ass may have hit the ground with a hard *thwack,* but my head has landed on something soft.

I'm in his arms.

And my heart is beating so hard I am sure that if I look down right now, I will see it very clearly beating through my shirt because, let's face it, that thin layer of material is serving no purpose at this moment.

"I think so." I stare at him as he slowly lets my body down the last few inches but keeps my face cradled in his hands. "But I stand by my claim last night on predestination. Otherwise, I might need to start worrying that the universe has my number."

He laughs. "Not while I'm around." I notice that his thumb strokes the side of my cheek.

I'm staring up at his eyes, and he's staring down at mine, and I'm getting that very same vibe that I was getting last night: There is something between us that is more than friends, more than roommates, even.

I want him to kiss me now. There is no wavering this time, no ifs, no buts. Although I could think of no place less sexy than Harmony's bathroom floor, I am willing to forgo all ambiance to feel his lips on mine. My hands are clinging to his shoulders—still in their discombobulated death grip—and I have this urge to bring him closer to me and complete what we left unfinished on the couch.

He leans down.

And I close my eyes.

. . . And then I hear the very distinct sound of someone clearing their throat.

15

"PLEASE TELL ME I'M INTERRUPTING SOMETHING."

My eyes fly open to see Koko staring down at us from the doorway.

I let go of Mackenzie's shoulders and scramble to my feet, this time with the sense to hold on to the vanity so I don't slip.

"We were fixing the pipe." I glance at my profile in the mirror, and as suspected, everything above my neck is glowing a fire engine red.

"Oh, yeah." Koko nods. "That's exactly what it looked like." She waggles her eyebrows at me, but I am spared the need to respond as Harmony appears behind her with the plug for the wet vac.

"This should have things cleaned up in a jiffy." Harmony leans over to plug it in.

"Whoa, whoa, whoa!" Mackenzie lunges for the plug, startling Harmony, who has failed to realize how close the plug is to pooling water.

"How about we move that cord somewhere a little drier? Just to keep us all in one piece." He takes the plug from her hands, catching my eye as he wheels the wet vac toward the much drier kitchen.

"Told you I got you," he says as he passes me.

It sends a weird flutter through my body that I tell myself is gratitude for avoiding yet another brush with death.

Ten minutes later, the majority of the water has been vacuumed, and the rest of the apartment seems to be back to normal.

Harmony leaves to return the vacuum, and Mackenzie excuses himself to head back to our apartment and change. I watch him leave, my eyes following the wet trail of footprints he leaves behind him until, once again, Koko clears her throat.

"So I need to get back downstairs to the store." She gives me a knowing look. "But I will be there all morning should you want to drop by and . . . I don't know . . . chat?" She winks, then lets herself out.

One of the many downsides of losing your mom at sixteen is that you lose the default person who is supposed to be the sounding board for life's critical milestones. My mom had explained the birds and the bees to me when I was seven, in perfect anatomic detail, using the correct terms and enough description that I spent my childhood with the well-informed opinion that sex was gross. However, that opinion changed the year after she died when I was asked to the Winter Formal by a boy a year older than my almost seventeen self. Hunter P. Anderson, my biology partner, had been dumped by his girlfriend of three years two weeks before the dance. His invitation was mumbled as we dissected a worm. I was elated and half in love by the end of class. I made the mistake of not clearing my browser history after googling "things to know about having sex for the first time" on a laptop both Larry and I shared. The night of the dance, Larry came into my room. He dumped a shopping bag with four different boxes of condoms onto my bed. He told me he respected my right to make choices about my body, and if I felt I was ready for sex, then his only ask was that I do it safely. "And if you change your mind at any time," he said, pausing awkwardly in the doorway, "know that it's okay. You never have to do anything you're not comfortable with. And I'll leave my phone on all night so you can call me. I'll always come." Then he left me to finish getting ready.

I called him just after two A.M. when my date was getting handsy, and I decided I didn't want to spend the night at the Howard Johnson Hotel. Larry picked me up, just as he said he would. He took me to the apartment, made me hot chocolate, and held me when I cried and recounted the not-so-gentlemanly things my date said when I told him I wanted to go home.

"Want me to call my buddy Moose?" he asked. "We could give him a nice, long talking to about how to treat a lady."

I made him promise not to, but from that night on, Larry became my confidant.

I don't have a Larry anymore.

But I think, with some effort, maybe I could have a Koko?

Ten minutes later, I open the door to Thrift Me, carrying two coffees and two bagels.

"Good morning, little miss wet and wild," Koko says as she takes the coffee from my hands and sets it on the counter.

"I'd been hoping you'd stop by. My imagination has been filling in all of the salacious details of what I stumbled into this morning, but now I want to hear them from you. But before we get into it, I need your help." She points at the clothing rack in the middle of the aisle. "Flip the lock with your toe and then push."

I'm familiar enough with Koko's store to know she wants me to take the rack onto the sidewalk. I flip and push as instructed. She follows me out with a second rack. When we get back inside, she hands me my coffee, and we both take a moment to enjoy the caffeine in silence.

"What do you do when it rains?" I tip my head toward the racks on the sidewalk. I've never considered this question until now. Koko's store isn't big, and other than the very tiny back office, every available space is already filled with clothing.

"I figure it out," Koko replies, understanding my question. "If I lived my life planning for rain, I'd drown in flannel button-ups. I prefer to assume it will always be beautiful out, and when it isn't I have friends." She winks and takes a long sip of her coffee, followed by a dramatic *ahhhhh.*

"Thanks." She holds out her cup to cheer with mine. "I needed that. I might have had three hours of sleep last night."

She walks out from behind the counter and heads down one of the crowded aisles. When I don't immediately follow, she turns and beckons me with the wave of her hand.

"Good date?" I ask, remembering her plans with Zee as she heads for the tiny office.

She flings open the door, revealing the desk that occupies three-quarters of the space. I have no idea how she managed to get it in there in the first place.

"Zee is an interesting guy. We don't have a lot in common. I can't see this lasting all that much longer, but my god, the sex. I swear we were at it for like six hours last night. I was fully convinced that I was going to be walking funny this morning, but you didn't notice, did you?" She pulls a gym bag from one of the drawers, sets it on the desk, and looks up. "Sorry, was that too much?"

She pauses a moment but doesn't wait for my answer. "I know I have this problem where I say exactly what I'm thinking without actually thinking it all the way through. I can usually tell I've done it after the fact when people give me . . ." She points at me. "Well, the same look you're giving me right now." She pulls out a stick of deodorant, removes the lid, and applies it under her shirt.

"It's fine," I answer, and she smiles.

"Good." She removes her shirt and exchanges it for one from the bag. "But I don't think you're here to talk about me."

She shuffles past me, now fully dressed and holding a toothbrush. She opens a tiny door, which I never noticed before, to reveal a very small bathroom with a toilet and sink.

As she squeezes paste onto her brush, I consider the best way to sum up the last twenty-four hours. "I think you were right, and I might be developing feelings for Mackenzie that aren't strictly platonic."

She spits a mouthful of toothpaste into the sink and looks up, her eyes meeting mine in the mirror. "I don't think that's the shocker you think it is, Lise."

She rinses her mouth and wipes it with a towel, then turns and gives me her full attention. "So, what exactly has happened between you two?"

I think about last night. The roof. The couch. The cake. How I went from perfectly functional to practically feral in the bathroom this morning.

"I don't know. We hung out yesterday and had a really fun time, but I can't tell if it was just a normal fun time or something else. Then this morning, he was wet, and I was wet, and I thought there might be something happening between us, but, well . . . you saw. I am not sure if I'm sending the wrong signals or the right ones or if I even *want* to be sending signals at all."

She cocks her head to the side. "Okay, but you like him, right?"

I nod. "I think so? I don't know. Yes?"

She steps past me out of the bathroom into the store. "And do you think he likes you?"

I shrug, having asked myself the same thing with no conclusive answer. "When we talk . . . it feels like he's really listening, you know? And he smiles all the time, but I think he does that with pretty much everyone. You should see how he charms that redheaded barista at Nana's."

Koko raises a brow. "The little angry one?"

"Yes." I let out a long groan.

"I get where you're coming from. The man is charming." Koko leads us back to the counter and picks up her coffee. "But how does it feel when you're around him? Do you ever pick up on some . . . I don't know . . . vibe that says . . . yup, something is happening between us?"

On the couch, when he was looking at my lips. This morning, on the bathroom floor.

I shake my head. "If I picked up on anything, it would be my confirmation bias—seeing what I want to see."

Koko shakes her head. "Do me a favor and shut the science brain off for a few minutes."

I nod, even though what she's asking is impossible.

"You like him," Koko says as if confirming. "What is the worst that can happen if you tell him how you feel?"

My mind filters through a dozen terrible outcomes. "He laughs in my face."

Koko rolls her eyes. "I literally watched the guy help an old lady cross the street yesterday. You know that's not going to happen. Realistic worst case?"

I know what it is. I've pictured it. "He avoids me for weeks because I get the sense that he hates any sort of confrontation, and therefore we live in awkward silence until I leave for school in January, or worse, it gets so weird that he breaks the lease and leaves me without a subletter."

Koko tilts her head. "I know what he's paying in rent for that room. He's not going to leave. But you're right. The worst case is probably a couple of weeks of awkward kitchen encounters, and then you'll both move on."

Her point is rational and very likely what would happen. We have opposite schedules. If I really needed to, I could eat lo mein in my room for a few weeks.

"Now." She slaps her hands down on the counter. "What's the best that can happen? You fall madly in love, get married, have three kids, and get a goldendoodle."

This suggestion paints a picture even more unlikely than Mackenzie laughing in my face.

"We're not going to get married. I'm leaving for school. I'll be overseas for at least two years. If we did get together, it would be temporary . . ."

Suddenly, I begin to regret coming down here this morning. What was I even thinking? I am leaving in under three months. That's barely enough time to start a relationship, and definitely not one that could last two years of long distance. My studies are going to be intense. I can't have a boyfriend to distract me, and I don't want one.

Koko claps her hands together. "We clearly have our answer."

I know I do, although the way she is grinning at me makes me think our answers are not the same.

"Three months of hot roommate sex," Koko declares, clarifying what I clearly needed to be clarified. "That's the best part of a relationship anyway," she continues. "When you can't keep your sweaty hands off each other. Then there's the park sex and car sex, and pool table at the Horseshoe Tavern sex."

I know the pool table she's referring to. I will not be having sex on it.

"Then you get to head on your merry way when things start to fizzle out." Koko leans forward, resting her chin in her palms. "The moment you realize you hate his going-out pants or how his spoon always clanks on his teeth when he eats soup, you're on a plane heading over the ocean. No hard feelings."

She holds up her hands as if she's just presented irrefutable evidence. "Now go on." She shoos me with her hands. "Get going. You really don't have much time to waste. Gotta pack that magical new love sex in while you can."

I pick up my coffee and head for the door, not because I'm rushing to share my feelings but because I know an easy out when I see one.

"Uh . . . thanks for the talk," I say to her as I push the door open.

She smiles. "Any time, my friend. Any time."

WHEN I GET out to the sidewalk, I stand there for a good five minutes, needing fresh air and a few moments to work up the nerve before returning to the apartment.

When my hands and feet begin to feel the chill of the cold October morning, I head back upstairs, pausing at my front door to listen for sounds inside.

I can hear music and Mackenzie's voice singing along to what sounds like a country song.

I worry the moment I open the door, he'll take one look at my face, and the choice will be out of my hands. Whether I want him to or not, he'll know exactly how I feel.

I turn the knob, and the door swings open. Mackenzie's eyes meet mine from across the room, and he smiles in a way that his entire face lights up.

"Hey," I say, knowing my face is giving every one of my feelings away.

He rushes toward me. "I have the best news. I just got off the phone with Zee. I don't know if you've heard of the band the Rydells, but they're on tour right now, and the band that was supposed to open for them broke up over the weekend. They've asked Midnight Station to fill in." He picks me up and spins me around, and when he sets me back down again, our bodies are so close I can see the tiny crumb from his breakfast toast still clinging to his stubble. "These guys are supposed to be the next big thing. There's like three labels fighting for them right now. Zee says there's going to be producers at one of our shows, maybe more."

"Wow." I try my absolute best to match his excitement. "Congratulations. That's amazing."

He runs his hands through his hair, literally bouncing on the balls of his feet. "Thanks. I knew this was all going to work out. I just had this gut feeling, but then I wasn't sure, and I started doubting everything, and now I *know* . . . I gotta go call my brother."

The rest of the details come out in hurried spurts over the next two hours as Mackenzie packs his bags and finalizes details over the phone with Zee. The Rydells are on a twelve-week tour. The band that was supposed to be opening for the northeastern leg, Bingo Jerry and the Rumpled Teasers, got into a major fight when the drummer hooked up with the bass's ex, who also happens to be the lead singer's sister. Mackenzie will be gone for four weeks, playing ten of the thirty shows in five cities in upstate New York, northern Ohio, and eastern Michigan.

He leaves tonight.

"I sent you next month's rent," he says as he slings his duffel bag onto the pile next to the door, which also includes his backpack and guitar case. "And I'll keep in touch while we're on the road."

He comes to stand in front of me. His eyes drop to something below my neckline, but I can't tell if that's just a reflex or if my T-shirt is doing weird things again. I look down just in time to see his fingers flex and his weight shift from his heels to his toes. Now, I think he might be going in for a hug but is waiting for me to give some indication or signal that I am going to meet him halfway. I almost do it. My arms come up, and I lean in, closing my eyes for a fraction of a second . . . and then I chicken out, pivoting on my toes and retreating to the kitchen, returning a minute later with a Tupperware container in my hands.

"I have something for you."

He doesn't need to open it. He knows what's inside. "But it's your favorite."

I nod. "Don't worry. I left myself a big slice on a plate in the fridge. There's a fork in here, too. It'll make for a good road trip snack."

He smiles. "Keep me posted on things. Let me know if Harmony bakes anything weird."

"Oh, that's not a matter of *if*," I correct him. "It's a matter of *when*."

"See you in a few." He holds out his arms. This time, the invitation to a hug is clear. I hesitate for only a moment before letting him pull me to his chest. My head finds the same spot it did last night, right under his chin, ear pressed to his heart.

I lied to Koko earlier. I don't think I like him; I know I do.

As for how he feels? I am still in the dark. But I swear our hug lasts a little longer than it should—confirmation bias be damned.

He only pulls away when a car honks from the street below.

"I better go." He slings his bags over his shoulder and picks up his guitar. As he steps toward the door, I notice his leather jacket hanging on the hook behind him.

"Aren't you taking that?"

He glances at the hooks and shakes his head. "Why don't you look after it for me while I'm away?"

And with that, he walks out into the hallway.

A moment later, he is gone.

16

I WAKE UP SUNDAY MORNING TO THE sound of a quiet kitchen. No one singing the same song lyric over and over and over until it's absolutely perfect. My apartment smells like lemon Pledge and my winter wonderland bathroom candle, not the subtle traces of Epic Thunder or Mega Mountain Mist.

By 9:56 I'm in front of Koko's store again, with two large coffees and two strawberry sunshine doughnuts in hand. However, the woman who rounds the corner at 9:59 is unfamiliar. She's wearing a short black skirt with ripped black tights and has pink hair in the most perfectly immaculate bob. She unlocks the front door with Koko's keys after greeting me with a "hey," assuming I am an eager Sunday morning shopper.

"Where's Koko?" I ask, having never seen anyone other than Koko behind the cash register.

"She had a family emergency," this new woman tells me. "Had to fly back to Japan last night. I'm here for at least three weeks. Were you looking for something in particular?"

She continues to tell me her name is Perstephanie. She only drinks green tea and has celiac.

When it becomes clear I'm not there to purchase anything,

she turns her attention to folding a pile of sweaters, and I take my coffee and my doughnuts and my sadness back upstairs. I even stop and knock on Harmony's door, but there's no answer other than a soft meowing from her cat.

My apartment feels so empty that I go for a walk, roaming the city for hours to avoid going back. I even stop into Nana's seeking the familiar grunt from the grumpy redheaded barista, but there's a guy behind the counter whose name tag says Todd and who smiles so widely that I turn around and leave.

I HAVEN'T FELT this alone since Larry died. I hadn't really noticed the way that Mackenzie and Koko had begun to fill the tiny cracks his death left in my heart until they, too, were no longer around to fill them.

"They're coming back," I say out loud, startling an elderly woman passing me on the sidewalk. She clutches her purse and steps away, but it doesn't stop me from repeating the phrase. "They're only gone for a few weeks. They're coming back."

I finally convince myself to go home with a bribe to order takeout from Rol San. But when I call the restaurant to place my order, the owner recognizes my number and asks if I want the dinner for two. I have to tell her I'm dining alone tonight and will be for the foreseeable future. When the delivery guy comes, there's a note scrawled on the paper lid: *Men are pigs. You go, girl!*

When I flop onto the couch, I'm not even sure a Christmas movie will pull me out of my funk. I flick the television on reluctantly, my heart giving a painful lurch when I click past Netflix and it pops up the option for *Schitt's Creek.* I scroll past to the Hallmark Channel and make my way through *A*

Princess This Christmas, The Christmas Princess Swap, and *A Very Royal Christmas* before I give up and decide to go to sleep.

As I plug in my phone for the night, I check my texts one last time, hoping for one from Mackenzie or even Koko, but there's nothing. There's just a single missed call from an unknown number.

"Good night," I whisper, feeling stupid the moment I do it.

My phone screen stays dark.

"YOUR PHONE IS buzzing."

Phillip doesn't break eye contact with the computer screen in front of him, but I can hear the annoyance in his voice.

"Sorry." I glance at the screen quickly before sending the call to voicemail. "It's one of those scammy robot voices telling me there's a warrant out for my arrest or something. I think that heating pad I ordered online last week sold my phone number to Big Data."

Phillip goes back to his computer. I know I should return to my growing pile of work, but after almost forty-eight hours alone, I'm craving conversation.

"What's new in your life, Phillip? Do you have any big plans for tonight?"

Phillip does turn away from his screen this time, his eyebrow arching as if he doesn't understand why I'm asking the question. It's an understandable reaction, as I'm pretty sure this is the first time I've ever asked it.

"I'm going to a bar with my girlfriend and her friends," he replies. "Why do you want to know?"

My mouth drops open, not entirely sure I heard him right. "You go to bars?" I shake my head. "Wait! You have a girlfriend! Who is she? How long have you been dating her?"

Phillip thinks for a moment. "Her name is Dara Kim. She's a PhD candidate in the biological engineering program at U of T. Apparently, we've been dating for three years, but I've only been aware of that fact for the last two."

That answer makes the entire thing believable.

"Do I get to meet her?" I'm suddenly very much intrigued.

"You would want to do that?" he asks like the answer isn't obvious.

The only reason I would say no is that my imagination is running absolutely wild right now, and I can't see how the real woman would stack up to the elaborate fantasy forming in my head. "I absolutely want to do that. Ideally immediately."

Phillip squints at something on his screen. "It's the middle of the workday, Annalise. Immediately is not feasible, but you're welcome to join us tonight. We're meeting at the Rivoli at nine."

The Rivoli is a bar and live music venue that I'm pretty sure has been around since the eighties. I cannot picture Phillip setting foot in the place.

"I still can't believe you're going to a bar on a work night. Who even *are* you?"

Phillip sighs and finally peels his eyes from his computer. "There's a band she's looking forward to seeing. Some sort of rock group. Not my cup of tea, but I indulge her."

Phillip tilts his head, looking past me to the paperwork on my desk that I'm only halfway through logging.

"You might want to get a move on. The lab needs those files by five."

The rest of the day flies by as I dream up the potential future Mrs. Button. Does she share his love for practical chinos and earth tones?

I am still thinking about her when I pack up my bag and nearly run into Phillip on his way back into our office.

"Whoa!" I teeter on my toes, but I manage to regain my balance and avoid an actual collision, which would be even more disastrous, as he has a urine sample cup in his hands.

"Please tell me that's empty."

Phillip holds it out to me. "It is for now, but I need you to fill it."

I eye the cup, wondering if this is a joke. "For what purpose?"

He sets a manila folder down on the counter. "I sent your specimens in with my last batch, and the lab screwed up. They need another sample."

I take the cup from his hands. It's labeled with an anonymous patient number, Phillip's name, and study information. "Do I need to do it now? I am not prepared to do what is required at this particular moment."

Phillip shakes his head. "Tomorrow is fine. Just leave it in the fridge and make sure you use this cup. I want to make sure there aren't any more mix-ups."

I leave the cup on my desk for the morning and head home.

The streetcar is full when it hits my stop, so I decide to walk the rest of the way down Spadina. When I finally get to my apartment, I am tired and cold and a little worried about what is happening in our lab, so I almost step on the package sitting on the mat outside my door.

It's a pie tin covered in silver foil with a pink Post-it on top. Scrawled in Harmony's neat handwriting are the words, *'Tis the season for holiday mincemeat! Enjoy!* I pick up what most closely resembles a pie and carry it inside. My stomach is grumbling from skipping lunch to finish my paperwork. In a momentary blip of low blood sugar, my hunger outweighs my good judgment, and I grab a fork and dig in before performing the proper sniff and poke protocols.

The first bite is so overwhelming with the combination of nutmeg and cinnamon that it numbs my taste buds. I don't get a good feel for what exactly is going on until the second bite, when I'm hit with something chewy—and the taste of oregano? And then I promptly spit out the entire mouthful into the garbage.

I want to text Mackenzie, but I worry that this Post-it thing we had going will seem stupid over text and that he's busy or, worse, hasn't even thought about me since he left.

What's the worst that can happen if you text him? This time it's not my uncle's voice in my head but Koko's.

"He doesn't text back," I say out loud, and as the words leave my lips, I realize my "worst" isn't actually all that bad.

And what's the best that can happen?

I hear Koko again and immediately know the answer. *We start talking and then we don't stop.*

I pick up my phone, but it isn't Mackenzie that I'm messaging. It's someone else who has been a far better friend than I have given her credit for.

ANNALISE:

Hey Koko. I stopped by the store and heard you're back visiting your dad. I hope he's doing okay. Just wanted you to know that I'm thinking of you, and if you need me to check in on the store or grab your mail, I'm happy to help. Take care.

I send it. Then, using the rush of serotonin that comes along with the whoosh, snap a photo of the pie, find Mackenzie's name in my phone, and send it to him.

ANNALISE:

Note says mincemeat. 80% sure it contains actual meat. 90% sure it's not supposed to. 3/10

I abandon my phone on the counter and get ready, although as I dress, I secretly hope to hear the soft ping of an incoming text. Twice, I swear I hear it, but my screen stays dark. A streetcar passes, its *ding* sounding a little too similar to my phone's.

When I head out to meet Phillip, I turn my phone off completely because *I* am an independent woman. Who goes to bars. On a weeknight.

However, as I climb the steps and push open the doors to the dark, crowded bar, I can't help but think how I am more the type of woman who seriously debates if she really needs to go to the grocery store when it's after seven—even after years of Larry's nagging that she's wasting her young, wild, hangover-free years—and how he would have loved to see me here tonight.

I find Phillip at a large high-top table, a club soda with lime half drunk in front of him. He introduces me to his girlfriend, Dara Kim, who is loud and funny and speaks at a speed of two hundred words a minute. She isn't even in the realm of what I expected except for the fact that I can immediately tell she is very smart and clearly adores Phillip from the way her hand rests on his biceps and how she smiles at him when he describes, with painstaking detail, the parameters of our current research project. Dara introduces me to her two friends, who smile at me politely and cheers their vodka sodas with my Diet Coke when I return from the bar. We make polite, surface-level conversation until the band comes on at ten after nine. The lead singer introduces them as Sid and the Crosbys. They are loud and only okay. Their drummer overpowers the lead guitar, and the harmonies of the lead singer and bassist sound like they're fighting each other.

I snort with a mouth half full of Diet Coke when I think how quickly I've gone from the girl who couldn't name a relevant band if she tried to one making judgmental commentary as if she were a music critic. And suddenly I'm thinking of Mackenzie again, and my hand is in my purse, reaching for my phone to turn it back on—just in case—only stopping as the fragments of Dara's friend's conversation cut through the music.

". . . Midnight Station . . . Thursday . . . No, not this week."

I whip my head toward them, my movement so sudden they stop mid-conversation.

"Um, are you guys talking about Midnight Station, the band?" My heart begins to thump hard for no apparent reason.

"Yeah," says the curly-haired blonde, whose name I'm pretty sure is Veronica. "We normally come here on Thursdays because they sometimes play here, but I don't see them on the schedule for this week." She holds up her phone. The web page for the Rivoli is up on her screen.

My mouth opens, and the words pour out as if I've been waiting for this exact topic of conversation to come up.

"Oh, they went on tour. They're opening for the Rydells. It was a last-minute thing." I manage to sound quite nonchalant.

Like the Rydells weren't a band I only learned about three days ago.

"That's wild," says the dark-haired one, who I also think is named Veronica. "How did you know? Did they post on Instagram?"

I feel legitimately cool as I shrug. "The drummer is my roommate."

The Veronicas look at each other. The blond one leans forward. "Shut the fuck up. He's your roommate? Tell me he's single. He's gorgeous."

A pain slices through me as Veronica Number Two stabs the maraschino cherry in her cocktail glass with a tiny plastic sword and pops it into her mouth.

"He's on tour, Vee," says the brunette one. "Single or not, he's probably banging everything that walks."

Their conversation continues, but I lose the plot. My Diet Coke is sloshing around in my stomach, and I no longer feel so good.

"I think I might head out," I yell across the table to Phillip, who does not seem the least bit upset at my sudden, unplanned departure. It's Dara who slides from her seat to come around and hug me. "It was so nice to meet you finally, Annalise. We should do this again soon."

I shoot a look at Phillip, who shrugs as if he's indifferent to the matter. "I'd like that," I tell her, and I'm not even lying.

17

WHEN I GET HOME, THERE IS A new pie with a new note waiting for me outside my door.

Made a little oopsie with the other one. Recommend you throw it out. Second time's the charm.

I pick it up and take it inside with me, thinking to myself that I'm pretty sure it's the third time that's supposed to be the charm. Just to be safe, Pie Number Two follows its predecessor straight into the trash.

As I stare at the crusty brown mess sliding its way to the dark depths of my garbage can, my emotions slide along with it from a place where I was feeling like I was maybe okay to one where I know that I'm not.

I don't know what is more pathetic—that with Koko and Mackenzie out of town, Phillip is the closest thing I have to a friend in the city right now, or that I hadn't even noticed or cared about that fact until tonight. When Magda and Gopi moved away, I had Larry. And when Larry died, I didn't have any room in my heart to deal with anything other than the pain of losing him, and now . . . now I'm alone again, staring at a pie in my garbage can.

My eyes wander across the apartment to the hooks next to the door. Mackenzie's leather jacket hangs next to Larry's old rainbow umbrella.

Before I can stop myself, I'm crossing the room and lifting it off the hook.

I am doing this for science, I tell myself. *Just a little experiment to see what will happen.*

But there's a deeper truth at play here. One I'm not willing to admit aloud.

I want something to happen.

Something that connects me to Larry or Mackenzie. Some memory, some story that isn't me, here, alone in my apartment.

I close my eyes as I slip it on, ready for whatever is about to happen.

And what happens is . . . nothing.

What the hell?

When I open my eyes again, it's to the sight of the empty hook, my apartment door and the rest of the room exactly as I left it.

I take the jacket off and put it on again.

Nothing.

I try a third time and even a fourth. Zilch. Nada. Zero.

"The Universe sends us what we're ready for at the exact time we need it in our lives."

I can practically hear Larry's voice in my head.

"Well, I'm ready," I yell to the universe. "Send me thy signal. I am telling you I need it right now."

The Universe apparently feels otherwise.

Or I'm wearing a regular, old jacket.

I take it off and throw it across the room, where it lands on the couch.

A sadness washes over me as I settle into the cushions and wrap myself in my favorite blanket.

Although it's late, I turn on the TV, find *Romancing the Christmas Duke* in my Netflix queue, and hit play.

Instantly, I am transported to a small town in Maine where a down-on-her-luck schoolteacher is trying to revive the town's annual Christmas pageant and carry on her grandmother's legacy. I make it through the first twenty minutes, but after a disastrous first pageant rehearsal, I begin to lose interest and pause it with an audible sigh.

My phone sits on the coffee table in front of me. I pick it up and swipe open the screen. There is no response to my earlier pie text to Mackenzie, but there is one from Koko.

KOKO:

You are a doll. Things are better now. He's home and eating soup and reminding me of all of the ways I've failed him as a daughter, so I'd say he's on the mend. Will be home in a few weeks. Persteph has things covered at the store but I appreciate you xo.

I heart her message, then exit to my home screen with the full intention of setting my phone down, but as my thumb hovers over the Instagram icon, Veronica's words from earlier linger in my head.

Before I can tell myself not to, I click.

The little magnifying glass appears, and I punch in the band's name. The screen refreshes, and I press on a little picture that looks like Zee singing at a microphone. My entire screen fills with pictures of the band. I scroll down a few times. There are some shots of the band onstage, one that I'm sure was taken at the Gladstone and even a solo shot of Mackenzie. I scroll through the comments for exactly three seconds before I abort, much preferring Veronica's PG-13 "he's gorgeous" to the thirsty ones under his picture.

There is a ring around the profile pic, and because I've turned down this dark road, I figure I might as well continue.

I click on it to display the band's stories and regret my decision immediately.

The first picture that flashes is one of the band taken at what appears to be a backstage area. The guys are sweaty as if they've just finished their set, and surrounding them are a group of women—all very gorgeous and all very young.

Mackenzie has his arm around one of them.

At least, I think he does.

Before I can confirm, a new picture pops up. It's of Zee and the bassist, Benjamin, and it looks like they are in a club with a bottle of champagne between them.

I click back to watch the stories again. This time I screenshot the first picture.

At closer inspection, Mackenzie's hand isn't around her. It's just hovering above her shoulders.

Relief rushes through me.

I try zooming in even closer just to confirm, but as I do, a notification pops up on my Instagram app.

> WASTED_WORDS:
> You alive?

I startle at the unexpected pop-up and accidentally throw my phone. It bounces off the corner of the coffee table and then slides across the living room floor.

I retrieve it with a loud "shit" and hold my breath until I confirm the screen isn't cracked and there are no other visible damages before scrolling to my messages and opening the unread one.

Wasted_Words.

Who the hell is Wasted_Words?

I click on the tiny profile pic and am taken to a page that I've never seen before. Most of the posts are of nature: a lake so calm you can see the perfect reflection of the brightly colored fall trees, a stone shaped like a heart, and a sky so bright with stars you can see the Milky Way. There are no face pics. Just one of a hand on the neck of a guitar.

I know that hand.

I click back to my messages and type.

> ANNALISE HARRIS:
> I am alive. It was touch and go for a while there earlier. Harmony made pie.

Three dots appear, then a message.

> WASTED_WORDS:
> Is it weird that I'm craving her seven-oat cookies?

> ANNALISE HARRIS:
> seeing as we've only been able to identify five of the seven oats, yes

A minute goes by, and he doesn't reply. I grow antsy and type what I'm really thinking.

> ANNALISE HARRIS:
> you look to be having a lot of fun

His next message takes seconds to appear.

> WASTED_WORDS:
> The shows have been great. I'm still getting used to playing for a big audience. The Rydells are great guys. But I'm exhausted. I don't know how Zee is doing it. He's out after every show.

My heart begins to pound harder.

> ANNALISE HARRIS:
> not your thing?

> WASTED_WORDS:
> Not really. I usually go out for a beer or two and then sneak back to the motel to write or watch a movie.

> ANNALISE HARRIS:
> Is that what you're doing now?

WASTED_WORDS:
I wrote for a bit but I've been scrolling the last twenty minutes for something to watch. I'm at the point where I need to pick something or give up and go to bed. What are you doing?

I consider lying but don't.

ANNALISE HARRIS:
I'm wrapped in a blanket watching a movie too.

WASTED_WORDS:
The Hudson's Bay blanket?

My hands instinctively pull the wool tighter.

ANNALISE HARRIS:
The very one

WASTED_WORDS:
That's my napping blanket.
It's a good one.

Without thinking, I pull the wool to my nose and sniff, and I swear there's the faintest trace of him.

> WASTED_WORDS:
> What are you watching?
> I'll watch it with you.

My face turns red, which is silly, seeing as he can't actually see the screen. I can easily lie, but he texts again before I get the chance.

> WASTED_WORDS:
> Is it murder or Christmas tonight?

I look around, my heart thumping wildly, half expecting him to be standing behind me, but my apartment is empty.

> ANNALISE HARRIS:
> Christmas and how did you know?

It's almost a full minute before he answers.

> WASTED_WORDS:
> The Netflix algorithm gives away all your secrets. And you've fallen asleep a few times. I watched the second half of A Pumpkin Spice Proposal one night while you snored away beside me.

> ANNALISE HARRIS:
> I do not snore

WASTED_WORDS:

Are you going to tell me what you're watching?

I hesitate only for a second this time.

ANNALISE HARRIS:

Romancing the Christmas Duke

WASTED_WORDS:

How far in are you?

ANNALISE HARRIS:

22 minutes. She just left the first Christmas pageant practice, and only half the cast showed up, and they did not look promising. He is on a runaway horse charging through the woods. She spotted the horse in her car on her way home and wandered into an abandoned Christmas tree farm. Now you're all caught up.

WASTED_WORDS:

Pressing play now

I hit play as well, not entirely sure if he's serious.

> WASTED_WORDS:
> Devastatingly handsome dude with the long hair is the Duke I presume?

> ANNALISE HARRIS:
> According to the preview, yes, but we don't officially know that yet.

He falls from the horse just as the schoolteacher spots him. She rushes to his aid next to the most beautiful Douglas fir just as tiny snowflakes begin to fall.

> WASTED_WORDS:
> Bet you he's going to have amnesia

His text comes just before the duke opens his eyes and asks, "Who am I?"

> ANNALISE HARRIS:
> Lucky guess

The heroine gets him to his feet and over to her awaiting car.

> WASTED_WORDS:
> Watch . . . it's not going to start

Sure enough, she puts her key in the ignition, and when she turns it, the engine whines and stutters.

ANNALISE HARRIS:
Have you seen this before?

I accuse him out loud as I type.

WASTED_WORDS:
Not this one specifically, but my mom loves these movies. She usually starts watching them on the first of November, and no one else is allowed to use the television in the family room until January 1, so I've watched a lot.

WASTED_WORDS:
Do you mind if we switch to text?

ANNALISE HARRIS:
Yeah. No problem

A text pops up on my screen.

UNKNOWN NUMBER:
Much better. Also, do you think I could pull off that jacket? I'm kind of into it.

I glance at the message and then at my television screen. The heroine has managed to get the duke back to the community center by flagging down a local pumpkin farmer. The duke has replaced his muddy coat with a pale blue and silver overcoat that looks like it was from an old production of *Cinderella*.

I stare at the text.

ANNALISE HARRIS:

What number is this?

UNKNOWN NUMBER:

Oh, yeah. I bought a US SIM card. It was cheaper than paying long distance.

All those scam calls from the last two days suddenly look very different.

ANNALISE HARRIS:

Did you call me? I thought you were a robot voice telling me I'd won a trip to the Caribbean as long as I give my VISA number for incidentals.

UNKNOWN NUMBER:

I hate to disappoint. That was just me checking in to see what you were up to.

I think about the pie.

ANNALISE HARRIS:

I hope they didn't give away your old number, or someone will be very confused about the pictures I sent.

I click on his number and scroll my phone to add this new number to my contacts. When I get back to our text thread he's replied back with three messages.

MACKENZIE:

Pics?

MACKENZIE:

What kind of pics?

MACKENZIE:

I like pics

All of my insides turn to Jell-O as it dawns on me what he's thinking.

ANNALISE:

They were of Harmony's pie. Although the text that went with it was one of my better ones.

MACKENZIE:

Send it all!

I find the photo and text from earlier and resend it to his new number. He immediately hearts it.

MACKENZIE:

Pic and delivery 10/10

I glance up at the movie. The couple have somehow made it onto Santa's sleigh at what looks like a parade.

ANNALISE:

We've been ignoring our movie.

MACKENZIE:

Yeah, I've lost the plot. Rewind or head to bed? It's getting kind of late. I'm assuming you're working in the morning?

I glance at the clock on my phone. It's almost three A.M.

ANNALISE:

Bed is probably the responsible call.

Three dots appear to let me know he's typing back. For some reason I hold my breath.

MACKENZIE:

We're on the road tomorrow. No show but we should be in Toledo by nine if you want to watch the end with me.

I can't help the smile that spreads across my face.

ANNALISE:

it's a date.

18

OUTSIDE, THE FIRST WEEK OF NOVEMBER TURNS drizzly and gray, but inside my apartment, it's starting to feel like Christmas.

The morning after my movie date with Mackenzie, I haul the Christmas decorations out from the back of the living room closet where they're covered in a thick layer of dust.

After my mom died, I lost interest in decorating for Christmas, but Larry would make an effort every year. He'd put up a tiny, apartment-size tree and hang two red oven mitts below the window. They were covered in tiny photos of Larry dressed as Santa—a gag gift from the Secret Santa game at the curling club where he worked. I think he felt like he needed to carry on some Christmas traditions for me. I had told him once that my mother and I exchanged ornaments every year, picking ones that reminded us of each other, and he insisted we do the same.

Last year, Larry was in the hospital and I didn't want to do anything for Christmas other than binge-watch movies. It was easier to get my serotonin fix from moonlit snowball fights and mistletoe kisses without the daily reminder that I'd be both putting up and taking down my apartment-size tree alone for the foreseeable future.

This year, however, everything feels different.

Every night after work, I come home, order takeout, and settle in for a Christmas project.

One night, it's stringing lights around the windows. The next it's cutting out patterns for two Christmas stockings.

I knit.

I decoupage.

I even attempt to bake a gingerbread house from scratch with a recipe I find online and ingredients like real ginger and allspice that I have to borrow from Harmony. However, my enthusiasm and patience wane when it comes time to stick the whole thing together, and my roof keeps sliding off. Eventually, I give up and purchase one of those premade kits. The store-bought icing is basically edible superglue. My final creation deserves its own Pinterest board. Instead, I snap a pic and send it to Mackenzie.

MACKENZIE:

Wow! Harmony is not fooling around.

ANNALISE:

Actually, you're looking at an original Annalise Harris. Just a heads up though—Christmas may or may not have exploded all over our apartment.

MACKENZIE:

Why am I not even a little surprised?

ANNALISE:

You aren't? I am. Wait, is this another Virgo thing?

MACKENZIE:

No. It's a you watch Christmas movies in October thing. I assumed the two went hand in hand.

ANNALISE:

Did you ever stop to think I might just be into guys in flannel?

Three dots appear. Then disappear. Then appear again. After another message-less moment, I give in and type:

ANNALISE:

I know it's weird, but I've always seen the two as mutually exclusive interests. Hallmark movies are a way to give my brain a break from reality. They're set in cute little towns with carolers and hot chocolate festivals, where nothing truly bad happens. And if there's problems, they're fixable little blips easily remedied with a sweeping grand gesture. Real Christmas is always a little bit of a letdown. If we get snow, it's a murky gray slush. All the carolers are in the Distillery market, which is too crowded with tourists. Half-assing a Christmas dinner with a rotisserie chicken and stovetop stuffing feels sad. I find it easier to accept that big, magical Christmases only happen in fiction and that it's easier to keep things low-key with minimal expectations.

MACKENZIE:

Ahhh, I get it now.

ANNALISE:

My general pessimism?

MACKENZIE:

No. You've just never experienced a Smith family Christmas. They're magical.

ANNALISE:

Let me guess: you wake up in matching pajamas to a room full of presents and then sit down to a full turkey dinner wearing paper crowns?

MACKENZIE:

We're more of a sweatpants and old T-shirts kind of crew . . . but yeah, pretty much.

All of a sudden, I'm picturing him in sweatpants. Except he's wearing no shirt, leaning back against the bed frame, that single lock of hair falling into his eyes as he types.

I begin to craft my next message in my head. *What are you doing? What are you thinking about? Are you wearing a shirt?* But before I actually text him, another message comes through.

MACKENZIE:

Zee is back, and he's wasted. We had to share a room tonight. He's got someone with him, and I need to make sure she gets home.

I feel a zing of jealousy slice my stomach even though I have no official claim on him.

MACKENZIE:

We are on the road tomorrow, but we're in Rochester on Saturday. Maybe we can watch something together then?

My insides soften at the thought.

ANNALISE:

Sounds good

MACKENZIE:

Good night Annalise

ANNALISE:

Good night Mackenzie

. . .

SATURDAY, WE WATCH *Romancing the Christmas Duke Two,* then a few days later, combine my love of romance and murder with a Christmas-themed mystery aptly titled *Mistletoe She Wrote.* They're the exact kinds of movies I love, but I find myself paying less and less attention to the plots and more and more attention to the text messages that accompany this new post-show ritual.

Mackenzie tells me about growing up in West Lake with his brothers and sister, who pranked, teased, and terrorized him daily but are still his best friends. I tell him about growing up in the city and the lackadaisical parenting that had me easily navigating the transit system like a pro by the time I was ten.

Our texts start to creep past our usual midnight-to-two texting window. One morning, while I'm at work, I get a pic of the world's largest weathervane (Montague, Michigan), then later that afternoon, a picture of his new custom Nikes (express delivered from All the Other Kicks in Hamilton). I send back a shot of the amazing sour and spicy cold jelly noodles I splurge on for lunch, then the next morning, a photo of Nana's Doughnuts' new flavor of the month: sriracha peanut butter.

I have slowly morphed from a person who would turn off her phone at work and proudly declare "we are losing our humanity to screens" to someone who smiles every time a notification bubble appears.

So when I sit down for dinner on the second Thursday of November, my back wedged between the base of my couch and my feet shoved under the coffee table, my smile is wide when I look down and see that I have not one but two messages waiting to be read.

I click open the first. It's from Koko. A pic of her arm holding out a beautiful vintage embroidered jacket. *Scored this at the market, do you love?* I heart her message and send back a smiley emoji and *yes* emphasized with three exclamation marks. The second text is from Mackenzie. It is also a picture. I click on it and zoom in.

It's a selfie taken in what appears to be a dressing room mirror. He looks good. No, he looks great, and . . .

ANNALISE:

Are you wearing leather pants?

Three bubbles immediately appear.

MACKENZIE:

We're doing a photo shoot. Zee thinks the band needs merch. These things are so tight I can't even sit down, but I'm counting that as a good thing, otherwise, I worry he'd make me wear them to our show tonight.

I had very much noticed the pants appeared tight, but that was not their defining feature. What made my breath catch and my heart complete a loop-de-loop was how low they sat on his hips, revealing the tops of his V-lines just above the waistband.

ANNALISE:

Where does one purchase this merch?

ANNALISE:

Are everyone else's pants equally as tight?

ANNALISE:

Too bad you left your leather jacket here. You could have had a whole three-piece suit.

He doesn't text back but instead sends another photo. Mackenzie is in the foreground, eyebrow arched in an expression that is clearly not impressed. Zee and the rest of the band are behind him seemingly unaware the photo is being taken and wearing identical pairs of leather pants.

ANNALISE:

Good luck. Send me the link for merch. I need a new hoodie.

The following day I get a pic of a donation clothing bin and a text.

MACKENZIE:

Took me 45 minutes to get them off last night. Maybe they will make some other Michiganian very happy. Getting on the bus now. Will text you later.

I send him back a "safe drive" but don't hear back from him until just after one A.M. as I'm climbing into bed. I reach for my charger and am just about to plug it in when my phone pings twice in my hand.

MACKENZIE:

hey

MACKENZIE:

are you still up?

I flip on the light, a giddy lightness flooding my body.

ANNALISE:

You caught me just in time. How was the bus?

I roll on my side seeing the three dots appear on my screen.

MACKENZIE:

Easy trip. Inspiration struck on the 75 South. I wrote something. Can I send it to you?

I don't know what exactly that means but I type back.

ANNALISE:

Of course.

Five minutes go by where I see speech bubbles appear and disappear three different times, but nothing comes through. Finally, I get a message, but there is no text, just a single video.

I click it, and it begins to play.

The footage is of Mackenzie. He appears to be sitting alone on a bed. The generic maroon patterned bedspread and coordinating yellow wallpaper make me think he is in some budget hotel. His guitar is in his lap, and the camera is sitting at an odd angle as if he has propped it up on a TV stand and hoped for the best. Then the first few notes trickle out of his guitar. His finger work is fast and yet the song feels slow and soft. It reminds me a little of the one from that night at the Gladstone.

When he starts to sing, my whole body goes still, which is odd because it's not like I haven't heard his voice before. But this feels different. It's as if this song was meant for me. A private glimpse into something I'm not sure everyone gets to see.

And I'm standing here, just waiting for the rain
Hoping it won't break, hoping it won't break
But I'm drowning in silence, pretending it's okay
I don't want the storm, just the calm before it comes.

I feel a sense of loss when the song comes to an end.

I watch the video a second time and then a third. A fourth is under serious consideration but before I can press play a text comes through.

MACKENZIE:

What did you think?

I think that I could listen to this song and only this song for the rest of my life and never get tired of it.

ANNALISE:

This is what you are meant to do.

He hearts my message, but no text comes through. I begin to think that's the extent of his response, but then a message pops up on my screen.

MACKENZIE:

I needed that tonight. Thanks.

I think I should text back more. Maybe something like I wish that he was here but that this video is proof that he's clearly born to be up on a stage sharing his talent. But before I get that or anything else out, a second text comes through.

MACKENZIE:

I know it's late and you need to get up for work tomorrow, but I really wanted you to hear it first. Get some sleep. I'll text you tomorrow.

Any courage I may have had a moment ago is gone.

ANNALISE:

Of course. Anytime. Good night Mackenzie.

MACKENZIE:

Sleep tight Annalise.

19

TWO WEEKS LATER, I GET HOME FROM work to find a package outside my door on the landing. At first I think it's another Harmony special, but then I see my name and address on the front and I realize it's actual mail.

I pick up the white bubble wrap bag and bring it inside, where I rip it open.

It's a sweatshirt—black and oversized, which gives ample real estate for the blown-up photo of the four leather-clad men posing on the front. I pull it over my head, scoop up my phone, and begin typing as I run for the mirror in the bathroom.

ANNALISE:

If I die from happiness tonight please let it be known that my last wish is to be buried in this thing.

I snap a selfie and send it, grateful that it takes only seconds to get a reply.

MACKENZIE:

It is so bad I couldn't not send it to you.

I laugh out loud, walking back into the living room and scaring the pigeons sitting on the windowsill.

ANNALISE:

What did Zee think of the new song?

It's a very long two minutes before he answers back.

MACKENZIE:

He hasn't had a chance to listen to it yet. He's been busy. I just need to get him in the right mood.

Two days later, it is an unusually warm November Saturday, so I decide to take a walk through Trinity Bellwoods Park, when a text comes through.

MACKENZIE:

So Zee is not a fan of the song. He said the band needs to ignite the crowd, not put them out with lullabies.

My heart feels like it detaches and falls straight to the pit of my stomach.

ANNALISE:

Well he is wrong. That song is incredible. I've listened to it every day since you sent it.

I don't get a text back, but my phone begins to ring in my hands.

I stare at Mackenzie's name on my screen and almost don't answer—thrown off by the shock of moving from text without ample warning.

"Hey." I finally press my phone to my ear and my hand to my heart, which is beating awfully fast considering we lived together for a month and talked all the time.

"Is this okay?" His voice is raspier than I remember. "I just wanted to hear your voice."

My knees legitimately wobble. I have to brace myself against the trunk of a maple tree for a moment.

"Did I make it weird?" he says when I still haven't said anything.

"No. Not at all. I just normally have more time to think between texts. My semantic fluency is a little out of practice, so don't expect any overly witty comebacks."

He laughs, and I realize how much I've missed that sound.

"So Zee is a total asshole," I say. "And I do prefer saying that out loud versus texting it. It allows me to really put the emphasis on *ass.*"

He laughs again, and I find myself wondering why we haven't been doing this all along.

"You really listen to my song every day?" he asks, and there's a vulnerability to his voice that makes everything inside me ache.

"Yes," I tell him. "And I think Zee needs to listen to it again because he's completely wrong about it, not to mention that he owes you for uprooting your entire life to join his band. I think you should remind him that he agreed to play your songs, and now he's going back on his word."

I can hear Mackenzie sigh long and hard. "It's fine. I don't want to fight with him."

I don't think it's fine at all, and I don't understand why Mackenzie seems so okay with it.

"Well, what about the other guys?" I change my tactic. "Have you played it for them? It's a band, not a dictatorship."

I can't see Mackenzie, but I can feel him shaking his head.

"I just don't want to be the guy that causes drama. Things are going well right now. The guys are all getting along. We've got less than a week before we're back. It just doesn't feel like a time to fight."

Something swells inside me that feels a lot like frustration. I don't understand why he's so reluctant to go after something he claims to want so badly.

I close my eyes. When I open them again, something on the paved path a few feet away catches in the sun. I walk over to it and bend down, and once I study it for a moment, I abandon all of my rules about touching things left on the ground in the city and pick it up.

It's a penny. As I study it in the palm of my hand, I realize it has been awhile since I've seen one.

Larry considered pennies to be the ultimate heralds for signs from the universe. He did not share my wariness about picking things up off the sidewalks, and any penny he found while he was out went into his pocket with a declaration that something good was about to happen. He had a big pickle jar in his closet filled with them. And when Canada stopped producing pennies and the sidewalk supply started to dwindle, he'd plant his stash around the apartment, leaving "luck" for me to find. They'd appear on days when I had a big test or a date and sometimes on days where I was just feeling down. I never thought they brought me any sort of supernatural power, but they did bring something far better—a reminder that someone cared about me.

"You know how you believe in signs?" I say to Mackenzie.

There's a short huff of laughter on his end. "Yeah."

I hold the penny up to the light. "Well, I just spotted a lucky penny. I think it means your song is something really special. I am going to hang on to it until you get back and keep it safe."

"Thank you," he says, and I get the impression he's talking about more than just the coin. "I have to run. I'm having a drink with Edwin Stark—he's the lead singer of the Rydells."

He draws a breath and I almost get the sense he's going to say something else, but he lets it go in one long exhale. "Maybe I'll play it for him."

I like the possibility I hear in his voice. "I think that's an excellent idea."

20

MY CALL WITH MACKENZIE GETS ME THROUGH a grueling few days at work. Phillip and I have come to the part of our study where we need to review the notes from our subjects' counseling sessions. They have all been in a six-week rehabilitation program focusing on managing their addictions. We are comparing their files with their MRI scans to see if their progress or regression can be mapped to their brains.

It involves reading very personal details. Although the files are anonymous, each one shines a light on a life plagued by addiction. The road for most of the patients in our program is rocky. And although there are several successes, many participants are struggling, and there are several others where the patient has dropped the program altogether.

The file in front of me hits a little too close to home. The patient is a single mother struggling with an opioid addiction formed after she was hit by a car and was given painkillers for a broken leg. She is working hard at recovering, but each page of her file paints a picture of two steps forward and one step back.

I worry about her kid. There are no details about them in

her file, and yet I still find myself wondering if they have a Larry-like adult who can step in if needed?

It's an answer I'll probably never know and one that weighs particularly heavy on me when I finally get home and crash on my couch with a tin of Harmony's surprisingly delicious butterless butter tarts and *A Merry Little Mix-up.*

It's a delightful, cozy movie about an advertising executive who doesn't believe she needs love and hides behind her ice queen exterior, and a traveling nomad who has never found a place that felt like home. They both accidentally book tickets to Sydney, Nova Scotia, instead of their intended destination of Sydney, Australia, and there's a winter storm grounding all transportation and a winter festival that's booked up all the hotel rooms except for one. The characters are beside themselves. She is late for a big presentation with a tuna farmer looking to rebrand, and he is missing the phenomenon of bioluminescent algae of Jervis Bay. But I know that despite logic or logistics or any of the other obstacles that plague reality, they are a single queen-size bed and a well-timed power outage away from the happily ever after they both deserve.

Onscreen, the characters are drinking hot chocolate and making googly love eyes at each other. I'm doing the same in my living room with my iPhone 12, and the text that has just popped onto my screen.

MACKENZIE:

Hey. You up? I should be home tomorrow before dinner. The guys are out celebrating tonight. I'd love to get going first thing in the morning, but I don't think it will happen.

The band is in Buffalo—two short hours away, on the other side of the border. Their month-long tour is done. Their last show ended a few hours ago.

MACKENZIE:

It feels like I left Toronto yesterday, but also like I've been gone for a year if that makes any sense.

It does.

ANNALISE:

Do you think you'll find it weird going back to playing at the Gladstone?

MACKENZIE:

Maybe. But I can deal with anything as long as I get to sleep in my own bed.

His bed.

Tomorrow night, he'll be back in this apartment, sleeping two thin walls away from me.

MACKENZIE:

By the way, did the Christmas explosion involve putting up a tree?

I glance toward the corner of the room, where my two-foot artificial one looks disproportionately tiny, even in my small apartment.

ANNALISE:

Just a little one. It's not big enough to put presents under. It's more of a symbolic gesture.

MACKENZIE:

Maybe we should get a big one? A real one?

I get way too excited at his use of the word *we.*

ANNALISE:

Maybe we should.

MACKENZIE:

We should do a lot of things.

My breath feels thick. It's like I need the full use of my brain to pull it in and out, in and out.

I'm desperate to type *Things? What kind of things?* But instead, I send back a very lame smiling emoji.

MACKENZIE:

I should *probably* pack, but I'll see you tomorrow

ANNALISE:

I can't wait

I set my phone on the coffee table and start to reach for the TV remote, but I stop myself. I'm tired but not quite tired enough to fall asleep. I consider making hot chocolate, but as I lift my head, my gaze lands on the hooks next to the door and Mackenzie's leather jacket.

I haven't tried it on since that night weeks ago when nothing happened, and I threw it across the room.

Tonight, as I take it off the hook, it isn't answers I'm looking for; it's just a reminder of him.

The leather still holds remnants of his scent. I cradle it in my arms, the collar pressed to my nose, like a total weirdo, and carry it back to the couch, where I snuggle under it like a blanket.

Closing my eyes, I picture his dark blond hair and deep blue eyes as my breath evens out and I drift toward sleep. I'm fantasizing about tomorrow. Him: opening the door to the apartment, holding out his arms, pulling me tight to his chest as I crash into them.

I swear I can feel the slight scratch of his stubble on my cheek—when everything around me goes black.

21

AT FIRST, I THINK I'VE SLEEPWALKED BECAUSE when I open my eyes, I am standing in my kitchen, staring across the room at my bedroom door. It's dark outside. As I look out the kitchen window, I can see that it has rained because the puddles on the street reflect the neon "Manny's" sign of the dry cleaners below.

The blood in my veins cools as my head snaps from the window to the rest of the apartment. The little tree is gone, as are the twinkle lights around the windows.

I might be in my apartment, but it's not the apartment I went to sleep in. If Manny's is still downstairs, then it's at least six months ago.

The door to my bedroom begins to creak. I brace, not sure what to expect as it slowly opens, and someone steps from the shadows of my bedroom into the living room lit by the streetlamps outside.

It's not until she almost reaches the kitchen that I can clearly make out her long, dark hair, the U of T sweatshirt, and the joggers with the hole in the crotch.

Whuuuuuuu. The sound is half "what," as in "what the hell?" and the rest is a wobbly, confused breath.

The person in my living room is me—which makes sense considering this is my apartment, but it also bends my mind in a way I am unprepared for.

"Hello?" I call to her, knowing she probably can't hear me.

Just like in the other times, she walks right through me, then heads for the fridge, pulling the door open, removing the Brita water filter pitcher, and filling a glass.

This action orients me to exactly where I am in time. It's last winter, one of the three months I was seeing Lucca. He had this weird thing about tap water and carbons and convinced me to get a Brita water filter. The thing took up too much room in my fridge, so I got rid of it the day we broke up.

I watch myself drink the water and set the empty glass in the sink. I do not look good. My hair is slicked back, not with product but with the texture that comes with at least three days without a good hair wash. I am paler than normal, too, with deep purple circles under my eyes and not the kind that can be corrected with a good night's sleep and expensive concealer.

Do I look like that now?

It's hard to tell. I've never seen myself this way before.

The other me shuffles back toward our bedroom. I'm wondering why I'm here. What sort of meaning should I take from a late-night drink of water? But as she passes the couch, she stops and bends down with a sigh, picking something off the floor.

It looks like a jacket, which she tosses onto the armchair, but she overthrows and it falls behind it into the corner. However, she doesn't notice because she is picking something else off the floor.

A memory begins to surface. It's just a wisp at the back of my brain, not fully formed, but as Other Me straightens, staring at a piece of paper in her hand, the memory comes back with movie-like clarity, and I can recall the details completely.

I found a coaster on the floor from the bar Lucca likes on King. It had a phone number written on it in black eyeliner underlined twice.

I recall thinking Lucca seemed odd when he came over after the bar. I had suspected something was up, but then he fell asleep watching something on his phone, and I didn't care enough to ask him about it.

I remember my heart pounding so hard when I found it. *Had he picked some girl up at the bar and then, when she wouldn't go home with him, called me?*

Our relationship might have been casual but in my head, he'd just crossed a line.

I needed confirmation, so I found my phone, called the number, and waited.

It was several rings before someone answered.

"Hello?" said a male voice thick with sleep.

I remember feeling confused and then angry on both our parts. She had a boyfriend.

"Hi," I replied. "Um, I'm looking for someone . . . a woman? She was at a bar on King tonight. She gave this number to a guy named Lucca?"

There was a beat, I remember, because I wondered if he might have hung up, but then there was a rustling sound like he was moving around, and then his voice came back on the line.

"I'm sorry. This is my number. I'm fairly certain I wasn't picking up guys at bars tonight. Where did you say you were? King City?"

"No. Toronto."

He laughed. "I'm nowhere near Toronto. I think there's been a mix-up."

My imagination pictured him—a sleepy, rumpled man sitting alone in the dark.

"So you *don't* know Lucca DiRossi?" I said, just to be sure.

"I'm sorry," he said. "I don't."

"And you didn't give your number out? On a coaster? Written in eyeliner?"

He let out a low laugh. "I'm really more of a mascara kind of guy."

"Oh . . ."

The emotions of the last few minutes vanished, returning me to my sad, empty state. Lucca didn't go out and pick some woman up tonight. I could crawl back in bed beside him and things would be the same as when we went to sleep. Nothing had changed.

I shook my head suddenly, feeling stupid for calling.

"Sorry for bothering you so late."

I could hear the creak of his mattress as if he'd shifted positions. I was waiting for the soft click of him hanging up, but instead he spoke. "Are you okay?"

There was a softness to his voice, and as strange as it sounds I could hear his concern through the phone line.

"No," I answered, then realized he probably meant the whole Lucca number thing. "I mean, yes. It's all fine. I'm fine."

There was another moment of silence until he cleared his throat.

"I don't know what happened but . . . I really hope it all works out."

"Thanks," I said, but I remember thinking that I didn't agree. I think I called the strange number that night because part of me was hoping it was a woman. Lucca was a nice guy and I knew he wanted more than the casual relationship we had. But I also knew I didn't. And instead of telling him that, I was letting things linger on, which wasn't good for either of us.

"Hey," the stranger said, "I know this is kind of out of the blue, but you said you were in Toronto, right? Do you like it? I mean, do you like living there?"

It was a question I could answer without thinking. "Best city in the world. Why?"

He let out a breath. "I've always wanted to live there but never quite made the move . . . I don't know . . . maybe this phone call is my sign?"

I was suddenly so tired.

"Who knows. Sorry again for all of this. Hope you have a good night."

My memory ends just as Other Me sets her phone back down on the kitchen counter and then returns to the bedroom and slips back into bed.

I know she won't mention the phone number or the phone call the next morning when she finally tells Lucca it's over. She won't think of this night at all—I guess until now.

My head begins to swim with the complexities of the past and present colliding. I am a mess of questions and half-remembered memories.

Larry gave his jacket to Zee.

Zee saw Mackenzie at the festival.

Lucca brought Zee's jacket home with a drummer's number.

Which means the person I called that night was Mackenzie.

And even though I don't need any further proof, I step toward the counter and read the number written on the coaster. It's the same nine digits he wrote on that Post-it the very first day he moved in.

What the hell is going on?

I feel like I'm putting together two different puzzles, but I'm missing half the pieces, and the ones I do have are all jumbled together. But before I can sort any of it out—make sense of what is real and where my brain is filling in the blanks—the room around me goes black.

When I come to, it's not like every other time the jacket has sucked me someplace else and then thrust me back to reality.

I'm not dumped back onto a street corner or into a thrift store changing room. I'm lying down, and my body feels heavy, and I'm not quite sure where I am because everything around me is pitch-dark.

"Hey," says a voice. "I didn't mean to wake you up. You just looked cold."

But I'm not cold. I'm covered in a blanket. So warm. So cozy.

"Go back to sleep," the voice says. I feel a hand brush my bangs from my forehead, and I swear I can smell . . . Iced Lightning.

"Mackenzie?" Somehow, it occurs to me that I'm on my living room couch. I'm aware of the familiar corduroy fabric against my skin and the way the cushions dip a little right where my butt sits. I want to open my eyes and verify all of this, but my eyelids are so heavy.

"Hi."

I feel fingers stroke the side of my cheek. I lean into them as a happy sigh escapes my mouth.

Just before I slip away completely, I swear I hear his laugh.

I AWAKEN WITH a kinked neck to the sound of an angry car honking somewhere down the street. I am cozy and warm under my Hudson's Bay blanket, and Mackenzie's jacket is folded on the coffee table beside me.

I roll off the couch and stumble into my room, where I shed my clothes in the hamper, wrap myself in a towel, and head to the bathroom.

There, I run a very hot shower and let the water massage away my non-ergonomic sleeping choices.

My mango-scented body wash wakes me up just enough to process last night's events.

I still don't know if these visions I get are dreams or memories or something else entirely. I think that all along, I've known deep down that they are my brain's way of dealing with everything that has happened—looking for deeper meaning in events that had very simple explanations: My mom was in the wrong intersection, my uncle's body couldn't fight the cancer cells, I was on the unfortunate end of two sets of improbable odds. But there are too many connections for it all to be coincidence.

Which means it's *not* just coincidence. It's something else.

I emerge from the bathroom in a cloud of mango-scented steam and then stop dead at the sight of a man in my apartment. He's sitting on my couch with a cookie in his hand halfway on the route to his mouth.

I once read a study that said our first emotional response to a new stimulus reflects our unfiltered, true reaction.

My reaction to seeing Mackenzie sitting on my couch is immediate.

I run—straight into his arms.

"You're back!"

He envelops me in a hug, pulling me tight to his chest. Exactly as I imagined it.

"When did you get home? Did you just get in?"

I try to pull away, but his arms tighten, so I stay.

"I got in last night, actually." His voice is gravelly as if he hasn't slept. "Ben's girlfriend came down for the show but decided to head home after the party. I caught a ride back with her late."

I pull away again, and this time, he releases his arms.

The loss of body heat causes goose bumps to prickle across my exposed skin, reminding me that I walked straight out of the bathroom.

"I am wearing a towel." I state the obvious and watch as his eyes dip from my face to my collarbone, then back up again. "Yes, you are."

"I think I better put on some clothes."

He opens his mouth but then closes it without saying anything. Still, I can feel his eyes on me as I turn and head toward my bedroom. Just before I reach the door, I hear him clear his throat.

"Hey, do you have plans for the day?"

I turn, shaking my toweled head. "Not really."

"Want to go somewhere? With me?"

My heart double beats. "I do."

"Okay," he says, backing up toward the front door. I'll be back in a little bit. Make sure you dress warm."

22

I DON'T STOP SMILING THE ENTIRE TIME I get ready. My ear is half trained on the door, waiting for the sounds of Mackenzie's footsteps on my creaky apartment floor, so when there's honking from the street below again, it takes a few seconds before I notice it.

It's not the angry traffic noise of earlier this morning but a friendly *beep beep beep beep beep* of a horn. I look out my living room window to see Mackenzie across the street. His upper torso is poking out of the driver's side window of a green hatchback.

I open my window and lean out over the ledge. "When did you get a car?"

He pats the outside with the palm of his hand. "I've got it rented for the day. Although now I see why no one owns cars around here. I've circled the block twice and still can't find a parking spot. Any chance you're ready to go?"

I glance down at my jeans and Uggs. "I think so."

He grins. "You might want a hat. Mine is hanging on the hooks next to the door if you wouldn't mind grabbing it for me. We're going to be outside most of the day."

I close the window, grab his hat and mine, plus two sets of

gloves, and head down to the car. Mackenzie gets out just as I cross the street and opens the passenger door for me, blasting me with a wave of heat.

"Are you going to tell me where we are going?" I ask as I settle in and buckle my seatbelt.

He smiles, flipping the left blinker. "If I tell you, then it wouldn't be a secret."

I groan, but my smile is wider than his as we pull into traffic.

We head west out of the city. Mackenzie's earlier "dress warm" plus our texts from last night make me think we might be heading to a tree farm. However, I question that assumption when we hit the hour mark and turn north, passing several signs for various tree farms as we drive through Kitchener into Waterloo. When we reach the city limits and again are back on country roads, it begins to snow. The flakes are teeny tiny, but they soon begin to coat the road, covering it in a layer of white.

"Subarus are good in the snow, right?" I ask, my city-dwelling self suddenly getting nervous as a blast of wind sends a blanket of white from the field next to us straight across our windshield.

"They are," Mackenzie reassures me with a smile. "Also, my brother taught me to drive in two feet of snow when I was fourteen. If my surprise today doesn't go over well, my backup plan is to take you to the parking lot of the Valu-mart and impress you with my doughnut skills."

He winks as he flicks his blinker to turn left.

As we round the bend, the empty country road gives way to buildings. At first, it's just the odd country home—a cute stone cottage or a ranch-style bungalow—but the farther down the road we get, the closer together the buildings get, until suddenly, we are in the middle of a quaint downtown.

"For the love of all things Hallmark." My jaw drops as we drive past an adorable bakery with a dainty gold-lettered sign and a lush green garland hanging across its entrance, complete with a giant red velvet bow. Across from it is a flower shop whose sidewalk is covered in silver buckets filled with fresh evergreen boughs and branches with bright red berries. Every store we pass is decorated with lights or bows or gold and silver Christmas balls. There are flower boxes filled with birch branches and twinkle lights. Fully decorated Christmas trees in store windows. There are even carolers on the sidewalk who look like they walked straight out of a Dickens novel and—

"Is that a horse and carriage?"

The black-and-white Clydesdale trots by. Its driver tips an honest-to-goodness velvet top hat in our direction.

"I was joking before, but now I seriously feel like we've been dropped into the middle of a Hallmark movie."

Mackenzie signals and parks in front of the most adorable post office I have ever seen.

"Welcome to St. Jacobs." He gets out of the car and comes around to open my door. "My mission today is to convince you that Christmas magic actually exists."

I move as if in a trance. My senses are overloaded as I take in every inch of this tiny, perfect town.

I breathe deeply. "The air even smells like peppermint."

Mackenzie laughs and inclines his head toward what looks like a zhuzhed-up lemonade stand with a sign for hot chocolate.

"We can get some if you like."

"Oh, I *like.*"

A burst of cold wind gusts down the street, bringing with it a tiny snow tornado. The freezing air hurts my teeth, but I can't stop smiling.

"I can't believe this is a real place."

He laughs and begins to walk toward the stoplight. "Just you wait. I will make a believer out of you, Annalise Harris."

I grab his arm, wrapping my fingers around the plushness of his down coat, tugging him in the opposite direction.

"Not before I make a jaywalker out of you, Mackenzie Smith."

We get distracted by two gift shops, a toy shop, and a store devoted entirely to brooms.

The hot chocolate tastes even better than it smells. We drink it inside a tiny blow-up igloo that insulates us from the snow and wind outside. I can hear the carolers harmonizing their way through a playlist of Christmas classics just outside. It gives me both an emotional and a sugar high as I tip my mug back and drain the last drop.

Mackenzie tilts my cup so he can see the bottom. There's nothing left other than some fine granules of crushed candy cane.

"So, what do you want to do next?" He pops my empty cup under his and shoots them like a basketball into a nearby garbage can. "There's a little Christmas market up the street we can check out or a bigger one just outside town. We also have to save some time to pick up our tree. I googled a place that's on the way back."

All of those options sound amazing, but his mention of a Christmas market has reminded me of something I have wanted to do for a few weeks now. "I'd love to find an ornament for our tree."

He smiles. "I think I can help with that."

We get back in the car and drive to a German-style Christmas market outside of St. Jacobs. Like the town, the moment it comes into view, my breath catches in the back of my throat because it feels like it came straight off the front of a Christmas card. The main area of the market is housed in a humongous red barn surrounded by what feels like a hundred wooden stalls selling everything from candied nuts to fudge to handmade jewelry and every Christmas ornament you can imagine.

The lingering storm clouds make the late-afternoon light feel darker than it should, but above us are strings of lights that create a magical, twinkling canopy as we walk from stall to stall. We wander for almost an hour before we stop to eat sausages covered in sauerkraut and giant salted pretzels, which we wash down with spiced apple cider pulled from a cauldron over a crackling fire.

At every stall, my eyes skim the rows of Christmas ornaments, but none of them are quite right.

"I need to hit the bathroom." Mackenzie nods toward the barn. "Then we should probably head out and grab our tree. Is there anything else you want to check out, or do you want to meet up in the square?"

"Why don't we meet by the Beaver Tails in ten?" I ask. "I'm going to wander down there." I point toward an area tucked away behind the barn.

Mackenzie nods and heads off. I wander down a small aisle we missed earlier, and that's where I find it—at the very last stall, my eyes are drawn to a tiny Santa Claus wearing a black biker jacket, sitting on top of a Harley Davidson motorcycle. Etched into the motorcycle's front headlight is the year 2025. Santa's jacket is eerily close to Mackenzie's, and Santa looks a little like Larry if you squint your eyes.

"I have a weird question for you," I say to the vendor as she wraps my Santa in tissue. "Do you have any ornaments left over from last year?"

"Sorry, hon," she says. "I usually sell out everything a week or two before Christmas."

Larry passed away three days before Christmas. I was too busy with work and taking care of him to buy my 2024 ornament, and when he died, I no longer had the heart. Grief-stricken, I decided that it was time to end the tradition. I had no one to carry it on with, and forcing myself to do it alone would only be an annual reminder of everything I'd lost. But as I cradle the little motorcycle Santa in my hands, I realize that although the pain is still there, it's peppered in between a lot of really good memories. I only wish I could also find something to commemorate last year.

I end up meeting Mackenzie back near the Beaver Tails as planned, and since we're already there, we decide to split the deep-fried Canadian treat.

"Did you find something?" Mackenzie asks as he licks cinnamon and sugar from his coated fingers.

I tap the side of my purse. "I absolutely did."

"All right, then." He holds out his arm. "Let's go get our tree."

We walk back toward the parking lot, crossing an outdoor picnic area set up with tables and a small stage featuring a single lone guitarist.

We stop to listen for a moment. He's pretty good. Not Mackenzie good—but his voice blends with the soft strumming of his guitar, and with the dark night and the twinkling lights, the experience feels almost surreal.

"Shall we go?" Mackenzie asks as the song ends. I nod and follow him, but just as we reach the edge of the square, the singer begins his next song, and the opening notes freeze me in place.

"He's playing Jimmy Buffett," I tell Mackenzie. "'Bring Back the Magic.' It was my uncle's favorite song."

The song's slow tempo draws a few couples from the crowd to the dance floor. They hold each other and sway along, a few more joining in with the next verse.

"I know you don't dance . . ." Mackenzie's voice is quiet, and although the question never leaves his lips, I answer it anyway.

"I would love to."

He holds out his arm as if telling me to lead the way. I weave through the crowd and find an open spot off to the side. I wasn't lying at the Gladstone when I told Mackenzie I was a terrible dancer. I have two left feet and no natural rhythm. I worry about where my hands will go, where his hands will go, if I'll actually make good on my previous threat and step on his toes. But when he takes me into his arms, all of those spiraling thoughts fizzle out. He's so sure of his movements. When his arms slide around my waist, it's as if they've been thinking about exactly where they'd go if given the opportunity. I follow his lead, reaching my arms up and around his neck, lacing my fingers together behind his head as we begin to sway. My cheek finds that spot just under his collarbone that I claimed that night on our roof.

His winter jacket is thick and puffy, but even through the layers of down, I swear I can hear his heart beating. It sounds like a drum, blending with the guitar, telling my feet when to move perfectly in time with his.

It begins to snow again, but there's no frigid wind this time, only big fluffy flakes floating down from the sky, making it feel like we're inside a snow globe.

It's the perfect ending to the perfect Hallmark day—except for one thing.

There's another reason I like Hallmark movies—one I didn't dare mention to Mackenzie because it's cheesy, cliché, and—given our situation—a little too on the nose. I watch them because the heroine is always a little broken. Sometimes, she's a workaholic or depressed and down on her luck. Sometimes, she simply doesn't believe she's ready to love. But the love interest still wants her despite her flaws, or even because of them.

"It will come when your heart is ready to carry it" was one of Larry's favorite sayings and those words play on my mind as the song comes to an end and the crowd bursts out in applause, myself and Mackenzie included.

"Are you ready?" He nods toward the parking lot, where the snow has turned the cars into indistinguishable mounds of white. "It might take us a little longer than we planned."

I know he means the car and getting the tree, but I can't help but think about him, the song, and whether I'm ready to carry anything more than I'm carrying already.

I adjust my purse and feel the weight of my new ornament. It makes me think of Larry and the day of the eclipse, how I missed out on another experience with him because I refused to be open, and how if I had the chance again, I'd do it all differently.

"Yes," I tell him. "I'm ready if you are."

23

WE STOP AT BENJAMIN'S TREE FARM ON our way home. It is so picturesque and adorable that I half expect a dashing duke to come galloping out of the forest. Mackenzie lets me pick out what I think is a small Fraser fir, until we have to bungee cord it to the roof of the car and I realize I may have gotten a little too excited.

It's so thick and heavy that we're sweating by the time we get it home and up the stairs to the apartment. We set it up in the stand, and Mackenzie leaves me to decorate while he returns the Zipcar to its spot in time for the next renter.

Having never had anything more than my apartment-size trees, my decorations are limited to the eighteen I have collected since I started my ornament collection tradition at the age of ten. Although I love how they all look against the blue-green boughs of the Christmas tree, there's a little pain in my heart knowing I'm still missing one.

"Hey." Mackenzie steps into the apartment with red cheeks and hands. I swear I can feel the chill waving off him from the other side of the room.

"I'm going to change." He nods at his bedroom door. "But do you want to finish our movie?"

My eyes dart from him to the couch and back to him again, my mouth suddenly going dry.

"Sure." The word comes out like more of a croak. I clear my throat. "Why don't I make some popcorn?"

He nods and disappears behind his bedroom door.

I retreat to the kitchen, not even sure if we have popcorn but grateful for the excuse to do anything other than overanalyze what is about to happen next.

We've watched TV together before. That protocol is established. The couch is big enough for us to both sit comfortably without unnecessary touching. But the touching feels necessary tonight.

I open the cupboard and find a pack of Orville Redenbacher, the origin of which is unknown to me. I tear off the plastic and pop it into the microwave.

Mackenzie and I have gotten closer these last few weeks. There is something about the nature of texting that makes it easier to share thoughts. Maybe it's having time to think before answering or the absence of a physical reaction. I don't know if that intimacy translates to our couch. According to the little green timer on my microwave, I have a minute and twenty-three seconds to figure it out.

The microwave beeps just as Mackenzie wanders back into the living room. Part of me was hoping that he'd emerge from his room shirtless in those low-slung sweatpants I have thought way too much about for the last four weeks.

The sweatpants are there, and they are as glorious as I remember, but he's wearing a dark brown beanie hat, a pair of wool slippers that look like they were knit by someone who loves him very much, and a thick cream fisherman's sweater with a collar fastened with a single wooden toggle. It's hands-down the hottest sweater I have ever seen in my life.

"I'm still freezing," he says when he catches me looking at him, then walks to the chair, pulls the Hudson's Bay blanket off the back, and sits on the couch, spreading it out on top of him.

I'm grateful he's busy with the TV remote because as I pour the popcorn into the bowl, my hands shake.

Up until a moment ago, I had things semi-figured out. The couch logistics were clear in my head, but now he's gone and introduced a blanket into the equation.

Slowly, I approach the couch, popcorn in hand, and assess. He has left me ample blanket real estate, therefore cutting off the option to simply flop down next to him and forcing me to make a call: sit on top of it or slide in underneath with him.

In a snap decision I opt for the safe route and decide to sit on top.

However, as I set the bowl down, he makes the call for me, peeling back the blanket and then tossing it back over my legs once I sit.

"Are you ready?" He looks over, his eyebrows raised. It's the same question he asked me at the market, with the same straightforward situational connotations, yet it makes me pause and think, *Is this really what I want?*

I nod, knowing my answer hasn't changed. "Let's do it."

He hits play. It's this one about the two Christmas travelers stuck in snowy Nova Scotia instead of beachy Australia. They have been crowned king and queen of the hot chocolate festival and are staring into each other's eyes as they share their first dance.

The plot is straightforward, but it's taking all of my concentration to follow along because I notice every time Mackenzie shifts in his seat, hikes the blanket higher, or reaches into the popcorn bowl. I have to stop myself from staring at the way his jaw flexes when he chews or the way his eyes crinkle when he laughs at the funny parts, which apparently there are a lot of in this movie.

When we both reach into the popcorn bowl and brush hands, I almost have a heart attack. And when he returns after taking the empty bowl to the sink and sits back down, I analyze the angle of our feet down to the millimeter to see if he's moved any closer. Finally, when he scoots his hand under the blanket, and it knocks into mine, I think, *This is it, here it comes,* he is finally going to cross the line from wherever we are right now to where we are supposed to be.

I am willing him to make a move. To brush his fingers against the back of mine, to look over and smile as he slowly laces our fingers together.

But nothing happens.

And when he removes his hand to reach forward and swipe his phone from the coffee table, everything inside me sinks.

What if I've been reading this wrong the entire time?

What if he's texting someone else right now? Not the wholesome "you up?" texts he sent me all month but a "you up" for sex.

What if—

My phone lights up next to me.

The notification flashes and disappears. I think I catch the name, but it happens so quickly, and I don't trust myself.

My heart begins to pound so hard I worry it's going to beat its way right through my rib cage as I reach over, slide open the screen, and click.

I read the message and blink twice just to make sure it's not some weird trick of my eyes, but when the message is still there, an electric thrill zips through my entire body.

MACKENZIE:

Hey

I pick up the phone, unable to look at him, and even more unable to contain the smile curling my lips.

ANNALISE:

Hi

MACKENZIE:

I am planning on kissing you in about three seconds, and I wanted to make sure you're okay with that.

I don't type back.

I set my phone back down calmly.

I close my eyes. I draw a breath. I let it out.

When I turn, he's already reaching for me.

His hand finds my chin just as my fingers curl around the collar of that glorious sweater. Our lips clash hard and frantic as if neither of us is sure if this is really happening, then slow as we both realize it very much is.

I groan a little as his tongue strokes mine. Then again, he reaches for my hips and lifts me onto his lap. I am half bewildered by all these new angles. My knees astride his hard thighs, my hands, which are now free to explore the planes of his body; the rest of me is absorbed in this kiss and the way that he cradles my chin so carefully and then kisses me hard like he can't get enough. But it's me that can't get enough. I rock my knees forward, pressing my breasts against his chest and finding him hard and ready under his sweatpants.

"Fuck, Annalise." His voice sounds pained as his hands find my hips, and he lifts me just far enough back that there's no longer friction between us.

"I have been waiting a very long time for this," he says between kisses. "But I don't want to rush. We have all night."

With that, he plants a kiss on my neck, just below my earlobe. Then he drags his lips to my collarbone, where he licks then kisses the tiny dip.

I very badly want to push his hands away and grind against him, finding that beautiful friction, but instead, I focus on his hands, which have traveled to the small of my back, fingers grazing the waistband of my jeans before sliding under the hem of my hoodie, where they become trapped in the folds of fabric.

"Can I take this off?" He waits for me to nod, then pulls the hem over my head, leaving me in a thin white tank top.

"Fuck," he swears again as his hands palm my breasts, his thumbs finding the peaks of my nipples, hard and stiff beneath the thin fabric.

"I've never heard you swear this much," I tease.

His tongue retraces its steps from my collarbone back to below my jaw before he kisses me firmly on the mouth.

"I swore when you walked out here in nothing but a towel. You just didn't hear me."

"You mean this morning?"

"No, this morning I was thinking about how badly I wanted you to drop that towel."

"So you mean . . . ?"

He grins and kisses me again. This time, it's slow and deliberate.

"The first day and every day since."

I don't know what to do with that information, so I kiss him back with every feeling stirring inside me. I want him very badly. But I also want to know his favorite kind of dog and how he likes his eggs, and if he feels leggings are an acceptable form of pants.

"Are you still freezing?" My hands scoot under his sweater, finding biceps and triceps and a slew of other muscles I've long ago forgotten the names of.

"Not in the least bit." He pulls off his sweater in a single fluid motion, tossing it so far that it almost hits the tree.

I reach for him, but his hands are quicker than mine. He tugs my tank top and pulls it off as seamlessly as he did his own; however, this time, he throws it in the opposite direction.

"Do you know how many times I thought about doing this?" he says as his mouth kisses its way along my collarbone. The swirl of his tongue nearly knocks all rational thought from my head.

I moan, although I'm not sure if it's at his lips or the way his hands are kneading my ass or some combination of the fact that I have spent the last month on this very couch wanting this to happen and now he is here and this is real and so much better than anything that happened in my head.

When he moves to my breasts, his lips leaving a trail of kisses across my skin, I grind my hips onto him, no longer able to help myself.

"Okay." He laughs, then gives my breast another kiss. "I can take a hint." He lifts my hips and flips me onto my back.

"Just so I'm sure, you're not freezing either, right?" His fingers skim along the waistband of my jeans. I want to tell him that my entire body feels like it is on fire, and yet I want as many parts of him touching as many parts of me. What I manage is: "I'm great."

He takes that as permission to undo the button of my fly. I lift my hips, and he slides my jeans down to my knees, taking one leg off and then kissing all the way up to my thigh before returning to the other leg to remove them altogether.

"Your skin is so soft," he says, returning his lips to where they left off. "It's even softer than I imagined."

"You've imagined my skin?" The thought weakens me in a way that makes me glad I'm already lying down.

"I've thought about your skin and if you're ticklish right here." He brushes his nose along the side of my neck. "I've wondered what you look like when you wake up first thing in the morning."

I think he's leaning in to kiss me again, but he brushes my bangs from my forehead and cups my cheek. "I know what I said earlier, but we can stop here if you don't want—"

"No. I want. I want all of it."

He leans down and kisses me like this is the answer he hoped for. His hand glides down from my cheek to my breast, down my stomach to my hip bone, where his fingers slide along the elastic band of my underwear and pause.

I lift my hips from the couch. I can feel him smile as he kisses me. His fingers pause for only a second before they slide under the lacy fabric.

Goose bumps spread across my skin as he slips two fingers inside me, and all I can think is how I could stay exactly like this forever. This man. This apartment. Where nothing bad can touch us. Sustained entirely by this euphoric feeling of falling fast and Harmony's questionable baked goods. We could be so happy.

My body, however, has different plans.

Those fingers. Those strong musician's fingers. They play

my body with the same delicate strokes as when he plucks his guitar.

I come, hard and fast, sinking my hands into his hair as I let myself come apart, and the world goes blurry for a moment.

He strokes my hair and whispers worshipping words that sound a little like one of his songs.

"I've got you, just let go . . ."

I close my eyes and let go of everything I have been holding on to these last few months—the good, the bad, the hard. The feeling makes my whole body shiver.

"You're sure you're not cold?"

I open my eyes to find him watching me, concerned, a hand resting on the blanket slung over the back of the couch.

"I'm perfect," I tell him, and I mean it. "But how do you feel about moving this to a bed?"

He doesn't actually answer but instead rolls off the couch and scoops me into his arms. I wrap mine around his neck and lay my head against his chest, where I can feel his heart beating wildly inside. And I know it's for me. I know it in the careful way he lays me down on my bed. In his quickened movements as he removes his clothes and slides under the covers next to me, like those few seconds apart were too long. Like our bodies were meant to be just like this, touching and stroking, feeling and tasting.

His hand finds my cheek in the dark, and he asks one last time if I am sure. I almost tell him that I have never been so sure about anything before in my life, but instead slide open the drawer to my nightstand and pull out a condom.

"Come here," I whisper.

He moves to straddle me. Arms braced on either side, he lowers his chest to mine and places a chaste kiss on my lips.

He rolls the condom on and then groans as he sinks into me. The sensation is so wild that I have to grip the bedsheets with both hands.

"Fuck, Annalise. You feel incredible."

I love the sound of my name on his lips. The profanity. The way it comes out, half moan, half whisper, as he begins to move. His tempo starts out smooth and rhythmic and then picks up like he's listening to my body as if it were a song, filling the moments between the beats exactly as I need them.

"I'm close," I say, although it sounds strikingly similar to his moan-whisper. He brings his mouth to mine and covers it with a hungry, feverish kiss.

When I cry out, Mackenzie's pace picks up, becoming faster and more urgent. I think he says my name. It's hard to tell because waves of pleasure are ripping through me, and I can't think of anything else aside from how good it feels.

Eventually, I start to notice my breath again and that Mackenzie has stilled above me, although I can feel him still pulsing inside me.

We lie there for a few moments before he pulls out and rolls away with a small moan, dropping his legs over the side of the bed to remove the condom. He bumps around in the dark for a few minutes, then climbs back under the covers, pulling me to him. I lie there and listen to his breathing as it becomes smooth and even and deep. It mingles with the city sounds outside—the reminder of the world still out there.

But tonight, we are cocooned in my bed, where everything is easy, good, and right. Nothing can touch us, and I let myself fall asleep thinking only of that.

24

I AWAKEN THE NEXT MORNING TO HIM kissing my temple. Our legs are tangled together with the bedsheet, and my comforter is across the room on the floor, having been thrown from the bed sometime during the night. We stay in bed until well after lunch, repeating the events of the night before but switching the order slightly and throwing in a couple new positions. Eventually, Mackenzie calls in our lo mein order to Rol San. It arrives thirty-six minutes later with a message scrawled on the front: *Next time you hurt her, you deal with me.*

Mackenzie shrugs when he reads it. I pretend I have no idea what it means.

The next night, we fall asleep on the couch, me sprawled across his chest, the Hudson's Bay blanket draped over both of us as another Christmas movie plays out on the screen. The following morning, when I shower for work I find an imprint of the TV remote on my stomach. It spent the whole night sandwiched between us.

The night after that we spend in his bed. Then, two more in mine because he has late shows and crawls in after them to sleep next to me when he gets home.

He texts me while I'm at work.

MACKENZIE:

what are you up to?

ANNALISE:

Mapping genomes

MACKENZIE:

I love it when you science

I text him while I'm curled up on the couch, and he's playing a late show.

ANNALISE:

Do you own a ruffled shirt? And if not, would you ever consider wearing one?

MACKENZIE:

Are you watching Runaway Duke again?

ANNALISE:

Possibly

By mid-December, we've established a routine: weekends, we hang out in bed, living off Harmony's baking and whatever takeout we ordered the night before until it's time for Mackenzie to head out for his show. Sometimes, I even go with him. There's an official Annalise seat at the groupie table, and the bartender, Jodi, knows my Diet Coke order.

On weekdays, I go to work. When I get home, we eat dinner together, and on the nights he has a gig, I go downstairs to hang with Koko in her store.

Koko returned from Japan at the beginning of the month. Her dad made a full recovery, and all of the vintage treasures she bought that wouldn't fit in her suitcase have been arriving in boxes through the mail.

Tonight, I'm helping her sort through the last of them even though it's a Monday and Mackenzie is home. I have left him upstairs working on a song that he's hoping to send to Edwin Stark from the Rydells with strict orders not to message me until he's done.

"You two are so damn cute it makes me want to vomit," Koko says when she catches me reading my phone. "Then cry because I will probably die alone or get a dog so it can alert the authorities so that they find my body instead of it eating me like a cat."

She flops down on the counter in front of me, dropping her head into my lap.

"Maybe you could call Zee?" I pat her head, unsure of the proper protocol.

She lifts her head. "Who? Oh, that guy from Mac's band? Yeah, no. I am not picking up what he's laying down. I need someone who understands the inner workings of my mind. Someone who gets me, ya know?"

I do. I knew before that I liked Mackenzie and found him attractive, but I never realized what it felt like to have someone make my coffee in the morning, just the way I like it. Or someone who knows that look I get on my face when it's been a hard day at work, and I need fifteen minutes to decompress before I'm ready to talk about it. Someone who understands that I might get quiet or even weepy over silly things like the sound of a passing motorcycle or the smell of vanilla perfume.

"So," says Koko, pulling out a sheer white shirt and holding it up to her body, "what are you and Mac going to do when you move?"

Koko's question startles me, and I have to ask her to repeat it.

"When you leave for school," she clarifies. "Is Mackenzie coming with you?"

She's called out into the light the one dark spot in our relationship. I am leaving in less than three weeks—across an entire ocean—for two years.

"I don't know. We haven't exactly talked about it." I think both of us are doing the same thing, acknowledging on some level that it's going to happen and then shoving that thought to the back of our minds as far as it will go.

"Our relationship will probably start to fizzle out soon enough, right?" I say, although I don't really believe it.

"What are you talking about?" Koko throws the shirt, hitting me in the chest.

"You were the one who said that relationships are only ever good for three months. All the magic wears off. I'll start hating all his pants, remember?"

Koko rolls her eyes. "I was talking about the lust-filled ones I always seem to find myself in. Not what you and Mackenzie have."

"I don't know how we'd even do it." I finally let myself think through the logistics. My PhD is going to be intense. I'll be at school all the time, and traveling home really isn't in my budget.

Koko leans across the counter and presses her palms into her hands. "Maybe he could move there and join a British rock band. British rock stars are infinitely hotter."

I start to tell her why that won't work either, but my phone pings with an incoming text.

It's a picture of a chocolate cake.

MACKENZIE:

Vegan Bailey's cheesecake. 11/10. Harmony rewarded me for finishing my song. Come quickly. I may not be able to stop.

"I should probably go," I tell Koko, who smiles as if she fully expected this.

"Tell him hi from me." She winks, slides off the counter, and disappears behind a rack of coats.

When I reach the door, I hear her call out. "Hey, do you have plans on December twenty-ninth?"

I shake my head, even though I'm not entirely sure she can see me. "I don't think so. Why?"

Her head pops up from behind a rack, though it is not remotely close to where I thought she was standing. "I'm going to have a little get-together here at the store. Just a few close friends, post-Christmas, before things get too hectic in the new year. Can you and Mac come?"

I wonder if she considers me one of those few close friends. I kind of hope she does.

"I'll have to check and see if he is working, but you can consider me there."

HE'S EATEN HALF the cake by the time I get upstairs.

"I'm sorry. I couldn't help it," he says, mouth half full as I walk into the kitchen. "I couldn't even stop myself to put it on a proper plate." He holds out a second fork. "Save me."

I take a forkful and bite. "Dear god. What did she put in this?"

"I don't know," Mackenzie says. "I love this too much to ask questions."

His words make me pause mid-bite. He's talking about the cake, but it's exactly how I feel about our relationship.

"Hey." He sets his fork down on the counter. "I want to ask you something."

The mouthful of cake I'm in the middle of swallowing gets stuck, and I have to cough to dislodge it.

"Wrong hatch?" He pats me firmly on the back.

I nod, swallow, and then take a deep breath. "I'm good." Unless, of course, he does want to talk about Liverpool; then I'm not at all ready.

"What are you doing for Christmas?"

I am so surprised by his question that I almost choke again. "Christmas? I don't know. Hanging out here. Why?"

"Well . . ." He draws the word out. "I was thinking you could come back to West Lake with me. My brothers are staying with my parents for a couple of days. Christmas is much more low-key than it was growing up, so it's not exactly the full Smith family Christmas experience, but we do eat a lot, and my mom would love to have you. I would love to have you."

"You asked your mom already?"

He nods. "She's already bought your matching pajamas."

My eyes must go wide because he laughs. "I'm joking about that part. We all wear whatever we want, remember? But I'm serious about the rest of it. My family really wants to meet you."

I remember when Lucca said the same thing; it made me panic, but I don't feel that way at all right now. Quite the opposite.

"I'd love to come. But what do I need to do? Or bring? French hens? Turtle doves? I am very new at this."

He stands and walks over to me, wrapping me in his arms. He tucks me under his chin. "You don't need to bring or do anything. We don't do presents anymore. Just a white elephant gift exchange, and I will take care of that."

I nestle my head against his chest, feeling the best I have all day. "I'm happy to help you. Just tell me what you need."

He pulls back, brings his hands to my chin to tip my face back, and kisses me. "All I need is you."

25

ON CHRISTMAS EVE, WE RENT ANOTHER CAR and drive the three and a half hours north to West Lake. Once in town, we stop in the Valu-mart parking lot under the guise of picking up ice. When Mackenzie mentioned parking lot doughnuts a few weeks ago, I had a vague sense of what he meant, but I am subjected to the full experience as he pulls the parking brake on our rented Ford Focus and whirls us around in snowy circles.

"This is how we impressed all the girls back in high school," he says as we drive toward the exit, and he flicks his left blinker.

"And that worked for you?"

He laughs as he makes the turn. "Not at all."

Downtown West Lake is cute and quaint. It feels like a tiny beach town under two feet of snow. Mackenzie points things out as we drive: the Legion, where he had his first beer, and the ditch, where his brother Clive got their minivan stuck the day his other brother Aaron tried to teach them both to drive.

My stomach seems to be twisting itself into an intricate sailor's knot, following each bend and curve of the road as it flips and folds until we finally pull off the country highway onto a long graveled road. The trees on either side of us are tall and thick with snow, and even though it's just past noon, it feels like the sky is growing dark. When we turn a bend and a house comes into view, I have to blink twice to make sure what I am seeing is real and not some Christmas mirage.

"That is *not* your house," I say as we turn down the driveway and pull up in front of the building in question. It's two stories tall with clapboard siding and a giant porch that reaches all the way around the front. Each post is wrapped in green garland and twinkle lights, with more garland running along the banister. The roof and the top of the porch are all trimmed in white lights, and in each of the six upper windows is a green wreath with a red bow. Off to the side is a detached garage that looks like a miniature version of the house, decorations and all.

"My mom has a bit of a problem." Mackenzie puts the car in park and cuts the engine.

"You and I have different definitions of what constitutes a problem."

He undoes his seatbelt so he can turn to face me. "You'll take that back when you see the bathroom tree." He cups my face in both hands, which are still warm from the heated steering wheel. His breath, however, comes out as a white puff, the car already cooling to the freezing temperatures outside.

"Are you ready?" he asks, placing a soft kiss on my lips.

"Nope." The knot in my stomach squeezes as if proving my point.

Ready or not, the Smith family greeting party comes at us full force as the front door bangs open, and two German shepherds and a pug run outside, followed by a woman in a

Santa hat and an apron covered in Christmas trees with the phrase I LIKE THEM REAL THICK AND SPRUCEY, written across the front.

"They're here!" She has Mackenzie's dark blond hair and kind blue eyes, and from the way she sings her greeting, his perfect pitch.

We get out of the car and are caught up in a swirl of snow, dogs, and hugs. I meet Mackenzie's dad, Michael, his brothers, Aaron and Clive, and his mom, Nancy, and her three "babies": the German shepherds Domi and Gilmore and their pug Potvin.

"Gillian is working out in Vancouver," Nancy explains before I can ask about Mackenzie's sister. "She couldn't get the time off, but we will FaceTime her later. She'll be so excited to finally meet you. We are all so *so* happy you could come, Annalise." She hugs me long and hard.

"Okay, Mum." Mackenzie taps her on the back until she releases me. "I'm going to get our bags from the trunk. Why don't you take her inside to warm up?"

Nancy loops her arm through mine, walking me inside and detailing the events of the next two days. "There will be a Christmas Eve dinner tonight for the family," she explains. "Then tomorrow morning, we will all wake up and do our gift exchange game. Christmas dinner will be served at three, then Mike and I will retire to the couch in our stretchy pants, and then all you kids will head over to Mackenzie's cousin Zoe's house for her Christmas get-together. Sound good, honey?"

I nod, but my attention has shifted from her question to the living room in front of me.

I clearly exaggerated when I told Mackenzie that Christmas exploded in our apartment. If our apartment was an explosion, then this living room would be a Christmas decimation.

There is a mat beneath my feet that reads, MERRY CHRISTMAS, YA FILTHY ANIMAL. A coffee table is covered in fake snow and an entire miniature ceramic Christmas village with working lights and a tiny operating train chugging through it. There's fresh green garland running up the banister to the upstairs and trimming every single one of the doorways. In a span of thirty seconds, I count eight angels, four Santas, and three Christmas trees: one made of glass on a credenza, one in the corner of the dining room, and a huge real one in the family room.

I had thought Mackenzie was joking about the bathroom tree. Now, I am not so sure.

"I'll show you to our room." Mackenzie takes our bags and starts to walk up the stairs, but his mom clears her throat.

"Not so fast, there, bucko," she says. "Annalise is in your room, but *you* are out in the garage with your brothers."

Mackenzie stops mid-stride. "Are you serious? We're adults."

She shrugs. "You know the rules. There will be no funny business under my roof."

Mackenzie lets out a long, hard breath, retreats down the stairs, and drops his bag by the front door. He then holds out his now free hand to me. "Come on. I'll show you to *your* room."

I follow him upstairs to the last room at the end of a long hall. I'm not sure what to expect as Mackenzie opens the door—maybe more Christmas?—but what I get is a perfectly preserved shrine to Mackenzie's teenage years.

"Oh. My. God." I take in the Lumineers and Florida Georgia Line posters and the Toronto Maple Leafs bedspread. The music awards, the black light, and the floor-to-ceiling poster of Megan Fox.

"That was Clive's," Mackenzie says, and I notice a second bed in the corner.

"Wait! I'm stealing both of your rooms?"

Mackenzie sets my bag down on his desk. "Don't worry, it's fine. The loft above the garage is fully finished. We used to sleep out there all the time at Christmas. It was easier to spot Santa when we were little and easier to sneak home after curfew when we weren't."

I take another glance around the room, spotting a picture of Mackenzie taken sometime in his teens. His hair is long and shaggy, and I think he's wearing a vest and what look like thick leather bracelets.

I pick it up. "Is this angsty poet Mackenzie?"

My hot musician Mackenzie nods. "In all his tormented glory."

I glance at the photo again. "What was Becky thinking letting you get away?"

He takes the photo from my hands, tosses it on his desk, then wraps my arms around his body before cupping my face in his hands.

"Some things are just not meant to be." He tips my chin up to kiss me softly on the lips. "How are you doing? We haven't scared you off yet, right?"

I shake my head. "Not in the least."

"Good." He kisses me again. "Just remember, you don't have to do everything. My mom gets excited to have us all home and goes a little overboard with the activities. If you need a break to hide out for a bit, tell me."

"Should we have a safe word?" I press up on my toes to kiss

him this time. "Something I can say that hints that I need you to bring me back up to this room immediately."

I raise an eyebrow and bite my lip.

He walks me backward, pressing my back against the wall. His leg finds the gap between my thighs as he kisses me longer and harder than a moment ago.

"If you look at me the way you did just there, I don't think we'll be needing a safe word."

"Good, because I was going to go with something along the lines of *yuletide* or *sugarplum,* but I worry those phrases come up in regular conversation in this house."

He leans in to kiss me again, but before he can, his mom's voice calls out from somewhere a little too close to the bedroom door.

"I am about to bake some cookies and could use an extra set of hands. Is anyone interested?"

Mackenzie shakes his head. "Remember, it's fine to say no."

I smile as I call out, "I would absolutely love to."

"CAN YOU PASS me the allspice, honey? It's the second one on your left." Nancy holds a silver flour sifter above a large metal bowl. In the past twenty minutes, I've learned more about baking than I accumulated in my twenty-eight years of life, including what a flour sifter is and why one would use it. Mackenzie's childhood kitchen reminds me of the ones from the Friday night sitcoms I would watch growing up. The cupboards are a light wood and the counters an off-white Formica, and there's a border in the gap between the top of the cupboards and the ceiling with painted mallard ducks floating on marshes and about to take flight. Christmas has infiltrated this room as well. On the table is a set of salt and pepper shakers shaped like nutcrackers and a set of placemats with Santa's sleigh being pulled by a team of fat, little pugs wearing antlers. The air smells like cookies even though nothing has made it into the oven yet. It's warm and cozy, and I feel completely at home.

I pick up the allspice she asked for but hold it out instead of handing it to her. "Is this what you want?"

She nods and holds out her hand.

I open the tiny bottle and sniff. The red powder looks nothing like the allspice Harmony lent me for my gingerbread house, nor does it smell like it.

"Quick question for you. Is allspice ever green and leaflike?"

Nancy stops stirring to shake her head. "When it isn't preground, it looks like little peppercorns, but they're brown, not green. Are you thinking of parsley, maybe? Or oregano?"

I shake my head. "I'm thinking I might have an explanation for a few of my neighbor's baking mishaps."

She nods as if she's following while also looking very confused.

The dough comes together the perfect shade of gingerbread brown and rolls out smooth and even with my newly acquired rolling pin skills under Nancy's expert direction.

"Pick one." She holds out four cookie cutters: one typical-looking gingerbread man and three others in what look like karate poses.

"They're *ninja* bread men," she says with a wink. "This one is Aaron." She points to the one doing a side kick, and then holds up one that looks to be in a deep lunge. "And this one is Clive."

I hold up the third, who seems to be mid-leap, "Which makes this Mackenzie?"

Nancy shakes her head, "No, that's Gillian. She's the feistiest of all of them." Nancy picks up the plain gingerbread man. "This one is Mackenzie. The other three would go at it like feral cats growing up, but Mackenzie was a peacekeeper—he was never one to fight."

She hands me the cookie cutter, and when I take it, her hand covers mine. "That boy of mine—he loves hard. Just throws his whole heart in without thinkin' twice. It's one of the things I love most about him, but I'll be honest, sometimes I worry he doesn't always think about protecting that heart. He'll give and give, even if it wears him down, because making the people he loves happy means everything to him."

She gives my hand a squeeze. "So if he ever seems like he's holding back or not speaking up, it's not because he doesn't care—it's because he cares too much. Sometimes he just needs a little reminder that it's okay to say what he needs, too. That kind of honesty'll make you both stronger, I think."

She steps away and back to the cookie sheet, leaving me alone to think. I feel like she's handed me a cheat sheet—a shortcut to understanding things about Mackenzie I was only starting to learn. Before I can thank her, he appears, leaning against the doorframe—cheeks pink and wearing an old plaid puffy vest over his thick wool sweater.

"I need to steal Annalise." He drops an arm around my shoulders and kisses my temple. "We have important business to attend to."

His mom claps her hands. "Is it time for your snowman contest?"

I think this might be another Smith family inside joke, but neither Mackenzie nor his mom is laughing.

"It's not a snowman contest. It's a snow sculpture competition." Mackenzie drops his arm from my shoulders and steps over to a kitchen cupboard and pulls something from it, which he stuffs into his jacket. Nancy and I exchange glances as he walks around the counter and pulls a very large knife from the butcher block, which he also tries to hide in his jacket, but his mom stops him with a "No. Absolutely not."

She meets my eyes and shakes her head as she takes the knife from Mackenzie and returns it to its place. She opens a kitchen drawer, pulls out a butter knife, and hands it to him.

He grabs my hand as we leave the kitchen.

I eye the bulge beneath his jacket. "Do I want to know?"

He grins. "Probably not, but you're about to find out."

26

IT TURNS OUT IT IS, IN FACT, a snowman competition.

Mackenzie decorates his to look like Jeremy Allen White circa *The Bear.* Aaron dresses his up to look like Dolly Parton. It's not entirely clear what Clive's snowman is supposed to be, but it doesn't matter—the competition ends in an epic snow fight that leaves Dolly hatless, Jeremy headless, and Clive's creation knocked over and used as cover.

I have snow in places snow has never been before, and although I enjoyed every single second, I'm happy when we move inside to the next activity: a communal couch nap by the fire. When it's time to eat dinner, I'm toasty, hungry, and certain the day cannot possibly get better. I'm proven wrong as we sit down at a table set with a Christmas tablecloth and matching green and gold napkins. My plate is made of actual china, and my fork is fancy—but not the sleek, pretentious fancy you see at Williams-Sonoma, but the kind of fancy where someone's grandma clearly picked it out fifty years ago and lovingly passed it along.

"Christmas cracker?" Clive hands me a green paper tube covered in tiny gold reindeer.

I take it from him with a "thanks," but he stops me when I try to pull it open. "You might want to hold on a second."

I'm confused until he crosses his arms and offers me the end of his Christmas cracker, and I realize everyone at the table is pulling together.

"It is cheesy, but we humor her." Clive nods at his mom.

"It is not cheesy," I tell him. "It's wonderful."

The delights continue as we each put on our paper crowns and then take turns telling the terrible jokes.

"Hey, Annalise," says Mike. "What do you get when you cross a snowman and a vampire?" I shake my head as he pauses for effect and then announces in an exaggerated voice, "Frost-bite!"

We all fake laugh, but my smile is more than genuine. As is my "ohhhh" that escapes when Nancy emerges from the kitchen with what looks like an enormous pie.

"Tourtière," she says with a perfect Quebecois accent as she spoons the steaming meat pie onto plates.

I lean in toward Mackenzie. "Are you French Canadian?"

He shakes his head. "Not even a little bit. Pretty sure the tradition began years ago when Grandma Beauchannen over-cooked the ham, and tourtière was the only thing left at the Foodland."

The tourtière is delicious. The pastry is buttery and crisp, and the meat is perfectly spiced. I almost ask for seconds until Nancy mentions the gingerbread we will be having for dessert.

I help her bring the cookies out on a giant platter shaped like a candy cane.

"I made this one for you." I hand Mackenzie one of the regular-shaped cookies. "Check out his hair and his little leather bracelets." Mackenzie squints to read the cookie's shirt. "I write *songs,* not tragedies?"

"Get it?"

He laughs, and when his smile settles, there's something quieter left behind that sends a flutter through me.

"Well," says Nancy after we've all cleared the table and finished cleaning up the kitchen, "you kids are welcome to do what you want, but I have a date with a dashing duke."

Aaron and Clive head out to the loft. Mike grabs his book and says good night. Mackenzie waits until we're alone before wrapping his arms around me and asking, "Do you want to watch for a bit or come out to the loft?"

I can hear the crackling fire in the living room. "You know how I feel about dukes."

He laughs and kisses me on the forehead. "I'll go make the hot chocolate."

When we get to the family room, Nancy is fully wrapped in a blanket, reclining on a La-Z-Boy with a mug of tea in her hands. She has left the three-seater couch open. It has an ideal view of both the television and the Christmas tree, and as I sink into the oversize cushions, I think I get another rush of happiness.

"Do you like Christmas movies, Annalise?" she asks as I tuck my legs under me.

"Yes. I'd go as far as to say they are a defining part of my personality."

She opens her mouth to say something else but stops as Mackenzie walks in. He hands me the mugs while grabbing a blanket from the arm of the couch, then fluffs it out and pulls it over both of our legs as he sits.

"*You're* watching with us?" Nancy says to him.

Mackenzie slings an arm around my shoulders. "I am."

Nancy smiles, glancing from him to me. "He must really like you, honey." She shakes her head. "I used to beg my boys to watch my Christmas movies with me, and they denied their own mother. This one even said he'd rather walk barefoot in a gas station bathroom."

I look at Mackenzie, shocked.

"That was Clive," Mackenzie says to me, then, noticing the arch of my eyebrows, leans in so only I can hear. "I may have stretched the truth that first night. But I have grown to love them."

I shake my head. "But why watch with me in the first place?"

He looks at me like he's surprised I don't know the answer. "Because I knew they made you happy."

About an hour into the movie, Nancy falls asleep in her recliner until one of her snores gets so loud that she wakes herself up.

"Oh." She looks around as if unsure of where she is for a moment. "I'm going to head to bed. Good night, you two. May you have visions of sugarplums dancing in your head."

"You too!" I grin a little too wildly at the mention of sugarplums, then even wider as Mackenzie's hand slides beneath the blanket and squeezes my thigh.

"Want to head upstairs?" he says when we hear the closing of her bedroom door.

I shake my head. "Your mother was very clear about what would and would not be happening under her roof."

Mackenzie kisses the side of my neck. "Her rules are more like guidelines. And their bedroom is at the opposite end of the house from mine." His nose grazes the spot just below my ear. "I can be very quiet." He kisses me again, and it dissolves the little resolve I had.

"Fine," I concede. "But no funny business, though. Ten minutes of cuddling and then off to the garage for you."

He pretends to be hurt, but I can see his smile.

"I'll take it," he says. "I'll take anything I can get."

The stairs creak worse than our apartment floors, making it very clear by the second step that the house was not designed for being covert.

"I have an idea," Mackenzie says, sliding his hands around my waist, then cupping my ass and lifting my legs so they wrap around his body. "They'll hear one set of feet."

His idea works in theory, but it's a loud and heavy set of feet as he carries me the rest of the way upstairs, down the hall, and into his old bedroom, kicking the door closed behind us. He drops me onto the bed and then climbs on top of me, pinning me between his knees.

His lips find mine, and though it's a long, languorous kiss that I enjoy thoroughly, I pull away when it's done.

"This is *not* what I call cuddling."

He kisses me again, but lighter this time and quickly. "I'm sorry, I couldn't help it. I'll stop."

His "stop" is yet another kiss—one that parts my lips with a sweep of his tongue. It's a preview of what could come next if I were to surrender to it.

His hands snake under my hips, cupping my ass as he presses his body into mine. I am about to take it all back—everything I said downstairs—when there's a loud creak from down the hall.

We both freeze.

When a few moments go by with no more sounds, Mackenzie exhales. "It's just the house. It does that sometimes."

Still, he slides off the bed, peels back the covers, and then waits for me to climb underneath them. Then he climbs in after me, pulling the covers up and over us both, tugging my back into his chest, a little spoon to his big.

"Night, Annalise." He slides his hand over my hip and kisses the top of my head, before collapsing into his pillow with a sigh, his breath evening out into a slow, steady rhythm.

I close my eyes, not the least bit sleepy, but hoping the action will trick my body into sleep.

All it does is make me hyper-aware of his fingers still lingering on my stomach. His pinky finger rests just under the elastic waistband of my sweatpants and he is pressed hard against my thigh.

I hold my breath, fighting the urge to arch my back and take what I want.

Instead I wait. My patience is soon rewarded as his hand begins to move.

His fingers glide along my waistband, back and forth. Once, twice, until the third time when I break.

"Enough." The word comes out less like an order and more like a plea as my fingers cover his and push them down.

He laughs. However, he emits little sound, just a hot rush of breath along the back of my neck as his hand slides below the elastic of my underwear and begins to stroke.

"I thought you just wanted to cuddle, Annalise." He presses his erection into me. His lips find my neck, and I fight to keep quiet.

"I kept picturing you in those sweatpants." I grind against him, needing more.

"Hmmm . . ." He removes his hand to hook his thumb under the waistband of my sweatpants and underwear and tugs them both down. "Funny . . . I've been lying here the entire time trying to figure out a way to get you *out* of yours."

"You liar." I nudge my butt against him.

He catches my hip and holds me tight to his body. "Haven't you figured it out yet? I want you all the time. Always."

And with that, he sits up to remove my pants the rest of the way, dropping them into some dark pile next to the bed. He takes his own off next, apologizing when he knocks the covers off, and the cool night air makes my whole body shiver.

I forgive him as he slides in next to me, welcoming the heat of his body as it covers mine, then slides down, pulling the covers up and over his head.

When his mouth finds me, it's both a release and an instant reminder of how quickly he has learned my body. The slow strokes of his tongue and the pressure of his fingers find all my spots within seconds.

Without meaning to, I begin to moan. I come quick and hard, my back arching off the bed as the waves of pleasure curl my toes.

"Shhhhh." He laughs, but he slides out from under the covers and smothers my mouth with a kiss.

"I'm sorry," I whisper when my brain finally has enough power to register where we are. "I got caught up."

"I love the noises you make," he whispers through kisses. "Every single one of them."

His mouth covers mine again, muffling whatever satisfied sound is escaping as he settles between my thighs and presses himself inside me.

My brain loses all thought as he begins to pick up his rhythm, grabbing the rungs of the headboard to keep them from banging against the wall. However, if his intention was to keep quiet, he has failed to anticipate the leverage the headboard gives him as he thrusts deeper and harder with every stroke. My second orgasm comes on even faster and more intense, overtaking my body and impairing my ability to keep back the moan rocketing from my chest. But it's not my voice that breaks the dark and quiet. It's his deep and low "*oh fuck*" that fills the room as everything inside me fills with a euphoric rush.

I close my eyes and succumb to the waves of pleasure taking over my body, still feeling floaty and light as he exhales and collapses on top of me, laying his cheek on my breasts until I catch my breath and begin to laugh.

"Please tell me the walls here are thick or your parents are very deep sleepers."

Mackenzie lifts his head just enough to look at me. "To be honest, I have no idea. You are the first person I've ever brought home."

He returns his head to my chest, and I stroke his hair, letting that new piece of information sink in.

I think again of his mom's words from earlier in the kitchen.

He loves hard. Doesn't protect himself. Even when it costs him.

It's the opposite of me in every way—I guard. I protect. Falling means getting hurt.

And yet, lying here next to him in the dark, I find myself falling hard.

27

I WAKE UP SOMETIME IN THE EARLY morning to a kiss on my neck and a "Merry Christmas, Annalise" whispered in my ear. But before I can say it back, sleep reclaims me, and I slip back into dreams. When I wake again, it's some time later. The sun is streaming through the window and the smells of coffee, bacon, and something cinnamony waft up from the kitchen downstairs.

I roll over in a bit of a panic. His house has a single staircase. A staircase that leads directly down to both the living room and the dining room, and unless he plans to Spider-Man his way out of here, we are going to have to do a Christmas morning walk of shame.

"Mackenzie." I reach for his back to shake. However, the pillowy mound beside me is just that, only pillows, and the mattress beneath them is cold.

I scramble out of bed, throw on clean sweatpants and my official Midnight Station hoodie, and head to the stairs, pausing at the top. The Christmas tree is lit up and beautiful, and there's already a fire crackling away. Aaron and Clive are lounging on the couch in matching Midnight Station merch with mugs of something hot and steaming in their hands.

Nancy is in her recliner with a book, and someone is, from the sounds of things, in the kitchen blending something.

"Good morning," I say. "Merry Christmas."

Nancy puts her book down. "Morning, sweetheart."

Clive and Aaron both raise their mugs. "Look at us, twinsies," says Clive. I open my mouth to ask if Mackenzie is up yet, but my answer comes as the front door swings open, bringing with it a shot of cold air.

"Merry Christmas." Mackenzie bangs his feet against the doormat, kicking snow from his boots as he closes the door behind him. He sheds his winter gear and meets me at the bottom of the steps, where he slides a cold hand around my waist and kisses my cheek. "Morning. How did you sleep?" His tone is nonchalant, but his mouth curls as he says it.

"Pretty good," I answer. "I was exhausted."

He nods at the tree. "Looks like Santa found us." The pile of presents spills out well past the lower branches, and the seven red stockings that were empty when we went to sleep last night are so full they've tipped on their sides.

Nancy pushes the footrest of her recliner in with a click and stands. "I swear I heard Santa on the roof last night, just after midnight."

My body goes still.

"He was making quite the racket," she continues. My stomach plummets, and I know my cheeks have flushed a bright red, which only deepens as Aaron and Clive start to laugh.

Mackenzie pulls my face to his chest, his own back shaking with laughter just as his dad appears in the doorway to the kitchen.

"Wha'd I miss?" he asks

As Nancy walks past me, she pats me softly on the back.

"Oh, nothing. We were just chitchatting about how last evening was a not-so-silent night."

Mike shrugs as if he finds this all perfectly logical.

"Well, that sounds nice. Who's up for pancakes?"

If I wasn't convinced the Smith family were the living embodiment of a fictional Christmas movie, their breakfast table confirms it. In addition to the two large stacks of perfectly round pancakes, there are platters of bacon and eggs, cinnamon buns, and freshly squeezed orange juice in an actual juice pitcher. I am so stuffed by the end of the meal that I can barely move.

After breakfast, we go to the living room. Although Mackenzie claimed it would be low-key, there is a stocking with my name on it, filled with good coffee, a new toothbrush, the latest issue of *Scientific American,* and a Ghirardelli chocolate bar.

"These are from Harmony." Mackenzie hands me a tin of cookies. "Peppermint patties, and I pretested them for you: ten out of ten."

I set them aside. "I don't think I can look at another morsel of food for at least six more hours, but we can save them for the ride home."

I reach under the tree for the small box I put there yesterday. In our joint effort to avoid all meaningful conversations about where our relationship is headed these last few weeks, we also neglected to set any sort of guidelines regarding Christmas presents, but I saw something in a window of a small stationery shop and knew I wanted him to have it.

"It's a music journal," I explain when he unwraps the leather-bound book and cradles it in his hands instead of opening it. "One side is for writing music and the other for lyrics."

His hand finds mine.

"I love it," he says. "And I got you something, too."

He hands me a box wrapped in shiny gold paper. I remove it and lift the lid to find a black jacket inside. I almost think it's Larry's, but when I lift it from the box, I realize the collar is different, and it's a lot smaller.

"You look good in mine," Mackenzie says as he watches me study it. "I thought about giving it to you, but Koko found me one in your size."

I slide my arms into the sleeves and try it on. It fits perfectly.

Mackenzie leans in and kisses me on the cheek, lingering just long enough to whisper, "Looks great on you."

I lean my head into his. "This is perfect. I love it. Thank you."

After a pause to refill the coffee mugs, we move on to what I learn has become a cornerstone of the Smith Family Christmas experience: the white elephant game. I've played a version of it before at the CAMH staff party. Everyone draws a number. The first person opens a present. The second person can steal an opened gift or pick from the unopened ones and take their chances.

I draw the number seven.

The game begins, and Aaron goes first, picking a small box that looks like a candy cane. It contains a winter-scented candle and a king-size Kit Kat, neither of which he seems particularly excited about.

Nancy is next. She picks a gift bag with an oversize coffee mug that says, I LIKE BIG BOOKS, and a gift certificate to the movies.

Mike goes after Nancy and steals her mug, although I suspect it's less because he's a mug guy and more because he knows Nancy loves to unwrap.

On her second round, she gets an animatronic bass that sings "Fishing in the Dark." She tries to hide it behind her housecoat. Clive immediately steals it. Nancy goes back for the mug. Mike steals the fish, then Clive cries, "Collusion, you two are working together." Mike and Nancy deny it.

Aaron tries to get Clive to steal his candle and collude with him. Clive says, "Fuck no," and opens a shiny red box. It has a very cool vintage Tragically Hip T-shirt that I swear came from Koko's store.

Mackenzie is next. He steals the shirt.

Clive opens yet another one, a Neil Young T-shirt that I know for a fact came from Koko's store. Clive whips off his Midnight Station hoodie and puts the Neil Young one on. I suspect no one will be stealing it from him now, especially since the only person left to pick a present is me.

My eyes do a quick sweep of all the opened gifts. Everyone seems happy with what they have, except maybe for Aaron, who has taken the lid off the candle and is trying to waft the scent in my direction. I like the smell but worry that stealing it will start a whole chain of chaos.

"If you pick that last gift, the game is over," Aaron taunts.

This has been the best morning. I don't want any of it to end, but something about the last present—the plainly wrapped brown paper box—is calling to me.

I pick it up and hear Aaron groan as I carefully remove the tape to reveal a simple white box inside. I open it. Inside is what looks like yet another white box, but as I pull it out, I realize it's a Chinese takeout food container.

"Aw, man. Who regifted?" Mackenzie asks.

When Aaron starts to laugh, Mackenzie balls up a wad of wrapping paper and throws it at him.

Aaron bats it away. "No regifting is not an official rule.

Also, I told her to take the candle. Also, I'm willing to tradesies if I can keep the Kit Kat."

I open the container, and inside is yet another Chinese takeout container, but this one is on a string. It's made of a ceramic material to look just like the one it was packaged in. There's a thin, red satin ribbon looped through one of the handles. As I pick it up, it begins to spin, then stops to display the year 2024.

My lungs constrict, and my heart begins to thump so strongly it feels like it's shaking my entire chest.

It's a Christmas ornament.

From 2024.

The missing piece of my collection.

"It's perfect," I whisper to no one in particular. It's a reminder of the fact that neither Larry nor I cooked and how I used to sneak him takeout food when the hospital food sucked or when I got home too late and too tired to pull something together. Most of my memories of 2024 are not good ones. They are sharp and painful to touch, but also my last ones with Larry.

I hug it to my chest.

"Well," says Nancy, not realizing the full extent of what just happened but maybe sensing on some level that it was meaningful, "shall we get cleaned up? We have more eating to do today."

AND WE REALLY eat.

An entire turkey dinner in the middle of the afternoon. Then a constant stream of sugar and pastry until seven o'clock, when we head to Mackenzie's cousin Zoe's house for her annual Christmas party. She serves lasagna, which I skip, and eggnog, which I also skip, and the most delicious butter tarts, of which I have three.

When we get back to the house just after midnight, I feel like I'm going to burst, both literally from food and figuratively from forty-eight straight hours of Christmas-induced serotonin.

Mackenzie walks me to the house's front door but pauses on the porch outside. "I think maybe I should sleep out in the loft tonight," he says.

The inside of the house is dark except for a single light left on in the entranceway. I suspect Mackenzie's parents are fast asleep in bed, but I was also going to suggest the same. "There are no reindeer to take the fall for us tonight."

He laughs and leans in to kiss me, but stops as a flash of light shoots across the sky.

"Shooting star," he says, pointing. "Make a—" He pauses mid-sentence, leaving the rest unfinished. "Sorry, I forgot. Not your thing."

But tonight, I wonder if it is. I am standing on the front porch of a house that feels like it was plucked off the front of a Christmas card next to a man who is kind and funny and more handsome than anyone has a right to be. I'm full of turkey and chocolate, and I'm happy—and for the first time in a very long time, my heart doesn't ache every time I breathe.

For so long, I thought feeling like this would be impossible, and now I wonder if maybe I was wrong and this is what they mean when they say the magic of the season.

I close my eyes, and for the first time in a very long time, I make a wish. When I open them again, he is looking at me.

"Annalise Harris, did you just wish on a shooting star?"

I don't answer, but I do smile.

He shakes his head. "That's a gateway to big stuff. Next,

you're going to be telling me you believe in Santa or soulmates."

I make a show of rolling my eyes. "Let's not get too ahead of ourselves."

He leans in, bringing his face close to mine. "God, I love you," he says.

My entire body goes rigid, because that was a big word, and I'm not sure he meant to throw it out there like that. However, now it hangs between us as if it's waiting for its match. It's reciprocal: I love you, too.

"It's okay," he says, brushing frozen bangs from my forehead. "You don't have to say it. I sprung that on you. It was the right moment for me, but I know you like time to process."

I want to say it back. What I feel for him is deep and unlike anything I have ever felt before. But it's also something I can't unsay. It's a line once crossed I can never turn back. If you love, there are only two ways forward: love forever or loss.

I reach up and bring his mouth to mine, hoping it tells him what I still haven't figured out.

I might not be quite there—on Santa or soulmates or the rest of it.

But I'm getting damn close.

28

WE WAKE UP EARLY THE NEXT MORNING to say goodbye to Clive and Aaron, who are heading into Owen Sound for Boxing Day deals. After breakfast, it's just Mike and Nancy who send us off with hugs and a Tupperware of turkey leftovers for our ride back to Toronto.

"You should come for Easter," Nancy says as she hands me a thermos of coffee, which I plop into the beverage holder in the center console between our two seats. I turn around just in time to hear Mackenzie say, "Annalise will be overseas, Mom, remember?"

It hits with enough force to break the spell of the last few days.

Mackenzie doesn't mention my leaving again the entire three-hour ride home. Or when we carry our bags back to our apartment, where our half-burned-out Christmas lights and floor filled with dead pine needles make the whole room feel neglected and underwhelming.

He doesn't say a word until there is Thai food in our hands, and we are sitting side by side on the couch, and he is pushing his noodles around instead of eating, and it comes out as a quick and abrupt, "Can we talk?"

His eyes don't meet mine; instead, they follow the path of his fork as he pushes it back and forth across his plate before finally giving up and setting it down on the coffee table.

"You're leaving in a week." He puts it so simply. "And I think we've both been avoiding having the conversation about what's going to happen to us, but I don't know that we can put it off any longer."

All I can do is nod because my throat is dry, and my tongue feels like it is glued inside my mouth. Instead of speaking, I set my plate next to his. For a moment, I consider taking them both to the sink to buy a few more precious minutes, but then he clears his throat, and I have no choice but to accept what is inevitably about to happen.

"When I came home from the tour, I wasn't thinking about the time we had left together. I just wanted to be with you." He takes my hand between his. "I think, maybe in the back of my mind, I thought we'd work something out, but I realized over Christmas that's not gonna happen, and I don't think I can do two years apart."

His palms have gone sweaty, or maybe mine are the problem.

"I want to be with you, Annalise," he says. "But with the band's schedule and the cost of flights, I don't know how much I'll be able to get to Liverpool to visit. I know your budget is tighter than mine, and realistically, we are looking at seeing each other two, maybe three times a year, and that won't be enough."

His hands begin to shake, so I tug mine away and reach for my water. The liquid frees my tongue, but even then, I'm afraid to speak. I worry what will come out of my mouth is a "why?" or a "no," or a "please." Or maybe just a sob because I was stupid enough to think this was special enough to work. That the universe had somehow pushed us together. It's the most idiotic thing I've ever heard. Actually, it's delusional. It's—

"I want to come with you."

His sentence is simple, but I still don't fully grasp it.

I have to turn his words over in my head twice, and even then, I don't believe I've got it right.

"You want to come with me?"

He nods. "Yes. I mean, not next week. It will take me a little while to get the right visas, but I looked into it, and since my grandpa was born in Glasgow, I'm eligible to apply for an ancestry visa. I'll have to find someone to sublet your place and wait until Zee finds someone to replace me in the band, but I figure I can be there in three months at most, which will give you time to settle in."

He pauses as if he wants to see my reaction, which is to stare right back at him and question whether I am hearing him correctly. But I realize he's serious. He's clearly done research. This isn't some whim he's concocted just now over a few bites of pad Thai. He wants to move to an entirely new continent to be with me. Pack up his entire life so we can build a new one together.

"Will you find another band?" I think about Koko and her British rock star suggestion.

He shrugs. "If I can. Or I'll bartend. Or busk. Or work at a coffee shop. I don't really care."

The good of the last few seconds is halted with a single thought. I'm going to Liverpool to take the next step in the career I've dreamed about for almost a decade, but if Mackenzie comes with me, it means he's putting his on hold.

"But what about your music? Your writing? I can't ask you to give that up."

He breathes out long and hard. "But you *want* me to come?"

I nod. "Of course I do. But you finally have a band to play your songs. You worked so hard to get here."

"I know." He lets go of my hand, reaches under my knees, and scoops me into his lap. "But Zee's not playing my stuff anymore. Ever since the tour ended, he's been singing covers because it brings in the crowds. I'm not writing, Annalise, and even if I was, I don't want to spend the next two years long distance. It was so hard to be apart for a month, and we weren't even together yet. I know you don't believe that things are meant to be, but I do—and I'm trying to find the line between not freaking you out right now and making sure that you understand that I think you and I are . . . inevitable." He leans forward and brings his forehead to mine.

I close my eyes and savor this perfect moment, holding on to it for a full breath.

"You know I'll be at school most of my waking hours," I tell him.

He weaves his fingers through mine. "And asleep next to me for the rest of them."

"I will always be stressed out and talk about intracellular signaling incessantly."

He brings my hands to his lips and kisses them. "Talking science is my second favorite thing to do with you."

I close my eyes and picture us together in Liverpool. "The flat I rented is basically a shoe box. We will be on top of each other all the time."

He leans in and kisses the side of my neck, the heat of his breath lingering against my skin. "Are we putting that one on the pros or cons list?"

"I want you to come." The words come out so easily that I almost don't realize I've said them.

"I think you're right about us," I continue. "That we're meant to be together."

He pulls back, his eyebrows raised. "So we're doing this?"

Who am I to argue with the universe?

"Looks like we are."

29

WE SPEND THE WEEKEND MAKING PLANS. Mackenzie calls Zee to tell him the news. Zee does not take it well. Although Mackenzie takes the call on the couch and I am in the kitchen, I hear the long string of surprisingly poetic profanities as Zee tells Mackenzie he's an "ungrateful asshole" and "the knife in his back he didn't see coming" and also "fired." I also hear the apology that comes an hour and a half later when Zee realizes he needs a drummer for their gig that night and wants to take Mackenzie up on the offer to stay on and help find his replacement.

"You know you don't always need to be the nice guy," I say as he kisses me on his way out.

"You know me," he says. "All lover, no fighter. Besides, I'll need the cash if it takes me a while to find something in Liverpool."

It's still the one piece of the plan I do not love. Mackenzie will be essentially starting his entire music career over from scratch, and although Liverpool has a huge music scene, neither of us has any connections.

It's one of the many worries weighing on me as I get ready for work on Monday morning. It's my final day at CAMH, and according to the numbers on my kitchen clock, I will be late for it.

"Dammit." I press my cheek against the living room window to get a better view of the streetcar tracks. I can't see one coming, but I can hear the bell, which means if I run, I might be able to make it.

I grab my bag from the kitchen counter and sprint to the door, where I slip my boots on and reach for my new leather jacket. Rushing to lock the door behind me, I don't question why the first arm slides into my jacket a little too easily. It's when I put my second arm through the sleeve as I start down the stairs that I realize my mistake. Just as I hit the landing, everything around me goes black.

When my vision clears, I am back in my apartment.

I know it's another jacket vision because I'm staring down at the couch, and Other Me is curled up in the fetal position, staring blankly at the television, which would be less concerning if it didn't appear to be off.

Harmony is here, too. She is also staring down at the couch, a large cardboard box clasped in her hands.

"Chickpea." Her tone is coaxing. "Mr. Taylor is going to take me over to the Salvation Army in ten minutes . . ." She sets the box onto the coffee table. "I've finished the bedroom, and I think I'm done with the living room. Just need you to double-check this one." She nudges the box toward me. "I don't want to give away anything you planned to keep."

I know where I am in time now. It's the week after I broke up with Lucca. While I didn't miss him, his absence had both opened the wound of Larry's loss that had barely begun to heal and left a hole in my already empty social calendar, which I was filling with late-night sobbing.

Apparently, the walls were thinner than I thought because

Harmony showed up at my door one Saturday morning with an empty box and a lot of dried sage. She told me we were cleansing my life, starting with the apartment.

"What about these?" Harmony is by the armchair now, pulling something from behind it. She holds up a large rugby shirt and a black leather jacket.

Other Me lifts her head just enough to look. "The shirt, yes, but the jacket belongs to Lucca. He left it here the other week."

Harmony turns the jacket back and forth. "No, honey, I'm positive this one was Larry's. I was with him when he bought it."

The other me barely turns her head. "Donate it then." She rolls onto her back. "Just take all of it, Harmony. I really don't care."

Harmony gives me that look. That same mix of pity and her own grief that she gave me all last year. I think she's about to come over to hug me, but there is a honk from the street below, and instead she tosses the jacket onto the box, then picks it up and heads out the apartment door.

I debate whether I should follow her or stay behind, but before I can decide, the choice is made for me. I blink, and I am no longer in my apartment; instead, I am standing in a parking lot behind the Salvation Army.

Harmony is there, too, with the cardboard box in her hands. She rings the bell beside the door. A full minute goes by before the door swings open, blocking my view inside.

"I can take that," a voice says. Two gloves appear from behind the door, but Harmony hands her box over too soon, and it falls onto the pavement between them, spilling open.

"Shit, my bad." The gloves reach down toward the pavement to pick up the clothing and put it back in the box. They pause, however, on the last piece—the jacket.

"Um, I love this," the worker says. The jacket disappears from my view for a moment. "Are you sure you want to give it away?"

"It belonged to a friend," Harmony explains. "He always felt it was lucky, but now it's ready to be loved by someone new."

"It looks a little big for me," the worker says. "But oversize is in these days."

I don't know what is familiar—her words or the way she says them—but I move to the other side of the door so I can get a clear view of the worker's face. Her dark hair is almost to her waist, and her outfit is baggy and shapeless, but I know this woman, just maybe not the version of her standing before me.

"Koko?"

She can't hear or see me, yet I repeat it. "Koko? Is that you?"

Koko picks up the box, oblivious. "Thanks for donating." She turns and heads back inside the center.

I'm unsure what to do: follow Koko or stay here with Harmony. But then the blackness comes, and I'm sucked right back.

WHEN I'M ORIENTED again, I'm halfway down the stairs and present-day Harmony is staring up at me as if she's just come through the front door.

"Everything all right, chickpea?" She closes the gap between us and presses a cool palm against my forehead. When

I don't answer, she reaches into her bag and pulls out a Tupperware. "Here." She pulls off the lid. "Have a bite. My famous maple syrup chew-chews. They will bring your blood sugar back up." She forces something into my mouth. It's crunchy and seedy and, yes, there is the faintest hint of maple.

"Better?" she asks, closing the tin and sliding it into my purse.

"Yeah." I snap out of it. "Yes. Thank you. I'm good. I just . . . need to catch the streetcar. I'll talk to you later."

I run down the remaining steps, out the door, and onto the sidewalk in time to see the streetcar continue on down the street.

I have to walk to work, which has me at my desk twenty minutes later than I should be, and Phillip makes his feelings about that known through a series of sighs and disgruntled exhales. By his third one, I'm irritated.

"I'm sorry I was late, Phillip. I had a small personal issue this morning. It won't happen again."

I fail to mention that it won't happen again because it's my last day. Really, he should be giving me kudos for showing up ready to work at all.

Despite my concession, Phillip sighs again. "I'm just concerned about you, Annalise. You have been different these last few weeks, and frankly, I'm worried you might be slipping."

My irritation flares. "I was late *once,* Phillip. My work ethic doesn't need to be questioned because I missed my streetcar."

He pulls a file from the pile in front of him and holds it between his hands in a way that I'm not sure if he's showing it to me or wants me to take it. "We got the results back from the tests we ran." He hesitates momentarily before opening it and laying a stapled piece of paper in front of me. "It provides a possible explanation for that issue of yours we were investigating."

It's a lab report. I know the familiar formatting. I've looked at hundreds of these throughout our study. However, my eyes snag on the name at the top—Annalise Harris—and then scan until they find the section marked *Final Results Summary*. My heart triple skips at the bullet points noted in the big gray box: "THC Marijuana—detected."

"What is this? Some last-day joke?"

Phillip frowns and shakes his head, his expression saying, *You know I don't make jokes.*

I scan all of the information again. My blood type and birthdate are correct. The lab report is legitimate and hasn't been mixed up with another Annalise Harris.

"There has to be some mistake." I set down the report and push it away, but that act clears a space for Phillip to put a second report down in front of me. This one also has my name on it, and the drugs included in the toxicology screening have tripled in number compared to the first. My eyes skim this one until they find the results for THC.

Marijuana: NEGATIVE

I breathe a very momentary exhale of relief before I read on to the result below it. A result that makes my stomach clench so hard I think I might throw up.

Psilocybin: POSITIVE.

Magic mushrooms?

My spinning brain may not be firing on all cylinders, but it pulls up the street name for psilocybin with little effort.

This result is even more ridiculous than the marijuana. I have never in my life taken psilocybin or anything related to it.

"Okay, this is definitely a mistake." I also toss the paper onto the desk and push my chair back, needing physical distance from it. "The lab must have mixed my tests up with someone else's."

Phillip picks up both reports and puts them back into the file. "That's what I thought, too . . . after the first report. That's why I asked you for that second sample."

I shake my head, still not fully believing what I'm hearing. "But I don't do drugs," I tell him, the volume of my voice increasing. "I'm serious, Phillip, I have never taken anything stronger than an Extra Strength Tylenol. This can't be my report."

Phillip reaches out his arm, then after a moment of hesitation, he pats me softly on the shoulder twice. "I am not going to show this to anyone," he says. "I am hoping you'll see this as a wake-up call. The next two years will be very challenging academically, and as your friend, I want to tell you that drugs are not the answer. Science is the only high you need." He gives me yet another pat, then nods to himself, returns to his chair, and begins to type as if the last five minutes hadn't happened. I, however, can't do anything but stare at the manila file folder in front of me.

Phillip is right. One result could be chalked up to a lab error, but two? The odds are minuscule. Unless someone was tampering with my tests? But why would someone do that? The only person who even knew I was doing them in the first place was Phillip, and it's obviously not him.

My stomach feels like it's filling up with battery acid. I reach for my purse to see if I have any Pepto Bismol, but when I dig into my bag, my fingers hit something hard. It's a tin container. I'm confused until I pull it out and remember the weird maple granola bars Harmony gave me this morning. I open the lid and look at them, and my blood runs cold.

Tiny green flakes cling to the maple syrup, holding the seeds in their bar shape. I didn't really look at them this morning, and even if I did, I would have assumed the green was sage or lime or some unidentified plant Harmony grows outside her bedroom windowsill.

"Oh my god." All the pieces click into place as I think back throughout the last few months. The cookies, the cheesecakes, the pies, and the flans.

She wouldn't.

There's no way.

But it's a *very* logical answer.

"I think I've been drugged," I say to Phillip, holding out the container. "My neighbor. She bakes. It always tastes a little off, but I eat it anyway."

Phillip nods as if he at least believes me. "How long has she been baking for you?"

"She's been dropping stuff off for years." I think back to the cookies she used to make Larry when we first moved in. "I stopped eating her food a long time ago because it was hit or miss, and I got sick of discovering the misses, but I started again when . . ."

When Mackenzie moved in.

"Oh my god."

I sink back down into my chair.

Harmony's been drugging us.

She's been drugging us for months.

30

PHILLIP SENDS ME HOME EARLY AFTER I do nothing but stare at the folder for another twenty minutes and try to recount what I might have ingested since September.

I don't recall feeling high.

As far as I know, I wasn't ever high.

But do I even know what high feels like? Between working where we do and the "say no to drugs" campaigns of my early childhood, the closest I ever came to any mood-altering substance was a single puff of a cigarette behind the portables in the tenth grade.

I whip out my phone on the streetcar and google *How do you know if you're high?*

My screen fills with a list of symptoms.

A happy or relaxed feeling—Sure. Fine. I have been both of those things lately. But is that being high or just finally being a normally functioning human being?

Faster heart rate—I haven't exactly taken my readings, but maybe I have had moments where I could feel my heart beat fast. Sitting on the couch texting Mackenzie. Kissing Mackenzie. Any time I am in the vicinity of Mackenzie. I'm suddenly conscious of the speed my heart has picked up these last few seconds. Am I just nervous, or is this the granola bar kicking in?

I read on.

Dry mouth. Shit.

Increased appetite. Shit.

Psychosis or seeing and hearing things that are not real.

I break out into a full-blown body sweat.

That has been happening to me.

That has been happening a lot.

My stop is called, but I am so preoccupied with my phone that I don't hear it and then glance out the window just as the doors are closing and have to run and beg the driver to let me out. My heart hammers hard as I stumble onto the sidewalk and stagger to my apartment door. It just makes the whole situation exponentially worse because I have no idea if the cause is panic or drugs or cardio.

I take the stairs two at a time, thinking that if I can get back to my apartment, I can figure all of this out, but when I reach the landing, Harmony is locking up her door. And all of the day's emotions pour out of me in a tornado of untethered rage.

"What the hell did you do to me, Harmony?"

She startles and drops her yoga mat, whipping around. "Annalise. Chickpea. What's wrong?"

My heart is definitely beating faster now. "Um . . . only the fact that you've been drugging me without my consent. That's what's wrong."

She bends down to pick up her mat, but her eyes remain on me. "When you say drugging you, what exactly do you mean?"

I don't know how to say this any clearer. "I mean, you've been putting *drugs* in my cookies."

Her face breaks into an expression I'm not expecting. It's not surprise, or fear, or denial, or any of the other wide gamut of emotions you'd expect in this particular situation. She just throws her head back and laughs.

"Well, of course I am. That's what makes them *special.*"

I am dumbfounded. I don't even know what to say.

"So you just drugged my cookies and . . . I don't know . . . forgot to mention it."

Now, Harmony's face changes. Her forehead crinkles, and the corners of her mouth turn down. "Oh, sweetheart. I thought you knew. *Special.* Wink wink. Nudge nudge."

"No!" I practically yell the word. "I did not know. I thought 'special' meant just for me. That is until I got a drug test back that told me I've been walking around high on marijuana and hallucinogenic mushrooms."

Harmony's face goes white. "Those mushrooms were an accident." She brings her hand to her mouth. "I got your minced meat mixed up with Mr. Taylor's from around the corner. He requested that particular ingredient. But I did tell you I made an oopsie."

I don't know how to even process what I am hearing. "Wait, you do this to the whole neighborhood?"

Harmony shakes her head. "Of course not. It's only ever been Larry, Koko, Mr. Taylor, Janice, my yoga instructor, and you." She reaches for my hands, pulling them both into hers. "I honestly thought you knew. I had been making them for Larry for years. I assumed you were in on the secret."

"Well, I wasn't." I pull my hands from hers.

She reaches out again and strokes the side of my arm tentatively. "You were just so sad for so long, chickpea. I thought maybe you wanted to take the edge off. Then, it seemed to do the trick. You were the happiest I'd seen you since he left us.

Although I don't think my cookies can take all the credit there. Some of it may need to go to that roommate of yours."

Mackenzie.

He's been eating the cookies as well, maybe even more so than me. I have to tell him what's happened.

"I need to go."

I push past Harmony and fish my keys from my purse, hoping she will take the hint and leave me alone, but I can feel her eyes on my back as I unlock my door and open it.

"I'm sorry, sweetheart," she says as I step inside. "I should have made sure that you knew. If it helps, I only use the highest-quality, organic ingredients."

It does not.

I feel drained as I step into our apartment, so I am grateful to find it empty, leaving no reason why I can't detour to my bed and crawl under the covers. At some point, I must fall asleep because when the front door bangs open, I awaken with a jolt until I hear Mackenzie's voice, speaking from somewhere in the apartment.

". . . Edwin, hey. Things are good, man. How are you?"

I roll over and blink until I'm fully awake and suddenly aware that the conversation has continued in the other room.

". . . Actually, I've decided to leave the band," Mackenzie says. "Zee is looking for a drummer, though. We're playing the Rivoli tonight; if you know anyone, send them by . . ."

He sounds like he's on the phone.

"Wow, congrats, man," he continues. "If anyone deserves a deal, it's you guys . . ."

The door to my bedroom is open, and I can hear every word as clear as a bell. I don't think Mackenzie realizes I'm home since it's the middle of the day, and I'm supposed to be at work. I almost feel like I'm eavesdropping on his conversation, so I sit up with the intention of making enough noise so that he realizes I am here. However, something in his tone makes me freeze.

"Are you serious?" His words come out loud and fast. "I mean, yeah, I definitely have a few songs that would work, and once I get a sense of the direction you want to go with the album, I'm sure I'll have a few more. When do you need them by?"

It is so quiet in our apartment I can hear the other voice explaining something but can't make any of it out.

"Oh, down in Nashville." Mackenzie's voice cuts in. "Yeah, you're right . . . It's easier to hear what's working when we're all in the same room. How long do you need me there for?"

Another beat.

"No, I get it. I've never made an album before, either." He laughs. "Yeah, six months seems reasonable."

Little black specks begin to form at the edges of my vision. They begin to multiply, and so I let my body collapse back into my pillow, no longer worrying if I'm making noise.

"Can I have a few days to think about it? I need to talk to Annalise."

Pause

"February. Wow. Okay."

He hangs up the phone, and the living room is again silent.

My mind, however, is a chorus of glaring alarm bells. *Was that Edwin as in the Edwin from the Rydells? And he what? Wants Mackenzie to write for an album?*

I don't have time to even formulate theories before I hear the door to our apartment close, and I realize he's left.

Although my vision has cleared, my heart is beating so hard and fast that I don't trust myself to sit up again. Instead,

I lie and stare at the ceiling feeling out everything that happened.

He got offered a job writing music for an album—this is his dream.

But down in Nashville—an entire ocean away from Liverpool.

My chest heaves with a pain that I haven't felt in months but is all too familiar. It's sharp at first, then leaves me feeling hollow, like everything good has been scooped out, and all that's left is emptiness.

My brain is throwing out very rational reasons why this news doesn't have to mean the end of us.

It's not that long in the grand scheme of things.

He will visit.

My heart, however, has been through enough to know better.

I'll be gone for two years. Maybe more.

As Mackenzie said, we both have tight budgets. At most, we will see each other two or maybe three times a year.

My brain throws a hail Mary—a last-ditch attempt.

We're meant to be together.

But are we?

There's a thought that's been forming all day. Until now, I've ignored it, mentally packing it into a tight little box, but now it's found a crack and has pushed its way out.

The jacket isn't magical.

It is just a regular old leather jacket.

And even though I let myself believe for a moment that it was part of something bigger than what my brain could comprehend, this afternoon, the very logical reason for my hallucinations was laid out for me in a typed, two-page report.

Drugs.

I started eating Harmony's baking again right around the same time the jacket visions started.

Yes, they seemed to fit together in a logical chain of events, but was that because those events actually happened? Or because I was so desperately lonely that I was seeing something I wanted to see?

This is where I'd normally turn to science. But the MRI I took showed nothing.

I need someone else from the visions to tell me they really did happen.

But who?

Zee? I can't imagine that conversation going well. *Hey, so . . . I'm stealing your drummer and taking him with me to Europe, but have you ever been to the West Lake watermelon festival?*

I guess I could call Lucca and ask if he knows Zee, but that's the last thing I want to do, and even if he does, I need to know if the memory happened exactly as I saw it.

What about Koko?

She got the jacket from Harmony. Maybe she remembers it.

I roll out of bed, grab my jacket, and run down the stairs two at a time, chastising myself for not thinking of this sooner. As I push open the front door, I have momentum behind me. I see the rack of clothing being wheeled out of Koko's store, but I can't stop myself in time, and a faux fur coat hip-checks me onto the sidewalk.

"Holy shit, Lise, are you okay?"

I blink twice and then get to my feet, rubbing the spot where the metal made contact. "I'm fine. But I need to ask you a bit of a weird question."

She pops her foot onto the rack, locking it in place. "Weird questions are my favorite, but can we do it inside? I'm freezing my ass out here."

She holds the door open with her arm. I step inside, but as my eyes find the counter, I realize the store isn't empty.

Perstephanie is back behind the cash register reading a novel.

Koko closes the door and makes a high-pitched *brrrrr* sound. "So, what did you need to ask me?"

Perstephanie has put her book down. Now, there are two sets of eyes on me.

I turn to Koko. "Where did you work before you opened this place?"

Koko opens her mouth to answer, but Perstephanie beats her to it. "Good old Sally's Boutique with the rest of us fashion school graduates."

Koko inclines her head toward Perstephanie. "Yep. What she said."

Everything inside me deflates. "Anywhere else before that?"

Koko shakes her head. "Not really. I was at Sally's for almost six years. Part-time while I was in school and then full-time until I opened this place."

If Koko didn't work there, then the vision was wrong.

Or maybe it never happened at all.

Koko hops up on the counter and crosses her legs. "Now that we've settled that, what time are you coming by tonight?"

I have no idea what she is talking about. "What's tonight?"

She holds up her hands. "My party, dude. You promised."

Shit. I did.

"Listen, Koko, today has not been a good day. I will catch the next one."

"Lise," she whines. "You're leaving tomorrow night. There isn't going to be a next time. You have to come. It's basically your going-away party."

I don't want a going-away party, and I don't want to think about going away, but I find myself nodding my head. "Okay. What time does it start?"

31

AT TEN O'CLOCK THE MUSIC BEGINS TO thump up through my floorboards. A few moments later, my phone lights up with a message.

KOKO:

> Don't make me *come* up there and get you. I am motivated and freakishly strong.

I sigh, knowing there is nowhere to escape. I grab my jacket, shove my phone in my pocket, and head down toward the party sounds.

I have always been in awe of how much clothing Koko can pack into her tiny store, but I am even more impressed at the number of people pressed into every nook and cranny of Thrift Me Baby.

"You're here!"

I hear her voice but fail to spot Koko before two bony arms wrap around my waist. Her hair is a bright electric blue, as if she has just dyed it again, and her sparkly silver dress catches like a disco ball in the light.

"I'm so happy you came," she says, lifting my arm to twirl underneath it. Then she cups a hand around her mouth and calls to a tall guy with braids sitting next to her cash register.

"Yo, Precious. Get my girl Lise here a Diet Coke."

Precious leans backward and when he straightens up, he has a can of Diet Coke in his hand, which gets passed through the crowd of bodies until it finds its way to me.

"This is quite a party." I check out the DJ with a turntable set up in the changing room, the pink velvet curtain swept to the side, and the area in front of the big mirror that has become a makeshift dance floor. Although the bodies aren't quite dancing, they are talking in tiny, tight circles and bobbing their heads to the music.

Koko leans in close so I can hear her over the noise. "Where's Mac?"

I instinctively reach for my back pocket to check if I still have my phone. "Playing the Rivoli tonight. They were opening for someone else. He should be here in a bit."

"So you're all mine until then." She swivels around and faces me. "I am going to miss you so much. We need a regular phone date in our calendars, and you need to let me know your schedule as soon as you get it so I can plan my visit for the summer."

I am equally surprised at both parts of that last sentence.

"You're coming to visit me?"

Her face forms an expression I best interpret as *Why are you even asking me this?*

"Of course I am. I know you'll be busy and stuff, but I can entertain myself at all the markets during the day, and when you're done with class, you can show me where to get the best lo mein. I figure you'll have it all worked out by then."

She hugs me, and my insides fill with a warm, gooey feeling that multiplies as she ushers me around the room, stopping at various groups to introduce me as "my girl, Lise," or "This is my friend I was telling you about."

"I started seeing someone," she whispers in my ear as we weave through the bodies. "It's still pretty new, but I haven't felt like this before."

We stop, and Koko lets go of my hand to snake it around the waist of a red-haired woman. I prepare to introduce myself, but when the woman turns around, her face is so familiar that I stop.

"Hi, I'm . . ." My hand freezes halfway between us.

She eyes it and me, then reaches out her hand, shaking mine up and down.

"Large Americano girl with an unpredictable pastry habit," she deadpans.

"Yes." I nod, still a little dumbfounded. "I also go by Annalise."

She glances at Koko and laughs; her smile transforms her face. "I'm Janette," she says. "Koko has told me so much about you."

The three of us talk for the better part of an hour, until the cops show up at the front door and Koko has to go work her persuasive magic. Her absence leaves a weird lull in our conversation, making it obvious Koko was the one carrying it and that Janette's social skills are the same level of awkward as mine.

"So . . ." I attempt to break the now too-long silence. "How long have you and Koko been together?"

"Just a couple weeks," she answers. "I mean, we started talking back in October, but then she went back home, and I had just got out of a long-distance thing with my ex, and I was not super keen on doing that again, but then Koko came back, and everything worked out from there."

Janette smiles but doesn't elaborate any further, and we are once again at high risk of slipping back into the awkward silence.

"So you and your ex were long distance?" It's a weirdly personal question, but on a topic I have been—given the circumstances—thinking about a lot today. Janette doesn't seem to mind it, either. She nods her head and drains the last of the liquid in her glass.

"Yeah. She was in the city when we met but moved back to her hometown to be closer to her family. It made what was once easy and fun a total pain in the ass. We probably could have drawn it out a few more months, but sometimes, it's best to pull the plug before things get messy, right?"

I nod my head again, thinking I know exactly what she means, but the truth is I don't—at least not yet.

The room is starting to feel too hot, and I keep getting bumped every time someone tries to get to the bathroom, so when Janette says, "I'm going to go grab another drink. Do you want anything?" I shake my head and instead sneak down the back hall to the rear exit, telling myself that I'm only stepping out for a few moments of air. However, I am not the only person who seems to have had this idea. Two guys are standing in the back alley, both vaping and in the middle of an intense conversation I get the distinct feeling I'm interrupting.

I consider changing my plans completely and heading home, hoping I've put in enough of an appearance to avoid disappointed Koko texts. But as I step away from the vapers and take a full breath of air, an idea forms, and I stop.

It's beautiful out. A little cold, yes, but the sky is clear. It's one of those rare Toronto nights when you can see the stars.

I make a quick direction change and instead head for the fire escape, climbing up the wrought iron steps until I reach the little landing outside the window. From there, I grab the ladder, gripping each rung carefully as I climb until I reach the roof.

There's a thin layer of snow covering everything but the two red chimneys. I brush off a small space at the base of one, sitting down and pressing my back against the brick. Immediately, the cold seeps through the denim of my jeans. I ignore it and stare up at the sky, which is as beautiful as I hoped it would be. My eyes trace the path of what is either the Big Dipper or a random square of stars until the groaning of the metal fire escape tells me someone has followed me up here.

I feel a small rush of panic at being alone on the roof in the dark until a familiar dark blond head pops up over the ledge.

"Hey," I call to Mackenzie as he climbs the last few steps onto the roof. "How'd you know I was up here?"

He walks over and sits down beside me, pressing a kiss to my temple. "I happened to glance down the alley as I was walking home. I thought you were a large raccoon at first." He reaches an arm around my back and tucks me to his chest. "How was the last day?"

I consider how best to put the events of the last twelve hours. "Not what I expected and a story you might need a beer for. We can head back down to the party if you want. I just needed some air." I try to stand, but Mackenzie pulls me back down beside him, pressing a kiss to the top of my head. "Actually, I need to talk to you about something."

I close my eyes and take a steadying breath as he clears his throat.

"I think I found someone to sublet your place while we're gone," he says. "His name is Andy. He's a friend of Clive's. He's a great guy. You can meet him tomorrow if you have time; otherwise I can introduce you guys over email."

I wait for the rest—the part where he says, "By the way, I'm moving to Nashville," but it doesn't come.

"That's it?" I surprise myself with the edge to my voice.

His eyebrows drop low, picking up on it. "I can keep looking if you don't think he'll work—"

"No," I interrupt. "He sounds great. But that's all you were going to tell me? You don't have any other news? Nothing life-changing happened to you today?"

Confusion clouds his face. "What do you mean?"

"I mean Nashville. The album. How they want you to write."

He leans back and stares at me. "How do you know about that?"

I feel my cheeks heat despite the cold. "I came home early. You are a very loud phone talker. I swear I was going to come out and tell you I was there, but then I heard what you were talking about and . . ."

Mackenzie stands, then walks head down in a slow circle as his feet leave imprints in the snow. When he looks up, his face is devoid of any expression.

"I'm coming to Liverpool with you. Nothing has changed."

My body rushes with such a strong wave of relief that it delays my ability to adequately process. "So what? They're letting you write remotely?"

The hope expanding in my rib cage lasts for all of a second until the first slow shake of his head.

"No. I've decided to turn them down. It doesn't really feel like the right move for now."

What doesn't feel right is the emotional seesaw happening inside me. I stand, needing exactly what he did a few seconds ago, to pace the roof for a moment and clear my head.

"But . . ." I whip around to face him. "All you've wanted

since you came here is for someone to play your songs, and now you have a band with an album asking you to write, and you're turning them down? Aren't you giving up everything you've ever wanted?"

He steps toward me, his hands reaching for mine. "*You* are everything I've ever wanted. And yes, this is big. But that doesn't mean something else big won't come along down the road. I can live with that gamble. What I can't live with is giving up on us. You and I are meant—"

"Don't say it." I rip my hands from his.

"What? Why not?"

"Because it isn't true. We weren't brought together by some magical force or written in the stars or meant to be anything, Mackenzie. We were just drugged."

He narrows his eyes, understandably confused. "What are you talking about?"

"Harmony's cookies," I explain. "She's been putting weed in them. She thought I knew about it. I didn't. We've been under the influence this entire time."

Mackenzie takes a step toward me. "Uh . . . okay. That is definitely something we should talk about more, but I don't see how it has anything to do with us."

I try to put into words all the thoughts that have been running through my head all day.

"The cookies and then your news helped me realize what I have known for a while. Why I avoided talking about what would happen to us when I moved to Liverpool." I can hear the thickness in my voice. "What you're feeling right now is a series of chemical reactions. It's what happens at the start of a relationship. Your brain is flooded with dopamine, and it's inhibiting your prefrontal cortex."

He shakes his head. "I don't understand."

"It's all going to wear off." The truth feels harsh as I say it out loud. "If you come to Liverpool with me, you might feel great at first, but eventually, those chemicals will start to wane, and reality will set in. You will realize you gave up something big and then you'll resent moving—you may even begin to resent me because I am at school all the time, or studying, or not as great as you once thought I was."

"Annalise, you're not—"

"And then you'll leave me."

Tears begin to rim my eyes.

"You will leave me, and I'll be back to being alone, and I won't be able to come back from it this time. I can't do it again, Mackenzie. I can't lose someone else. I don't have anything left."

I blink, and the tears fall. Like cascading raindrops, they coat my cheeks.

"I'm not going to leave you, Annalise." He tries to cup my cheek, but I turn my head.

"You don't know that for sure. What if a year from now, you're waiting tables, and the album comes out, and it's a huge deal, and your songs aren't on it, and it makes you miserable, and every time you look at me, you know I'm the reason."

"I won't be—"

"Really? Because even the idea of that happening makes *me* miserable. I hate that it comes down to such a rudimentary decision, but that's what it is—your dream or mine."

He opens his mouth as if to argue but shakes his head.

"So then we do long distance." His thumbs attempt to wipe my tears, but they fall too fast.

"No. We will just be drawing out the inevitable, and I think that's almost worse. You're the one who said it. My program lasts two whole years. We'll barely see each other. I won't be able to watch movies and text you like I did when you were on tour. I can't spend the next two years wondering what you're doing or who you are with, sneaking onto Instagram when I'm supposed to be studying, hoping for a glimpse of your life. I can't afford to be a wreck whenever I see a picture of you with someone else, and I am an entire ocean away."

He doesn't say anything, so I continue.

"These past few weeks have been the best of my life," I tell him. "They have healed me in ways I can't even begin to explain to you. But I want to keep them this way. Good and pure. I want to look back on this perfect, magical December you've given me and smile every time I think about it. I want to know that when we walked away from this, it was for the right reasons, to give both of us a shot at the things we always wanted."

He drops his hands to the side. "What are you saying?"

I take a deep breath. "I am saying that I get on my flight tomorrow night, and you call up Edwin and tell him you want the job. You kiss me goodbye, and I wish you all the best—and when I say it, I mean it with every cell in my body. But then, that's it. We don't talk or text or make this any harder than it needs to be. Instead, we leave this perfect—with you loving me and me loving you, because I love you, Mackenzie, I do."

He reaches for me again, and this time, I let him take me into his arms. I cry against his chest as he strokes my hair, and when I finally try to pull away, his arms tighten, and I stay there, holding on to the last of my perfect moments.

"This doesn't feel right," he says when we finally part.

I close my eyes, worried that if I look at him right now, I will break. "I know, but it's what I need."

He cups my chin in his hands and wipes the still-falling tears with his thumbs, waiting until I open my eyes again and look at him.

"You're wrong about us," he says. "We are meant to be together. Maybe not now, but I don't believe this is the end."

I wrap my arms around him, not quite ready to let this all be over. Squeezing my eyes shut, I search for any last remaining magic beans, any semblance of the girl who could toss all logic aside and believe in magic and that life would simply work itself out.

But I find nothing.

THE NEXT DAY, we say our goodbyes in the living room. He offers to see me off at the airport, but I argue the logistics are too complicated. The truth is, I want to remember him here, with his hair a little rumpled, that errant lock of hair falling across his forehead and that sleepy, content look he has right before he falls asleep.

"One text." He breathes the words into my neck as I cling to the final moments of our very last hug. "Just let me know you're there and you're safe."

"Okay," I reply, but a part of me wants him to ask for more. Two texts. Maybe a phone call, or maybe we forget this stupid idea altogether. Maybe we try. See how it goes. Fight for this.

But he doesn't say anything more.

His lips brush my temple, and I feel a tear slide down my cheek that isn't my own. I close my eyes and let it absorb into my skin, another tiny piece of him I get to keep.

"I love you," he whispers. "I am so incredibly proud of you."

His words bury deep into me, finding the tiny crevices of my heart where I know they will stay for a very long time. "I love you, too. One day, a song is going to come on, and I'll know immediately whose words I'm hearing."

And it just might kill me.

We hold each other until my phone begins to buzz and I know my Uber is waiting downstairs.

"Goodbye." I kiss him one last time. I bend down, pick up my bag, and use all of my willpower not to turn back as I descend the stairs. But when I reach the bottom and pull open the door, I pause for a moment just before I step out onto the sidewalk.

I'm listening for footsteps behind me.

Hoping for them.

The only sound is that of our apartment door closing.

He doesn't come.

32

LIVERPOOL IS RAINY.

My flat is smaller than it looked in the pictures, and there is a giant gaping hole in my heart that aches whenever I think about Mackenzie.

I text him as promised once I'm moved in and settled. He texts back a single "I love you," which I cling to throughout the entire first month of school as I meet my new professors, advisers, and fellow PhD candidates.

As the weeks roll on, I develop a strategy. Whenever I think about him, I distract myself by reading journal articles. When I glance at my phone, hoping for a text, I open my laptop and instead work on my thesis. If I see a passing cab and consider taking it straight to the airport to catch the next flight to Nashville, I walk to the library or the lab and throw my emotions into my books.

By the spring, I am at the top of my class, but the rest of me is hovering just above rock bottom.

In early June, I am talking to Koko on the phone as I leave a copy shop in town, the latest draft of my thesis in hand.

"What are you doing tonight?" she asks as I step out onto the sidewalk, the late-afternoon sun still bright and warm.

I consider my lack of plans. "Probably heading home and watching a movie. You?"

There's a sound of honking horns on her side, leading me to suspect she's also walking outside.

"I'm heading over to Ramone's now," Koko says. "There's a band he wants to check out later."

The word *band* shoots a sharp pain through my body. "Oh . . . that sounds fun."

I haven't socialized much since I moved to Liverpool. In the beginning, I used the excuse that I needed time to heal from Mackenzie. Then, the cold temperatures and rain gave me a reason to hibernate through the winter months, but now that it's almost summer, and people are out and about, I'm regretting those decisions a little.

"You know, they have bands in Liverpool, too," Koko says, as if reading my thoughts.

"Yes. They do."

"And I'm pretty sure it even works the same as it does here," she teases. "You buy a ticket. Sometimes all you need to do is show up."

"Koko." I try to sound annoyed, but she's right.

"Don't *Koko* me," she says. "I just want you to be happy."

"I am happy," I counter with a laugh, but it's met with a long pause.

"Are you?" she finally says.

I don't answer. Mostly because the real answer, the truthful one, is complex. I like school, but I am homesick. I know it's the right thing for me to be here, but—

"I know you miss—"

She can't finish the sentence, because I cut her off with a "Don't."

She sighs. "I could have been saying I know you miss *me*."

She could have, but we both know she wasn't.

"I do miss you," I tell her, admitting to that.

"I miss you, too," she says. "But hey, we have less than two months until I'm there for an entire week, and we are going to have a glorious time." Her side of the line quiets as if she's stepped back indoors. "But until then I think you should try and go out a little more." Her voice softens. "Find your people. Have fun."

When I reach my bus stop, I sit down on the empty bench, perching on the edge so I don't have to remove my backpack.

"I will try my best. But I can't make any—"

"Hey! Annalise!"

I stop my thought and look up toward the voice calling my name.

On the opposite side of the street is a little green painted pub with a small patio of picnic tables. A few of my peers are sitting at one, holding big pints of beer. One of the guys, Simon, is waving at me.

"Who's that?" Koko asks through the phone, reminding me she is still on the line.

"Just some of my classmates. They're having drinks across the street."

"So go over there! Sit down with them, order some hot wings. Talk. Laugh. Maybe even put your brilliant heads together and cure something."

"I don't know." I shake my head.

"Just go say hi," she urges. "Come on. We were just talking about this, and then you get an opportunity. It's a sign from the universe."

I don't believe in signs.

But as that thought leaves my brain, I don't like the ache it leaves in its wake.

I know there is no scientific evidence to support that signs from the universe exist—it's just pattern recognition and confirmation bias—but I miss the girl who, for a brief moment in time, did believe in them.

That Annalise wished on stars and found small miracles under the Christmas tree. She went to new places and opened up to people, with no guarantees that she wouldn't get hurt.

That Annalise was happy.

My gaze drops to the sidewalk in front of me. There is a wad of crushed gum, an indiscernible black stain, and something shimmering in the sunlight in between.

I bend down, pick up a bright copper 1p coin, and smile, once again thinking of Larry.

He would want me to go over there, too.

The jacket may not have been magical, but my uncle, in his own way, was. He had a way of connecting with everyone, whether it was his moody teenage niece or a busker in the subway. He had an uncanny ability of knowing exactly what you needed before you needed it—even if it was only a late-night hot chocolate. He brought out the best in people. He brought out the best in me.

When I stopped believing in the jacket, I stopped believing in Larry's magic, too.

I close my eyes. "Okay, you win," I say to Larry as I slide the coin into my back pocket.

"I love this for you!" Koko answers. "Go have fun. Stop overthinking everything. You're cool, you're funny, and they're going to be thanking the universe you even bothered to walk over there. Trust me."

I don't know if anyone thanks the universe, but I do have a good time. I also score an invitation to their regular weekly meet-up.

That invite turns into one for a lecture series in London and then a spot on the pub quiz team every Tuesday, which inspires me to start volunteering at the local mental health center.

By mid-summer, I have a budding yet still low-key social life, and I can feel that energy translating to my work. My thesis starts to really come together, and I find myself excited about my work in a way that I haven't felt in a long time.

When Koko finally arrives in August, the entire taxi ride back to my apartment is a scene of laughs and nonstop talking (mostly from her). She declares my flat to be *smashing*, my tiny bedroom *posh*, and the space I've made for her in my closet to be *brilliant* as she unpacks her things to change out of her plane clothes.

"That dress is incredible." I nod at the yellow polka-dot sundress she's just pulled over her head.

"Estate sale," she says as she cinches a green crocodile belt around the waist, immediately turning it from shapeless and matronly to edgy and chic.

"The jacket is what makes the outfit, though." She pulls a cropped leather biker jacket from her bag and throws it over her shoulders. It looks nothing like Mackenzie's, but the sight still shreds up my insides.

I turn away, hoping Koko will be too preoccupied with her reflection to notice me, but as soon as I do, two arms come around my waist.

"I know that look." She rests her chin on my shoulder. "That is a *I am thinking about a certain someone who I pretend I am not thinking about* look."

"Koko." I step away, not wanting to have this conversation. Koko takes the hint and instead flops on my bed.

"I know we're not supposed to talk about him, but I really think you should call M—"

"No," I cut her off. "Don't say it. I—"

My chin wobbles, and I can't get words out. But she nods knowingly. "Okay. Okay. I promise. Just you and me and fun this week."

During the day, Koko combs Bold Street and Renshaw for vintage treasures to take back to her shop while I grind away at more of my thesis. At night, we head to Duke Street for noodles or Cantonese or my new favorite Tianjin cuisine before we head home to my tiny flat and talk until it's time to fall asleep.

Koko makes good on her promise. She doesn't mention he who shall not be named until the very last morning, when she catches me staring wistfully at my phone again.

"You do remember you told him *not* to text you, right?" she asks, meeting my surprised eyes with a knowing single-eyebrow raise.

"I know." I flip over my phone. "It's just . . . I wish for once he'd argue with me."

Koko zips up her carry-on bag and slides the straps over the handles of her suitcase. "What does that mean?"

"I know I told him that I needed space and that we should make a clean break, but I guess a part of me also hoped he'd disagree with me for once."

Koko flops down on the end of my bed. "I am totally getting why it would have been utterly romantic for him to have chased you through the airport yelling "Come back, Annalise," but we both know he wouldn't have made it through security, and more important, he was doing what you asked him to do."

I nod. "I agree. It's stupid."

Koko sits up and reaches for my hand. "Stupid or not, I *do* know that he misses you terribly. He talks about it all the time."

"You talk to him?" The idea makes my lungs feel heavy and the rest of me lightheaded.

Koko nods. "Not as often as I talk to you, but yeah, we catch up about once a month. He usually lets me drone on about store stuff before he casually slips in some sort of way to ask if I have heard from you. I am very aware I'm being cajoled for info, but I'm willing to take one for the cause."

There's a reason I've not let myself think too long about him—it's because of exactly this. In less than three seconds, I am back where I was up on the rooftop, heart ripped wide open and questioning everything.

"And just in case you wanted to know, he's in Pensacola now, not Nashville," Koko says.

My geographical knowledge takes a moment to kick in. "Florida?"

She nods. "He's staying with Edwin until September, wrapping things up. Just thought I'd put it out there, since we are heading to an airport, and I know you don't have any reason to be back in Liverpool until Thursday."

I glance at my dresser, where my passport sits in the top drawer.

"I can't." I shake my head as if it will erase the thoughts quickly forming inside my brain.

"Why not?" Koko gets up from the bed. "You are clearly not over him, and he's very much still in love with you. This has happily ever after written all over it."

My heart begins to beat faster, and I don't know if it's the fear or the idea that what she is saying is even possible.

"Come on, Annalise. Don't you still love him?" Koko asks.

"More than anything."

"We have time to pack a bag."

I take two steps toward the closet and stop. I love him. I

had thought being apart all these months was going to dull that feeling, that the dopamine would wear off, and my rational brain would kick in, and maybe it has, but it's saying the same thing as my heart.

We are meant to be together.

And maybe it's not some cosmic force determining that. Maybe it's just that he makes me happy, and I make him happy, and although there are no guarantees that will be enough, it's enough that I know I don't want to be without him.

Koko reaches for her bag. "Do you need a sign?"

I laugh and shake my head. "Nope. I think I just need to pack."

Koko squeals as I grab the suitcase from my closet and begin to fill it with anything that makes sense.

I pack my toiletries and passport while she hops onto my laptop.

"Where is your credit card?" she calls as I pull out a bathing suit and every pair of clean underwear I own.

I toss her my wallet.

"Window or aisle?"

"Honestly, I'll take anything. Just get me there as quickly as possible."

She clicks and types and, a few moments later, shuts my laptop just as my phone pings.

"Direct flight to Castellón! Apparently, Pensacola doesn't have an airport, but Google says it's super close, and I got you a great last-minute deal," she says, slinging her bags over her shoulder. "But we have to move. Your flight leaves thirty minutes before mine. We're cutting it close."

We pile our bags into the back of a Ford Fiesta, telling the Uber driver to *step on it* because I need to make it to Florida to get my man back.

Our driver, Thomas, drives a very reasonable 112 kilometers an hour, gaining us zero extra commuting minutes but not losing any either.

When we're almost at the airport, Koko reaches into her purse and pulls out a yellow piece of paper. "This was going to be my backup plan if you didn't come to your senses."

I take it from her and unfold it. The paper is thin and aged with visible creases, and my heart stops at the words written in blue ink in very familiar handwriting.

This is your sign.

I can barely breathe. "Where did you get this?"

Koko takes it from my hands, folds it back up, and returns it to her bag. "I found it in the pocket of this leather jacket I scored from the Salvation Army. It was kind of a major moment for me—one that I was going to dramatically recount for you had you not come to your senses and packed a bag."

My throat is so dry I can barely speak. "I want to hear it."

Koko checks the map on her phone and shrugs. "Well, the short story is that I was working there last year, and someone brought a bunch of stuff in to donate. There was this incredible vintage leather jacket in the box. The kind people pay good money for, and I thought, *I could totally find lots of pieces just like this. Curate a collection and start my own store.* It had always been an idea in my head, but I never really thought about it seriously, then when I got home I put the jacket on and found this wallet. It only had a license and twenty dollars and this slip of paper that said *this is your sign.* I went to return it to the guy, who, believe it or not, lived in your building, but the guy who runs the dry cleaner told me he passed away, so I just kept it. Anyway, as I was leaving he also told me they were moving locations and the space would be up for lease, and I knew Thrift Me Baby was supposed to be there. I was being sent literal signs from the universe." She holds up her hands and smiles. "Wild, right?"

My head begins to spin, and I can barely get my words out. "But you never worked at the Salvation Army."

Koko's eyebrows scrunch. "What are you talking about? I worked there for almost six years. Right up until I opened my store."

I shake my head. "You said you worked at some boutique. Sammie's or Mandy's or something?"

Koko thinks for a moment, then laughs. "Sally's Boutique? Sally's. As in the *Sal*vation Army. It's a nickname. Like how people call Target Targé. Everyone knows that."

"I don't know that."

Koko throws her arms around me. "You precious unbaked cinnamon roll. I love how uncorrupted you are. Yes, I worked at the Salvation Army. Why?"

I just wanted validation that my leather jacket was trying to tell me something.

And now I know it was.

Our arrival at the airport is chaotic.

Thomas drops us at the wrong end of the airport. The security line is too long, and by the time we get through, I have only minutes until my gate closes.

"Thank you." I pause long enough to throw my arms around Koko's neck. "I wouldn't be here without you."

She hugs me back. "When I moved to Toronto, my parents were so far away that I had to make my own family in the city, and I am so happy that you are a part of it."

I can feel tears threatening, and Koko must sense it, too, because she breaks away, adjusts the strap of my carry-on, and says, "Go! You'll miss your flight. Tell Mac, 'You're welcome.'"

I run.

And I reach the gate just in time to get an annoyed look from the attendant who has to scan my passport. They close the door as soon as I am on board, and I am forced to stick my bag under the seat in front of me since there is no more overhead room.

The plane begins to taxi as I finally fasten my seatbelt and lean my head back with an exhausted sigh.

I close my eyes and slow my still-rampant heart as the captain's voice comes over the system.

"Good morning, ladies and gentlemen. This is Captain Javier Diaz speaking on behalf of your entire crew. I'd like to welcome you aboard this flight from Liverpool's John Lennon Airport to Castellón–Costa Azahar Airport. Our flight time will be approximately two hours and thirty minutes."

My eyes fly open. *Two hours.* There is no way that's enough time to fly across an entire ocean to Florida.

I scramble for my bag, earning a huff from the elderly woman next to me as I frantically search the pockets for my boarding pass.

I pull it out.

It says my name and the same airport the captain just mentioned.

Koko said Castellón. I remember it distinctly. *Pensacola doesn't have an airport, but Google says it's super close.*

I pull my phone from my pocket, and my seatmate gives me another dirty look.

It takes a moment for it to register the network, and then another for me to open Google Maps and type Castellón in the search bar. The page loads just as the captain concludes his speech.

"Thank you for choosing to fly with us today. Enjoy your stay in Spain."

33

"WHAT DO YOU MEAN, YOU'RE ALL BOOKED?"

I stare at the gate agent as she frowns at the computer screen in front of her.

"I made a mistake. I need to get to Florida. Isn't there anything you can do?"

She rolls her eyes, because this is not the first time we have discussed this.

"You can go on standby for the flight tomorrow afternoon," she says, tapping her pen on her monitor. "The odds are low that I will be able to get you on, and you will have to spend the night, but I encourage you to consider finding lodging before you decide. There's a lot of tourists flying in. Most of the hotels are all booked up."

My other option is a flight back to Liverpool leaving in an hour.

It's the logical thing to do.

Except I'm done with logical.

"I'll take my chances with Florida," I tell the woman, who gives me a look that tells me I'm picking the wrong option in her opinion.

I don't care. I will spend the night in one of those uncomfortable orange airport chairs if I have to.

Once I'm on standby, I take my bags and phone and find a vacant orange chair, where I sit to figure out what I'm going to do next.

I slide open my screen and begin to scroll. The gate agent was not exaggerating when she said it would be hard to find a place to stay. My options are either very far away or very much out of my price range—all except for one.

My finger hovers above a Booking.com listing. It's a single room in a small B&B, forty-five minutes away in Peñíscola, above Restaurante El Peñón.

I stare at the tiny exterior picture, wondering why the name is so familiar.

Best suquet de peix you'll ever have, says Larry's voice in my head.

I look up, suddenly paying attention to the passengers disembarking a nearby plane. There are some in business suits. Others in sundresses. And a family with two little kids who are pretending they can't see—because their eyes are covered with bright cardboard glasses.

I open a new browser on my phone and type the question my heart already knows the answer to.

When is the next solar eclipse?

That day on the sidewalk, Larry wanted to go to Spain, and I rolled my eyes at the idea, thinking it would never happen.

As the answer loads on my screen, I begin to laugh hard and loud. My back shakes, and my face turns what I'm certain is a bright red, given the looks I'm getting from passing travelers.

Okay, Larry. You win.

I click, and then my details and credit card are autofilled. Within minutes, I'm booked and heading for the airport taxi stand.

"Where to, miss?" says the driver as I slide into the back seat.

"Peñíscola, por favor." I've got an eclipse to catch.

34

PEÑÍSCOLA LOOKS LIKE IT POPPED STRAIGHT OUT of a fairy tale or at least the glossy pages of a travel magazine. The city feels like it's in denial that it's mainland, jutting out as far as it can into the Mediterranean Sea. Its big stone walls protect it from the crashing waves, giving it the vibe of a medieval fortress, but the whitewashed buildings and cobblestone roads soften its edges, making it feel warm and inviting.

My driver blares some techno mashup that is a little too heavy on the air horns as we navigate the narrow streets and tourists already donning brightly colored paper eclipse glasses. Whether it's his driving or the Spanish heat, or the day, I'm feeling a little queasy as we pull up in front of a tiny whitewashed restaurant with a big awning with the word RESTAURANTE on the front.

I get out of the car and wait as my driver pops open the trunk and retrieves my bags, setting them down in front of me.

"You have a nice vacation, miss," he says. "Remember not to look at the sun." He gets back in his car and drives off with a friendly *toot toot* of his horn as I make a slow three-sixty turn to take in my surroundings.

The plan I concocted less than an hour ago had two items

on the itinerary. *Get to hotel. Watch eclipse.* But there is a big black hole for the hours in between.

I pull out my phone and recheck my booking confirmation, which says to check in inside the restaurant with a man named Pedro. I pick up my luggage and step onto the restaurant's patio, but my search for Pedro stops at the sight of a man sitting at one of the tables.

Mackenzie?

I don't actually say his name out loud. I think part of me is worried that if I do, he will turn, and then it won't be him, and this beautiful illusion I've built up in my head will burst because it can't be him. It's simply not possible.

A solar eclipse in your own backyard. It's a time for spiritual awakening.

Again, I hear Larry's voice so clearly in my head.

Let the universe take you down a path. Trust it to guide you where you need to go.

"Those were some very literal directions there, Larry," I whisper, glancing down at the cobblestone walkway leading right to his table.

"Mack—" I start to say his name, but stop. Right now, I can pretend that the love of my life is sitting at the table in front of me, that some sort of universal magic has brought him here, and I am a mere ten feet away from telling him every single thought that has run through my head these last few hours—no, these last few months—starting with I miss him and I love him and I was stupid to think what he and I had was something I could tuck away and forget like it hadn't fundamentally changed who I was forever.

He lifts his head, and I know this is the last moment that I can hold on to this beautiful illusion.

Please be him. Please be him.

Not because I need to believe in some universal force—that doesn't matter anymore. Because I can't stomach the idea of still having an entire night and a nine-hour plane ride before I see him again.

He turns, as if he can sense that I'm behind him, and as he does a lock of hair falls onto his forehead, and my heart throbs so badly it hurts.

"Annalise?" He stands as he meets my eyes, the quickness of his movements knocking his chair down with a metallic *clank*.

He ignores it.

I ignore that my bag has toppled over, because he is walking toward me. Three wide strides. And then he's pulling me into his chest and burying his nose in my neck. And all of the pain of the last six months evaporates in a single moment.

He smells the same. Like Electric Pulse or Voltage Strike. Like home.

"What are you doing here?" My words are muffled against his shirt. He lets go just enough for me to look up.

"What are *you* doing here?" He cups my cheeks and bends so his forehead presses to mine.

"I was on my way to see you," I say, "in Florida. I take back everything I've said about Hallmark movies being unrealistic. It turns out it's far easier than you think to get Pensacola, Florida, mixed up with Peñíscola, Spain."

He laughs, and it's the most beautiful thing I've heard in a long time. "Well, I was on my way to see you too, but then—" He shakes his head. "I don't even know how to explain it. Even if I did, I'm not sure you'd believe me."

I pull away so I can look at him. "Try me. I have become very open-minded as of late."

He swallows, then closes his eyes for a moment. "This is

going to sound like I'm losing my mind, but I swear . . ." He opens them again. "I booked a ticket to come see you in Liverpool. I know that we agreed to give each other space. And I get why we did it. I do. I don't ever want to resent you—or you me. But the second you were gone, it didn't feel right. It felt like I left half of my heart up on that roof."

He brings his hands to my face, his thumbs stroking my jawline. "You were right about me going to Nashville. I needed to try. But the longer I was there, the more I kept thinking . . . it doesn't really mean anything without you, Annalise. You're not the person I needed to leave behind to live out my dream. You're the one I want with me while I'm doing it."

A tear escapes, rolling down my cheek. He wipes it with the pad of his thumb. "I know I should've told you all of this six months ago," he says. "I should've fought harder, or at least said more up there on that roof instead of nodding and pretending I was fine with all of it. But I'm saying it now."

He tips my chin upward, holding my gaze. "I'm still so unbelievably in love with you, Annalise."

My entire body reacts—pulse pounding and a rush that leaves me a little lightheaded.

"I got on a plane because I needed you to know that," he continues. "I needed you to know that I want this, you, all of it—even if it's messy, even if it's long distance for a while, even if we have to make it up as we go along. And I was hoping maybe you still feel the same."

I want to tell him that I do—that the words he's just said are the same ones I've felt in my bones ever since that night on the roof. But instead, my eyes fill with tears. Really happy tears, and when he pulls a crinkled Kleenex from his pocket, they come even harder, only this time I'm laughing.

"It wasn't your fault," I say, taking the Kleenex from him

and dabbing my eyes. "It was my stupid idea. Breaking up. Saying we needed space. I think I thought that if we made a clean break, it would hurt less. One painful, terrible moment instead of a hundred little ones."

I draw a deep breath for the next part, for as much as it's painful to say, I need him to know. "After Larry died I was so broken. I was determined to live my life and not let anyone into it again. Nothing was worth the pain of losing someone I loved. But then you walked through my door."

The tears fall harder. I abandon the Kleenex and let them. "I was never supposed to fall in love with you—but I did. You made me happy again. You made me want to love. You are magic, Mackenzie Smith, and I'm sorry I didn't believe in that."

He brings his lips to mine. "I don't need an apology. I just need you." He kisses me softly. It's the same kiss I remember, the slow press of his lips and sweep of his tongue and the low growl that escapes the back of his throat as I relax into him and his arms wrap around me tightly. It feels perfect and right, as if we are meant to be like this. Like we should never kiss anyone but each other forever.

I'm not sure how long we stay like that, but when we finally pull away, it's with tearstained cheeks and pink lips, and only then do I remember he didn't finish his story.

"Wait. If you were coming to see me in Liverpool, how did you end up here?"

Mackenzie glances back toward his table, and on the tipped-over chair lying next to it is his black leather jacket.

"I was at Edwin's place waiting for my Uber to the airport." He turns back to me. "I had my bag, put on my jacket . . . and then, just like that, I was back in Toronto, standing on the sidewalk in front of our apartment. And you were there. But you couldn't see me, or hear me, and then there was this guy on a motorcycle talking to you. I think it was your uncle, and he was wearing my jacket. He was talking to you about the eclipse, telling you to meet him at this restaurant. Made you promise. Said it was the—"

"Best suquet de peix I'll ever have?" I supply.

Mackenzie's eyes widen. "Yeah, how did you . . ."

He shakes his head. "Anyway, next thing I knew, I was back in Florida, totally confused, no idea what had even happened. But I couldn't get the last thing he said to you out of my head."

I try to think back, but the memory is too fuzzy. "What did he say?"

"He told you he'd always look out for you—no matter what," Mackenzie says, and my heart squeezes so tightly it hurts to breathe.

"I know he's not here anymore, but I think that dream—vision—whatever it was—was telling me it's my turn to take care of you now. I'm the 'no matter what.' So, I changed my plane ticket, flew here . . . hoping I wasn't imagining everything and that you'd keep your promise and come."

The band around my heart breaks and fizzles into a million different pieces.

"And now I'm here," I complete his story, and he shakes his head as if he still can't quite believe it, either.

"Wild, right?"

I smile. "It is."

"I can't think of a logical explanation."

I think back on this past year and all the tiny miracles that got us to this place. "I don't think there is one."

He leans in and kisses me, whispering, "I love you," every time his lips leave mine. When I say it back, it's with every single piece of me—the healed parts of my heart and the parts that are still working their way back to happiness.

We do eventually have to stop as the restaurant tables start to fill and the streets grow busier with tourists seeking out their spots for the phenomenon to come.

I track down Pedro, who takes me to a simple one-bedroom apartment above the restaurant with a double bed and a small bath. We make up for months of being apart, then just before six, join the rest of Peñíscola outside to watch the moon fully eclipse the sun, with a plate of suquet de peix between us.

The sky grows dark, blanketing us in an eerie twilight.

"Wow," Mackenzie says. "It really is incredible."

A breeze seems to pick up off the ocean. I'm not sure if it's the sudden cool air or the phenomenon happening above me, but a wave of goose bumps prickles up my arms.

"Are you cold?" Mackenzie removes his leather jacket from the back of his chair and hands it to me. I hold my breath as I slide one arm in and then the other, and . . . nothing happens.

"You okay?" Mackenzie's arm comes around my back and rests on my shoulders.

I reach for a piece of the crusty bread on the plate in front of us and sop up the last of the flavorful broth. I take a large bite and chew as the eclipse concludes and the sun returns full and bright.

"I am absolutely perfect."

Epilogue

THERE IS MUSIC THUMPING THROUGH MY FLOORBOARDS.

It's a new hit song from a new hit band that I know very well since I've recently become somewhat of a connoisseur when it comes to music.

"She texted you again." Mackenzie holds out my phone. "She says you have two minutes to get down there before she comes up here to get you. There's a smile emoji, but I get the sense it's meant to be a threat."

As soon as he says it, there is a knock on our apartment door. I walk to it and fling it open, expecting to give Koko my excuses, but it's not her on the other side; it's Harmony.

She holds out a stack of knitted dishcloths.

"Welcome home, chickpea."

I take the stack from her hand and examine it. The stitching is uneven, but the colors are bright.

"My new hobby," Harmony says as if offering an explanation. "I decided to give the baking a rest for a bit."

Over the last few months, through a steady back-and-forth of emails and Stanley Tucci Instagram reels, Harmony and I have repaired the confidence that was broken a year ago. I don't know if I will ever fully trust any baked goods that show up on my doorstep again, but I have come to understand that our root cause was a communication error and my uncle's deep love for THC brownies.

"You look good." Harmony's hand finds my cheek. "Happy."

I automatically smile because I am happy, really, truly happy, and it's no longer just a fleeting moment or a good day—it's just simply how I am.

Harmony's phone pings. She glances at it quickly and then holds it up. "I'm being summoned."

I can see a string of emojis under Koko's name that look like the one Mackenzie described a moment ago.

"Distract her for me for a few minutes?" I ask. Harmony winks and then heads downstairs.

I turn and take another look at our apartment. Most of our personal stuff is still in the UK or in boxes, but Mackenzie will soon start to unpack his stuff, and since we're no longer subletting, I'll begin to unpack some of my stuff, too.

I still have another year of study in Liverpool and then a thesis to defend before I can call myself Dr. Annalise Harris, but CAMH has already offered me a full-time role when I return to Toronto next year.

Mackenzie spent the last four months with me in Liverpool, working remotely with Edwin on some new material while busking the streets of Liverpool and acquiring a very sizable following on Instagram.

However, the buzz from the early release of the Rydells's first single has several bands looking to collaborate with him on songs. Although Liverpool has a great music scene, the bands he is working with are in North America, so he has found a studio in Toronto where he can work. Since the next few years will bring a lot of travel, he plans on calling Toronto home.

Our schedules will be busy and not ideally compatible for the next few months, but we have committed to making them work. Although the magic of the universe might have nudged us together, our love and our commitment to it will keep us that way.

"Ready to go?" I call to Mackenzie, who is now in the bathroom brushing his teeth. He pops his head out the bathroom door, gives me the "two minutes" signal with his fingers, then asks with a mouthful of toothpaste, "Would you mind looking for my leather jacket? I think it might be in one of the boxes by the couch."

He disappears back behind the bathroom door, and I hunt through two cardboard boxes, finding it folded at the bottom of the second.

I have tried it on a few times since the last eclipse in Spain, but nothing particularly otherworldly has happened, and although I have thought about the jacket many times as I lie awake late at night, trying to piece together some sort of logical explanation, the only thing that has come close is one of Larry's favorite sayings.

"The Universe sends us what we're ready for at the exact time we need it in our lives."

The jacket showed me the things I needed to see in the moment.

But now . . . all I need it to be is a reminder of a man who looked after me no matter what.

I slip the jacket on, close my eyes, and let my own memory transport me back to the sidewalk out front and that warm and sunny day with Larry on his motorcycle.

That's how I like to remember him now, removing that pair of eclipse glasses from my face and smiling his brightest Larry smile.

Do an old guy a favor and chat with a stranger sometime. Take a moment to gaze at the stars every once in a while and think of me when you're dancing to my favorite song or drinking a Diet Coke. I'll be watching you, Beans.

The memory fades as I open my eyes to my apartment and Mackenzie standing in front of me smiling at me in a way I have always wanted to be looked at.

"Are you wearing that tonight?" He tugs at the cuff that comes almost to my fingertips.

"Nope." I shake my head, taking it off. "It looks far better on you."

I hand him the jacket, and he puts it on and then tugs me close and kisses me. I almost suggest we skip the party completely, but then our phones ping simultaneously, and I know that isn't an option.

"I'm afraid for both of us if we don't go down there now," I say.

Mackenzie laughs and takes my hand, kissing my palm before we walk hand in hand to the party downstairs.

Koko's store looks exactly as I remember it. There are too many clothes and too many people, but it's filled with the family she has found for herself here in the city.

"There's my girl," she calls as Mackenzie and I step inside. I get a bony hug from her and a wave from my favorite barista.

We talk and laugh, and when someone hands me a Diet Coke, I crack open the tab and look up.

Acknowledgments

I CAN’T BELIEVE THIS IS MY FOURTH published book. It feels like both yesterday and a lifetime ago that I was writing my first set of acknowledgments for *This Spells Love,* starry-eyed about the whole experience, with a still-vague sense of what it means to publish a novel. Here I am four-ish years later, still in awe with a slightly less vague sense of how it all works.

I am eternally grateful that I found my way into Bibi Lewis’s slush pile and charmed her enough to represent my books. Bibi, my Tetley tea leaves may not have predicted you, but you and I are meant to be! Talia Cieslinski, our very first chat, you totally got the heart of this story and my Diet Coke–loving protagonist. Your care and genuine excitement for the story shaped this book in ways I never could have pulled off alone. Emma Caruso, as with every book, you have this magical ability to see exactly what I’m trying to do and to point out, with perfect clarity, what needs to happen to actually do it. The part of my brain that asks “What would Emma do” gets stronger with every book.

I’m incredibly proud to publish with an imprint that truly makes space for love in all its forms. Whitney Frick, your leadership sets the bar, and I’m grateful to be part of a list built with so much care and intention. Huge thanks to the creative team who made this book look so good, especially Donna

Cheng, and to the marketing and publicity teams, Jordan Forney, Avideh Bashirrad, and Debbie Aroff, who show up for every one of my stories with so much enthusiasm and belief. And to the copy editors who polished every last sentence—four books in, and my comma usage is still . . . a work in progress.

I started my writing journey by myself, writing YA portal fantasy that will never ever see the light of day, and now I am surrounded by the best people in the world. From readers who have shared my books, recommended them, reviewed them, and planned impromptu pottery and photography sessions on their lunch breaks, to booksellers and librarians (with a huge shout-out to the Toledo, Hamilton, and Grimsby libraries)—you are the kinds of people we need more of in this world.

My writing people—you know who you are, and if you don't, I likely have terribly photoshopped proof of our deep, unshakable bond. You and your emotional support cocktails/hot dog bao/Bavarian pretzels are the best part of all of this. I am a writer of love, and yet I fail to find the perfect words to sum up how much I love you. Might just have to put it on a commemorative T-shirt.

Finally, to my family and friends—thank you for loving me enough that I have the emotional stability to write every day, while providing enough chaos to keep the story ideas coming.

SOLAR ECLIPSE
OF THE
HEART

KATE ROBB

Love Stories
for the
Open-Hearted

Uncle Larry's Famous Hot Chocolate

Bad day? Cold day?
Or just in the mood for a sweet treat?
Uncle Larry has just the thing!

INGREDIENTS

1½ cups whole milk

½ cup heavy cream

2-ish teaspoons icing sugar (more or less according to taste)

½ teaspoon espresso powder

2 bars Ghirardelli Intense Dark 72% Cacao Dark Chocolate Bar* (3.5 oz each), chopped

1 pinch of salt

1 dash of love

INSTRUCTIONS

- In a medium saucepan over medium heat, whisk together the milk, cream, icing sugar, and espresso powder until hot, but make sure you don't allow the mixture to boil.
- Remove from the heat and add the chopped chocolate.
- Stir until melted.

- Adjust the sweetness if needed and add a pinch of salt.
- Serve immediately, topped with your favorite garnishes: marshmallows, whipped cream, chopped chocolate, or crushed candy canes.

*Feel free to get fancy with this one; try a peppermint chocolate or a salted caramel chocolate.

Kate's Guide to Living Your Life with No Regrets

(UNCLE LARRY STYLE)

1. Crack that Diet Coke at 3:00 with a little bowl of something salty (I will not judge you if you need this at 10 A.M.).
2. Hold on to every hug for one second longer and memorize that feeling of happiness, store it in a corner of your mind for when life sucks and you need a little joy.
3. Ask to pet the dog: worst case, the owner says no; best case, you get a big kiss from a good boy.
4. If Celine Dion comes on your Uber's radio, belt it loud and proud (it will give your driver a good story). Also applies to Whitney, Shania, and any other beloved power ballad.
5. Treat yourself to that dessert you pass all the time in the bakery window, ignore all the reasons why you shouldn't have it and think only of how delicious it tastes.

6. Say no to that thing that you think you have to do, but you don't really have to do, and instead have a hot bath with cucumber slices over your eyes (nineties rom-coms did not steer us wrong on this one).

7. Let the people you love most in this world know how you feel: Call them, write them, shovel their driveways, or make their coffee exactly how they like it.

8. If hiking to the top of a mountain for the perfect sunrise is your thing, that's cool, but don't beat yourself up if your thing is sleeping in while wearing flannel pajamas and drinking coffee in bed.

9. Don't be afraid to cry when you're sad, laugh when something's funny, or toss out the odd profanity when life calls for it (I have found the odd "blow it out your shorts" to be very cathartic).

10. Don't hold back from doing that thing you've always wanted to do because you think you're not good at it. One day, you can be sitting in your cubicle dreaming about writing a book and not so long later, you'll be writing subpar life advice in the back of your fourth published romance, reminding your readers that this is their sign!

IF YOU'VE READ MORE THAN ONE OF my romances, you've figured out that they are stand-alone and not part of a series. I also don't pre-introduce my romantic couples in earlier books (although I love when authors do that); however, I do like to think that all of my characters live in the same universe where their lives may be messy, but love and magic are hiding in dreams and birthday candles and chicken drumsticks—as long as you look hard enough. I've left some easter eggs along the way that interconnect my characters. I've made a list below in case you've missed them (and I'm sure there are a few more I wrote in and have forgotten completely!).

- Uncle Larry is the bartender from the Victoria Curling Club in *This Spells Love.*

- Nana's Doughnuts (Kiersten from *This Spells Love*'s marketing project) was so successful that it expanded to Toronto and is now Annalise's favorite coffee spot and the site of her and Mackenzie's first nonofficial date.

- Mackenzie is Zoe Beauchannan's cousin (Jules's BFF in *Kitty St. Clair's Last Dance*), and Mackenzie also grew up in West Lake.

- When Zee's date calls her new friend from her med school class, who is from West Lake, she calls Jules from *Kitty St. Clair's Last Dance,* who gives her Mackenzie's phone number.

- Mackenzie falls asleep watching an episode of *Carson's Cove* (the setting for *Prime Time Romance*).
- Mackenzie sends Annalise a picture of his new custom Nikes from All the Other Kicks (Dax's store in Hamilton).
- Clive, the mechanic who comes to pick up Jules's flat tire in *Kitty St. Clair's Last Dance,* is Mackenzie's brother (and Clive owns the garage where Mackenzie used to work).
- Mackenzie plays drums at the West Lake Watermelon Festival, and a group of elderly women from the retirement home dance in front of the stage dressed in watermelon-themed clothing (a tribute to Kitty St. Clair, who was known for wearing pink polka-dot capris pants to the festival every year).

PHOTO COURTESY OF DALLIMORE MEDIA

KATE ROBB is the author of *This Spells Love*, *Prime Time Romance*, and *Kitty St. Clair's Last Dance*. She dated a lot of duds in her twenties (among a few gems), all providing excellent fodder to write weird and wild romantic comedies. She lives just outside of Toronto, Canada, where she spends her free time pretending she's not a hockey mom while whispering "hustle" under her breath from the stands, a Pinot Grigio concealed in her YETI mug. She hates owls, the word "whilst," and wearing shorts and aspires to one day be able to wear four-inch heels again.

katerobbwrites.com

About the Type

This book was set in Caslon, a typeface first designed in 1722 by William Caslon (1692–1766). Its widespread use by most English printers in the early eighteenth century soon supplanted the Dutch typefaces that had formerly prevailed. The roman is considered a "workhorse" typeface due to its pleasant, open appearance, while the italic is exceedingly decorative.